Praise for *First Rodeo*

"*First Rodeo* is a sizzling read about a young woman who goes in search of herself out West. In this place filled with wide-open spaces Kate faces her real challenge, torn between head and heart, and choice over family or her imagined new future. A page turner destined for the screen."

—Peter M. Kershaw, Director & CEO Duchy Parade Films

"Readers will love to saddle up with Kate Marino, the sassy, sexy heroine in Judith Hennessey's debut novel. From wrenching relationships with rowdy ranchers to frank female friendships, Kate's story gallops along, always in an entertaining tone and always, always in a stylish pair of cowgirl boots. A fun read!"

—Kelly Standing, Standing Media
and author of *I'm Still Standing*

"*First Rodeo* takes us on a rollickin', rip-roarin' ride as disillusioned single mom Kate takes off to Wyoming, swapping martini cocktails and Manolos for snakeskin boots and smooching with her younger cowboy under a blue moon. Hennessey handles her uber-feminine portrayal of a thirty-something crisis and love affair with a deft touch. There's real tenderness here and plenty of 'ouch' moments."

—Helen Jacey author of *The Woman in the Story*
and renowned screenplay-writer

"An engaging story of a successful St. Louis business woman who finds love, adventure, and her true calling in Wyoming's high country."

—Laton McCartney, author of *The Teapot Dome Scandal*

"Part old favorite *Northern Exposure* and part uber popular *Sex and the City*, Hennessey's debut novel is an intoxicating tale filled to the brim with authentic settings, compelling characters, and smart twists."

—Chris Wiedman, Director of Regional Sales CoxRep

"*First Rodeo* is an inside look at a business woman who's boredom in the boardroom spurs her to embark on a string of wild adventures. Bucked, twisted, and spun in all directions, Kate finds herself in such a different state, literally; she must discover her instincts then find the courage to follow them. Expect the unexpected in this well written, entirely original story, filled with incredible visuals; it screams for the big screen."

—Shawn Jordan, Exec Vice-President, Director
Griffin Communications

"Fans of Janet Evanovich will love feisty Kate Marino of *First Rodeo*, book one in The Spur Series. Hennessey delivers a cast of colorful characters, non-stop action and a heroine you will find yourself rooting for until the very last line. Don't miss this must read!"

—Lisa Farkey, President FarMor Media

First Rodeo

THE SPUR SERIES ✳ BOOK 1

Judith Hennessey

First Rodeo

A Novel

SparkPress, a BookSparks imprint
A Division of SparkPoint Studio, LLC

Published by SparkPress, a BookSparks imprint,
A division of SparkPoint Studio, LLC
Tempe, Arizona, USA, 85281
www.gosparkpress.com

Published 2016

Printed in the United States of America

ISBN: 978-1-943006-03-8 (pbk)
ISBN: 978-1-943006-04-5 (e-bk)
Library of Congress Control Number: 2016937053

Cover design © Julie Metz, Ltd./metzdesign.com
Author photo © Suzy Gorman
Formatting by Katherine Lloyd/theDESKonline.com

For Jon,
I hope your trail has led you to love and happiness.

*

For my mother, Dr. Vera June DiSalvo,
who will always be my inspiration.

*

And for my son, Louis,
you are the best parts of me.

"The important thing is this:

to be ready at any moment

to sacrifice what you are

for what you could become."

—*Charles Dubois*

Kate

FAIRFIELD ROAD WAS ONE OF THE busiest thoroughfares in St. Louis, yet this early April morning it was miraculously void of traffic. Even after dropping off her five-year-old son, Sam, at school, Kate would make it to Marino Motors in record time. The red, white, and blue sign glared at her a block ahead. Other than the new cars, lined up like soldiers on a front line, the parking lot was deserted. Kate smirked as she pulled into the space right next to the front door, a space reserved for her father, Joseph Marino. Ordinarily, Kate wouldn't have behaved so defiantly, but this was no ordinary day. She killed the engine of her Jeep, and grabbed her steaming double-shot cappuccino with one hand and Gucci briefcase with the other.

There was no one to be found as she glided through the double doors, not one salesman, but more importantly, no signs of her father. She unlocked her office door and prayed he had a meeting, something—anything—to keep him out of her way.

Kate's office was dark and cold. No matter how much light poured in from the showroom floor, the three-hundred-square-foot space always seemed to feel and look like a cave. The dirty brown shag carpet, cocoa-colored paneled walls, and outdated metal desk certainly didn't help. In the past, none of this had bothered her; she'd been too busy to notice. But now it occurred to her how depressing it all was.

She put down her coffee and placed the briefcase on the filing cabinet that flanked her desk. The briefcase was made of beautiful Italian leather, a gift from her father. She pushed both of the brass latches with her French-manicured nails; the briefcase unlocked with a loud pop. Papers and various business cards littered the inside. The letter rested on top, like a snake ready to strike.

It had taken weeks to write that letter. So much had happened; so much had changed. Her father's words accused her of unspeakable acts and hurt her deeply. Kate worshipped her father. They had worked side by side at Marino Motors since she was old enough to answer the phones. And now she felt as though everything she had worked for was ruined, including her relationship with her father.

Kate took a rubber band out of the top drawer of her desk, pulled back her long brown hair, and looked through the gold-tinted glass that ran along the left wall of her office. A service customer stood in the hall on the other side, waiting for the cashier. He tapped his fingers with impatience. Kate knew the signs of another high-maintenance customer, wanting something for free. Janet, the cashier, came to the window and handed the man his bill. While he studied it, Kate stretched out her left foot under the desk and fished for the Jimmy Choo pump she'd shed just moments ago.

The customer raised his voice. Kate could barely make out his words but guessed it went something like, "This is the second time I've been in for the same repair! I want to speak to a manager!"

Kate raced to the door of her office and eased it shut. Back behind her desk, she swiveled around so her back faced the see-through wall. She stared at a monochromatic black-and-white photograph of a finely tooled Western saddle hanging out of the side of an old railroad car. It was Kate's work, and one of her favorites—a wonderful still life, moody, and so rich in texture. Another one of her pieces hung in the new-car sales manager's office, a beautiful shot of the San Juan Mountains. They were both taken while on vacation in Santa Fe years ago with her best friend, Stella—before Kate was married, before she had Sam. She and Stella used to travel every chance they could get. They were perfect travel companions. Both loved hiking, horse-back riding, skiing, and four-star hotels. There was no need to rough it after a long day playing in the great outdoors if there was a Ritz-Carlton or a Four Seasons nearby. They always chose destinations west of the Mississippi—Colorado, Utah, and New Mexico. The landscape made Kate feel as though she were living in a postcard, and she took hundreds of photographs. When she returned from her adventures, occasionally one shot would be so special that she would be inspired to paint. The black-and-white medium was perfect for the project. It gave Kate the freedom to feel the energy of the subject and use color accordingly. When she painted, she was transported; nothing mattered but the art she created.

But things were different now. There was no time to travel with Stella, and certainly no time to paint. Kate had responsi-bilities, big responsibilities, and they had gotten bigger now that she was a divorced single mother. The agitated customer's voice yanked Kate back to the moment.

"I tell you, I want to speak to the owner, someone with authority!" he repeated.

The tall leather chair devoured her tiny frame, the perfect

emergency hiding spot. Kate was not about to be the person in charge, the woman that listened to the complaint, not today, maybe not ever. She'd let James, her brother, handle it. He was always eager to be in charge.

Janet ushered the irate customer past Kate's office toward the showroom floor. The huge room displayed more of Mr. Marino's antiques and hunting trophies than automobiles. A swordfish hung on one wall, several ducks and a snow goose frozen in midflight across another, and an impala head hung next to the entrance to his office. But it was the buffalo head perched above the reception desk that seemed to get the most attention, more double takes than the latest model Jeep. Hunting, fishing, and traveling—those were Joseph's passions.

And there were pictures, lots and lots of pictures: a proud Joseph Marino showing off a twenty-pound sockeye salmon in Alaska; riding an elephant in India with his best friend, Dr. Morgan; and a more local shot at his farm in Gatlin, Missouri, with a record-size turkey dangling upside down from his right hand. When James and Kate were young, he would take them there to fish in the pond. As James got older, he lost interest, but Kate was still eager to go. She shared her father's love of the country, and they spent hours exploring the woods in their 1940s Willys, making new trails and putting out corn for the turkeys and deer.

Out of all his memorabilia, Joseph's pride and joy was an original watercolor, a caricature of him in a fishing vest and waders, holding a fly rod in one hand, and in the other, a suitcase with stickers from all over the world plastered on the sides. He was smiling and wearing a green army hat. A photo of him with his Army Air Corps buddies in front of a B-52 bomber was the focal point of the used-car manager's office. The Missouri Department of Conservation had given him this work of art as a thank-you after serving his term on its board back in the eighties.

Joseph Marino also used the showroom as a place to display his antique oil lamps, printing press, wood-burning stove, turn-of-the-century furniture, and the photograph of him shaking hands with President George W. Bush. The decor definitely gave the business a more personal feel.

Kate waited a good ten minutes before she went back to her door and cracked it an inch. She saw that Frank, their sales manager, had come to the rescue. Despite his gangster-type looks, he had a calming effect on customers. He listened, furrowed his brow with concern, and then spoke. Magically, the seemingly unhappy customer laughed as if Frank had told some hilarious joke.

Thank God, she said to herself and pushed the door back open. Besides being dark as a cave, her office had zero ventilation. Perspiration pooled under her armpits. She didn't need to add one more thing to her pyramid of dry cleaning, so she grabbed the paper napkin from under her coffee cup, pulled up the side of her cashmere sweater, and quickly blotted the sweat from under each arm.

It was Friday, so there would not be a sales meeting; there would be a managers' meeting instead. She studied the huge green chalkboard where daily and monthly sales were posted. This four-by-seven-foot slate surface faced her every day. For ten years she had worked in the sales department. The chalkboard had been the benchmark for her success. The funny thing was, Kate didn't even like the car business. It was flooded by men pumping too much testosterone for Kate's taste. And if you happened to be one of the few women that had infiltrated this egotistical man's world, you'd better grow balls. Car dealers were ruthless. They'd sell their mother for a car sale.

Joseph Marino was an exception to the rule; years of hard work had brought him from a used-car salesman to owner of one of the most successful franchises in North America. He worked bell to bell. If the doors were open, he was there, usually working sixty hours a week. Joseph was competitive yet fair; people trusted him, and his reputation preceded him. Customers drove for miles to buy their vehicles from him, knowing they'd get his personal attention and the best possible deal.

And now Kate found herself standing in her father's shoes, a pair she wasn't so sure she liked anymore. The money was good, no doubt. Kate mentally scanned her outfit—Jimmy Choo black suede pumps, $600; Ralph Lauren wool trousers, $950; matching cashmere turtleneck, $750; and crocodile belt, $1,200. The belt was a gift, but nevertheless, her ensemble totaled $3,500, a nice chunk of change. And that didn't even count the diamond stud earrings or the Ebel watch. *Holy shit, somebody might mug me just to get my clothes!*

This month Kate would be getting a huge commission check, most likely into the mid–four figures. The board showed a total of 125 Jeeps for March, a big month for Marino Motors—a *very* big month. Kate's name was at the top of the list; nothing unusual about that. What was unusual, extraordinary even, was that Kate had managed to outsell the entire sales force, delivering sixty-five out of those 125 vehicles. All those lunches, dinners, birthday cards, and Christmas gifts had finally paid off. Kate was tired of being "on," the constant entertainer. But going the extra mile for her clients made the difference between being good and being number one.

Since the fight with her father, food wasn't looking very appetizing. This morning the scale tipped below one hundred pounds, six pounds lighter than Kate's fighting weight. The whole thing was totally absurd. It had to be James, her brother, who had planted the story, and she just couldn't believe her father believed him. And obviously he did; otherwise, he would never have confronted her. The scene in her father's office was burned in her mind, a nightmare that wouldn't go away.

Almost a week had passed since Joseph Marino summoned his daughter to his office. He had been sitting behind his huge antique mahogany desk, the king of his empire, yet he appeared surprisingly uncomfortable. The man was confident and always in control. Kate had sat wide-eyed as she listened to him nervously sputter.

"There has been talk. A few people have said that you're getting, how do you say—" He paused and cleared his throat. "They say you are getting a *reputation*." He spat out the last word as if it were poison.

Kate tried to form a reply, but nothing came out from her lips, even though she was sure they were opening and closing. Maybe her ears had deceived her. Kate managed to finally whisper, "I'm sorry, I'm not sure I understand what you are saying."

"They say you are being loose. You know, sleeping with your clients." He paused, lowered his voice, and continued as if some evil spirit had possessed him. "And something was said about your doing drugs, too."

Kate would have burst out laughing had her father not looked so serious. She waited, thinking he was going to say it was some horrible joke. Instead, he just stared at the wall behind her. The clock ticked off the longest minute of Kate's life as she realized her father was serious. She was too stunned to reply. Mr. Marino might as well have slammed his fist into his favorite daughter's face. It would have probably hurt less.

"You did sell a lot of cars. I mean, how did you do that?" he asked, as if defending himself.

"Economy Plus is a big company. I've come to know most of the account executives very well. I've worked hard to build relationships. They like me, so they call me first when they're ready to buy a car." It was so simple; what was this all about?

Father and daughter stared at each other as Kate tried to make sense out of the surreal scene.

"It was James, wasn't it? He told you this, didn't he?"

"I'm not saying who it was. It was told to me in confidence."

"It was him. I know it." Tears of frustration poured from her eyes. She had never been so humiliated. "How could you believe this craziness?"

Mr. Marino closed his sad gray eyes and pressed his head against the rich leather chair. Kate willed him to get up from his god-awful throne, hug her, and say it was all a mistake. She was his favorite, the good girl, the one who had always done what was asked of her. When her mother, Jenny, left her father, a separation that lasted three years, Kate gave up starting college at Colorado State in Fort Collins and attended classes at Washington University in St. Louis instead. Kate felt it was her duty to stay at home with her father. Her own social life was replaced with running their family home and going to business functions with her father. His last request was the most difficult for Kate. He asked her to give up art school.

"The only good artist is a dead artist. You'll never make any money painting." Mr. Marino was very aware that Kate was unsure of her creative talents. "A business degree is what you need. Then you can take over the dealership when I retire. Minor in art. When you're older, it'll make a fine hobby."

Kate had been appalled. First of all, James was older and deserved to run the business. He *wanted* to run Marino Motors. James loved selling cars; it gave him something his father could not give. And Kate loved art. Yet Mr. Marino would hear none of it. He had selected Kate as his successor. It was a tough pill for James to swallow, and even harder for Kate.

As she sat there under her father's scrutiny, Kate wondered what had driven her father to this. They had argued lately, mostly about when he was going to retire. Kate was as ready as she would ever be. And it was perfect timing. Sam had started kindergarten that fall. Joseph Marino loved his only grandson probably more than his own children. It had been an ideal situation for Kate. Her father gave her as much time as she needed to raise her son. Sam always came first.

James wasn't exactly thrilled about that, either. He constantly badgered Kate about their father's favoritism. Grace, Kate's younger sister, never worked at the dealership but shared James's ugly jealous streak, although she'd never admitted to it. Grace left the Marino nest years ago, landed a cushy job as a financial advisor in Naples, Florida, and soon after married an attorney. Her life was pretty perfect right about now.

No, it had to be James. He had spun all the lies about her; Kate was sure of it. James was desperate to get what he thought was rightfully his.

Kate could barely catch her breath she had cried so hard, right in front of her father—an emotional luxury she didn't often indulge in. Snot dripped from her nose. She wiped it with the sleeve of her expensive sweater, got up, and left her father's office without another word.

In the days that followed, Kate went numb. It was easier not to feel anything than to process what had happened, avoiding the fact there was another crack in her perfect little world. She was not sure she was up to another round of self-help. Round one had occurred during the divorce from Michael. Even though it was fairly amicable, the dissolution of the marriage was painful. Fortunately, after five years, they had become good friends and raised their son with little friction. It was the breakup with Ted, the final breakup, that just about did her in.

Ted had pulled Kate in and out of his life for nearly a decade. Kate could never figure out exactly what it was about Ted that kept her hooked. Ted could be charming and attentive, but on the other side of the coin, deceiving and downright mean. Dating Ted was like being on a seesaw: she was either floating up in the air, screaming in delight, or slammed down on the ground, crying. Kate didn't want to think about what had passed between them over the years. Sometimes she thought maybe she had ended up marrying Michael just to get away from Ted.

Yet marriage didn't stop Ted. It actually seemed to spark his interest even more. He would call her at work and tell her he missed her, still loved her—the usual mumbo jumbo. Those calls certainly stirred the pot, but Kate remained faithful. That was the battle of the century, common sense versus "Kate, the Ted addict," which was why this whole thing about her sleeping around was so ludicrous. She could barely have sex with her husband during their three years of marriage, much less several other men after her divorce. Even though Ted hadn't been totally responsible for her leaving Michael, he had certainly ruined her chances for finding romance elsewhere. It was a blessing Ted lived a thousand miles away in Denver. Kate now focused on her son and career, leaving love for braver hearts.

Kate returned calls left over from the day before, then made the last few calls to her larger fleet clients to follow up on the important letter she had mailed to them. Most of her contacts were out to lunch, so she left detailed messages asking them if they received the note and had read it. The even more important letter sat waiting for her father, but noon came and went without a Joseph Marino sighting.

Kate opened the small cooler she brought with her every day and took out an egg salad sandwich. She grabbed her new purchase from Barnes & Noble, Gene Kilgore's *Ranch Vacations,* thinking it would help her relax. The book, a dictionary of guest ranches, was almost as big as a bible. It felt heavy in her small hands. She smiled for the first time in days, thrilled that someone loved these places so much that he wrote an entire book about them. And apparently Mr. Kilgore had visited each and every property, tucked away in beautiful and remote locations across the United States. Kate was sure he could help her find what she was looking for.

She paged to the index and found Colorado, the obvious choice for her summer trip out West. Out of all the places she'd visited, Colorado was still her favorite. She'd been having a love affair with the state since her first ski trip her senior year in high school. The Rocky Mountains instilled a sense of peace in her that she never felt when back in the city. Fifteen years later, Kate still yearned for those mountains, pining away for them like a heartsick lover.

Whether she could pass through the state and avoid seeing Ted was the question. Most of the ranches were not even close to Denver, so she could most likely pull it off, although it was a wee bit tempting. She sat back and refocused on the letter she was about to deliver to her father. Was she making the right choice?

Thank God I've got Sam, Kate said to herself, *now more than ever.* He touched her in a way no other person ever had. Lately, it was as if Sam knew that she needed him more.

"Mom, I love you more than you love me," Sam would say to her as she tucked him into bed.

"No way. I love you more," she'd reply, sounding very grown-up, but inside feeling overwhelmed about being a single parent and, soon, unemployed.

"Nope, I love you more," Sam would say, hugging her.

"That's impossible!" Kate would squeeze him hard, then start tickling him.

"Why?" He giggled and squirmed in her arms.

"Because I'm bigger than you!" And they'd both laugh.

As she walked to her room she felt happy and light, but by the time she climbed into bed and the cold sheets scratched her skin, the emptiness returned. There was a void from Ted, no doubt, but deep inside something else tugged at her heart. Kate had begun to understand that she hungered for something more, something a love affair couldn't feed, something she could not name.

Kate focused on Gene's descriptions of the various dude ranches, amazed that there were so many. They came in many shapes and forms, some hosting nearly one hundred guests, others housing only ten or twelve. Accommodations and amenities varied from cabins with woodstove heat and limited electricity, to beautifully furnished lodges with spas and gourmet meals. Kate wanted authenticity, but electricity was where she drew the line. There had to be lights, heat, and running water, and decent linens would be a plus. The ranch also needed to have a kids' program, someone who could teach Sam to ride and care for horses. She had grown up with horses at their farm, and it had crossed her mind more than once lately that maybe it was time she started riding again. Sam was old enough to ride with her, but it was important that he learned from experts in a safe environment. If he fell off, it would be hard to get him on another horse. But it also had to be fun. The cool cowboys and ranch experience would surely win him over. It would be their first vacation together. She wanted it to be perfect.

Surprisingly, none of the ranches in Colorado really struck Kate. She paged through Idaho and Montana. Still, nothing really caught her eye, or her idea of the right place for her to introduce Sam to the great outdoors. Toward the end of the book she came to the chapter on Wyoming. Kate picked up the phone and dialed Stella's number. Stella picked up on the second ring.

"Where in the hell is Wyoming anyway?" Kate asked.

"Well, hello, Kate. How are you?"

"Oh, sorry, didn't mean to be so short, but I'm researching a dude-ranch vacation for me and Sam, and I'm at work. You know how Dad is. He could barge into my office any minute. If I start talking about business being slow and we don't have the budget to advertise, you'll know he's come in."

"You mean you haven't told him yet?"

"You sound like a goose! I told you, I wrote him a letter, and I'm giving it to him today!"

"You are unbelievable."

"Stella, I have no idea how he is going to react. I wanted time to get all my clients lined out before he blew his top."

Kate had worried endlessly about her clients, knowing they would not get the same attention she provided. But there was nothing she could do about it now. Her sabbatical, as she called it, a term she found more positive and less permanent, was about to begin. And that was why she wanted to make sure that each of her cherished customers had read the letter she had sent out. It assigned them a temporary sales contact, a representative of Marino Motors whom she had handpicked.

"Are you nervous? You *have* to call me afterwards and tell me what happens!"

"I will. Can we please talk about Wyoming?" Kate begged.

"No problem. Wyoming is north of Colorado, you idiot. You

know, the Grand Tetons, Yellowstone National Park, ever heard of any of those places?" She laughed.

"I've seen pictures of Yellowstone ... and the Tetons are there? God, they are incredible!" Kate closed her eyes, and a slide show of photographs taken by her idol, Ansel Adams, flashed through her mind. Most of her favorites were taken in or around Yellowstone National Park. Kate inhaled, slowly let out a deep breath, and looked back at her photo of the saddle behind her desk. And at that moment she realized just how much she missed her art. She shook her head sadly. *What the hell happened to me?*

"Kate. Are you still there?" Stella couldn't hear a thing—not even the loudspeaker of the intercom that usually interrupted their conversation.

"Sorry, yeah, I'm still here. I was just thinking." Kate decided to stop thinking about photography and concentrate on the fun vacation she needed to plan.

"Wyoming," she repeated out loud. The place might as well have been on the other side of the world. Mr. Kilgore listed a plethora of quaint dude ranches across the state, many historic, most describing a real Western experience. As a matter of fact, there seemed to be more ranches in Wyoming than anywhere else. Kate wondered why she had never been there.

"I wonder how in the hell you get there?" She continued scanning the ranch descriptions with one eye and watched for her father's imminent interruption with the other.

"I would assume by plane," Stella said with her usual dry humor.

"I *know* that. Where would you fly into? What's the biggest town?"

"I imagine Jackson Hole would be where you'd want to go, depending on where the ranch is located. Where is it?" Stella was passionate about photography and the West, like Kate. Although she had many suitors, she had never married, and the lack of ties left her with plenty of time to travel. She was also gainfully unemployed for the moment. Wyoming was definitely on her radar, but it wasn't easy to get to from St. Louis.

"I'm not sure . . ." And then she saw it: the Prickly Pear Ranch. Adorable red-roofed log cabins, full private baths, thirty-six-guest capacity—not too big, not too small, rides skirting the Tetons, wildlife viewing, rafting down the Snake River, and a wonderful kids' program. There was even a Saturday evening excursion into Jackson Hole to see a real rodeo. Sam would go crazy!

"Stella, I think I've found it!"

"John Frazier from KTZR Radio is on line five!" Janet yelled through the intercom.

"Shit," Kate said under her breath, her visions of mountains and cowboys in tight jeans and boots erased. "Tell him to hold a minute."

"Stella, I've got to go. But would you help me figure out how to get to Moran, Wyoming?"

"Sure, no problem. Call me after work!"

Joseph Marino never showed up that day, as if he knew something unpleasant was about to happen. At exactly five o'clock, Kate delivered the letter to her father's empty office. She placed it right next to his Dealer of the Year Award.

"They'll have to carry him out of here in a coffin," Kate whispered to no one in particular.

Call of the Wild

JOSEPH MARINO TOOK THE NEWS of Kate's three-month leave of absence much better than she expected. The letter she had written must have gotten through to him, Kate thought. The first part of the letter had announced her leaving the dealership for a few months, and the second part addressed James's lies. She told her father she was not sleeping with her customers or doing any drugs other than an occasional prescription Xanax to help her sleep. She closed by telling him she found it extremely painful and embarrassing to have to explain her personal life in such detail, especially to him of all people.

Joseph Marino ended up agreeing to pay Kate full salary during her leave of absence without blinking an eye. Kate knew she had won the battle but felt a huge loss. She missed her father. As a peace offering, she asked him if he wanted to join her and Sam in Wyoming for a few days. He said yes, as Kate knew he would. Joseph Marino would never pass up an opportunity to be with his grandson.

"Maybe we just need to spend some time together away from the office," Kate told Stella. They were at The Vine, a restaurant and bar where the local upper crust hung out when they weren't at the country club, or in Florida or Michigan.

"I doubt that. Whatever. I can't believe you invited him to go to Wyoming!" Stella spoke into her glass as she drained the last drop of Côtes du Rhône.

"Ted called." Kate knew this little tidbit of gossip would distract Stella for the moment.

"No shit! What did the bastard want?"

"Well, actually he called the dealership first. Janet told him I wasn't there, of course; she knows him. I've trained her how to dodge his calls for years. Anyway, he asked when I'd be back, and she finally told him I was taking a leave of absence. She didn't know when I was coming back."

"Good one! I bet that blew his mind. How'd he track you down?"

"He called me at home. For some reason my caller ID said private call, so I picked it up."

"And?"

"At first he said he wanted to buy another Jeep. Someone in his office wanted his old one and made him an offer he couldn't refuse. But then he jumped all over me for leaving the dealership!"

"Correction, you're just taking a break."

"I know that. He told me I was crazy. He said, 'Why in the hell do you need time off? Are you stressed? The most stressful thing you do, Marino, is decide which pair of Manolos to put on in the morning!'"

"The nerve! What an asshole!" Stella said.

"I know! Can you believe him?"

"He just doesn't get it. I remember when I used to work for *my* dad. It was a nightmare. People think you've got a cushy job, but they have no idea how hard it is." Stella had worked as a paralegal at her father's law firm for years.

"Well, he seems to think it'll just give James more leverage to take over Marino Motors when it's time."

"Oh, give me a break. What? Does Ted think he's your father or something? He's certainly old enough to be." Stella brought a spoonful of vichyssoise up to her mouth.

Kate sat back, tempted to defend Ted. He was only eleven years older, and even though he occasionally preached to her, and it totally bugged her, there were times when he was right.

"Well, he's just looking out for me. James will definitely take every opportunity to make himself look good while I'm gone. So, it's a good thing I'm having my dad come with us to Wyoming!"

Kate slid a blue-cheese-stuffed olive off the toothpick that had been marinating in her vodka martini. "He's only going to be there for a few days. We're going to fly into Salt Lake City, drive to Jackson Hole, and spend a few days in Yellowstone and Grand Teton National Park. I've got him flying out of Jackson Hole on Monday before we go to the Prickly Pear Ranch." Kate took a bite out of the olive thinking about how she and her father would, she hoped, rebond in the simplicity of nature. It had been six weeks since she left the dealership, and they rarely spoke. And when they did, Mr. Marino just rattled on about how busy it was and how hard he was working. He did manage to come by Kate's house to see Sam, his droopy hound-dog eyes looking even sadder. In a way Kate felt sorry for him.

"I think you're absolutely out of your mind," Stella insisted.

"I don't know. Dad seems really excited about going to Yellowstone. He's never been there before." Joseph Marino had primarily traveled abroad, to exotic locations—Europe, Asia, and Africa—all trips he had won through sales or service contests.

"I'm telling you, he'll drive you nuts," Stella said, finishing her soup.

"I've booked separate rooms at all the hotels," Kate said, praying Stella was not right.

ON JUNE 5, KATE AND SAM met Joseph Marino at St. Louis International Airport. He scolded Kate for not being at the airport at least two hours in advance. "Things could happen," he said.

Sam looked up at the old man and smiled angelically. "But everything is okay, isn't it, Grandpa?"

On cue, Mr. Marino curled up the corners of his mouth, patted Sam's back, and said, "Sam, have you ever flown first class?"

"What's first class, Grandpa?" Sam asked as they got in line to check their bags.

Kate answered before her father could reply. "It's a place in the front of the plane where the seats are bigger and you get to drink all the soda you want!"

"Wow!" Sam jumped up and down.

"But it's very expensive, Sam. Your mother couldn't afford it," Mr. Marino said with a chuckle.

"But you can?"

"I can. But I had to work very hard," Mr. Marino said, serious as a priest saying mass at church on a Sunday.

The airline attendant waved them forward, diverting Kate's temper just in time. It took all her strength to drag her oversized Hartmann tweed suitcase to the desk and hoist it onto the scale. The bag weighed in right at the limit. Her father's advice rang in her ears: never pack more than you can carry. She had heard that over and over again when her father took her to Europe for the much-anticipated high school graduation gift. That trip had been a disaster. Now that she thought about it, their yearly jaunts to Florida were pretty painful, too. Nothing was ever right or good enough, making it impossible to relax and have fun. She handed over her driver's license while Mr. Marino put in the upgrade request.

Kate wasn't necessarily eager to introduce Sam to the joys of "flying in the front of the bus," as she called it. Once you flew first class you found out what you were missing in coach. The only time she had found coach palatable was when Ozark Airlines had had their Wine Cellar in the Sky program, many moons ago. Now, that made traveling much more enjoyable: free wine and cheese for all passengers. It made you forget about being stuffed into a seat the size of shoebox next to someone you didn't want to tell your life story to.

"We do have three seats available in first, two next to each other and the other a row behind," the sixtyish platinum blonde reported.

"Not three across, one across the aisle?" Joseph Marino frowned.

Kate smiled. Not being stuck next to her father for over three hours was very attractive. All previous deliberations about whether or not to fly first class were tossed aside.

"That'll be fine! Dad, you can sit with Sam. I'll go ahead and take the seat behind." Kate knew Sam would most likely nap for at least half the flight. The other half would be spent in a trance with one of his many computerized toys. There would be a few hours of blissful peace before the next leg of their journey.

It was fortunate Kate slept on the plane. The rest prepared her for the eight hours of hell in the rental car, Mr. Marino's choice, a Ford Taurus—a four door and safe. As they inched across the Utah border, from the backseat he yelled at Kate to slow down, keep her eyes on the road, or adjust the air conditioner. At first Kate turned up the radio, but then he complained about that being too loud. But once they crossed over into Wyoming, Kate found it easier to ignore him. The starkness of the gentle sloping hills, as far as the eyes could see, big as any ocean, drowned out all his negativity. Antelopes grazed freely, sagebrush tumbled across the road like feathers, light, following the breeze, which turned into some pretty strong winds as they got closer to Rock Springs.

Rock Springs was about the ugliest town Kate had ever seen—a blur of dusty buildings, not a hint of green. It was apparent the town was lacking in pride; trash littered the street, businesses seemed old and run-down. The place reminded Kate of her office—and of her father. *God, I hope this isn't what the rest of Wyoming looks like,* she thought.

Fifty miles later, Kate passed through the one-stop-sign town of Farson—only she missed it; her eyes were glued to the rearview mirror a minute too long, checking on her father, who had miraculously shut up. What she saw made her stop and think. He was resting in the backseat, head leaning against the window, eyelids closed. There was a softer side to him, Kate knew that, and she also knew the reason he was so bitter. Anthony, her father's firstborn, had been thrown off his minibike at their farm. He hadn't been wearing a helmet. Anthony died on the way to the hospital in Joseph Marino's arms. He had just turned ten the week before. Kate was a newborn when it happened. James was five. Her mother was pregnant with Grace. It had been very hard on James, although he never talked about it. No one in the Marino family did.

The more Kate thought about it, the more things made sense: her father picking up the tab on Sam's tuition at Oak Hill School, a private and very expensive institution; the trust fund that was already set up and funded for his college education. Kate could have afforded these expenses, but her father insisted on being the provider. And then there were the endless gifts, the miniature battery-powered, candy-apple-red Jeep being the latest. Sam drove it up and down and around Grandpa's neighborhood. Of course, Grandpa was following, at a slow trot, right behind him, beaming the entire time. Kate had never seen her father so happy. It was subtle yet obvious to Kate. Sam was receiving all the pent-up love Joseph Marino was unable to give his late oldest son.

Kate looked at her own son, who was sleeping in the passenger seat. Her parents' ongoing grief was a difficult thing for Kate to accept. After all, they had three surviving children. But after she had Sam, Kate better understood their pain—it had to be a living hell. She couldn't imagine surviving Sam, much less watching him die in her arms. Even now, Kate guessed her mother still blamed her father for what was clearly an accident. She reached for Sam's coat, pulled it over his shoulders, and decided she would not think depressing thoughts, not for one more minute. This was supposed to be a vacation. Kate shoved back the past, tucked it safely away in a distant memory, and concentrated on the moment.

The odometer told Kate they were at least two hours away from Jackson Hole. How much farther Yellowstone National Park was, she did not know. What she did know was that she was determined to make it to the Old Faithful Inn before dark. Kate couldn't wait to see the famous geyser. She checked the rearview mirror once more, then accelerated the rental to seventy-nine.

About twenty miles outside of Farson, the landscape changed dramatically. Magnificent mountains edged the distant horizon, and pine trees and aspens replaced much of the craggy sage. The highway followed a river; the pavement led into a stunning gorge. Sheer cliffs sprouted from the earth, bordering the rushing water. It was the most beautiful scenery Kate had ever seen.

By the time they arrived in Jackson Hole, the unpleasantness of Rock Springs was completely forgotten.

Jackson Hole was everything Kate had imagined. Wood plank sidewalks skirted turn-of-the-century buildings, with windows displaying beautiful artwork, furs, and cowboy-chic clothing. Sam woke up and announced he was starving. Kate tried to talk him into trying one of the fun lunch spots, but he insisted on heading for McDonald's, whose golden arches reached all the way to Jackson Hole.

"Okay, but after lunch we're going to that store over there." Kate pointed to Best of the West. "We definitely need cowboy hats."

"Can I get a black one?"

"Absolutely!"

"You don't need a silly cowboy hat," Mr. Marino said to Sam.

"They are not silly!" Kate turned her back to her father and looked at her young son. "Cowboys wear them for a reason. The brim protects their heads from the sun, and when it rains, it keeps them dry. Isn't that cool?" Kate turned back to face her father. He didn't reply.

Once in McDonald's, Mr. Marino ordered a quarter pounder with cheese and fries. Fast food was his weakness, and the greasier the better. Kate didn't share her father's taste and chose the least repulsive item, a McChicken sandwich. Sam was ecstatic with his Happy Meal.

AFTER LUNCH, MOTHER AND SON walked out of McDonald's and headed for Best of the West. Half an hour later they emerged, Kate in a straw cowboy hat and Sam in brand new cowboy boots, spurs, and a coal-black hat. Sam and Kate hopped back into the Taurus, where Mr. Marino had waited.

Her father was quiet as Kate maneuvered the car into the long line of motorists and tour buses that had already bombarded Jackson Hole, all circling the town square like a wagon train. The long day of travel finally caught up with her. Kate scanned the streets for a caffeine fix. A sign reading "Shades" with a coffee cup etched below rocked back and forth in the breeze just a few car lengths ahead.

"I have a feeling this is the last stop for cappuccino. Dad, I'll just run in. Would you mind staying in the car with Sam?" she asked, with a sweetness she didn't exactly feel. Why couldn't he just loosen up?

"I guess so." He sighed as if it were a huge imposition.

"Would you like anything?" she said, keeping her smile.

"I better have a coffee. You might need me to drive soon." He took out a two-inch wad of bills from the front pocket of his khaki pants.

"Dad, I can get this."

"No, you need to save your money." He handed her a five out of a stack of hundreds.

Kate took the money. Inside, she ordered a double espresso for herself and a decaf for her dad. There was no way she was going to let him get behind the wheel, no way in hell. The cute cowboy in Best of the West had told her the entrance to Yellowstone was only a half hour away, and the Old Faithful Inn two hours farther. It was four o'clock, and she fully intended to see that geyser explode before sunset. And after the torturous day with her father, she felt she deserved one very large cocktail.

As they headed west on Cache Street, the retail stores were replaced by small ponds with trumpeter swans and wild ducks. The traffic began to thin out, the road splitting into four lanes, then back into two. The pavement was now a narrow line traveling across wide open space, acres and acres of grass and sage under the dome of a clear cobalt sky.

"Look, there's the National Elk Refuge!" Mr. Marino said, rolling down the window.

Kate drew in a deep breath and thanked God he was finally appreciating the beauty of the place they were in.

"What's an elk refuge, Grandpa?" Sam unhooked his seat belt, kneeled, and turned backwards on his seat.

"It's a place where the elk come and stay during the winter. They get fed and are safe from the hunters and the other wild animals that might hurt them," Mr. Marino said in a gentle voice. It was a tone Kate hadn't heard in a long, long, time.

"What's an elk look like?" Sam looked at his grandpa as if he were the most important person on earth.

"It looks like a deer, but much bigger."

"Will we see one?"

"I don't know, son, maybe if we're lucky."

"I bet we do! You'd better get your camera ready!"

Kate smiled, more for her father than for her son.

"You'd better turn back around and put that seat belt back on," Mr. Marino said, patting Sam on the head.

"Dad, I read about a museum somewhere right around here, a wildlife museum I think. Maybe we can check it out. We should have time on Monday before your flight takes off," Kate suggested.

"I'd like that," he said as he returned his attention to the famous scenery that passed, frame by frame, outside the car's window. The Grand Teton Mountain Range ruled the landscape by its simple yet complicated beauty.

Kate steered the Taurus into the first pullout. Sam grabbed his camera and jumped out of the car before Kate could open her door.

"Mom, this is awesome!" Sam snapped picture after picture with the Fisher-Price camera Kate had bought him the Christmas before. Kate was using her old Olympus OM-1, her first camera, given to her by her father for Christmas when she was twenty-one. There were certainly better cameras on the market, and all digital, but Kate didn't care. She couldn't imagine replacing the old 35mm, familiar in her hands, like looking at the world through her very best friend.

When they got back in the car, Kate drove so slowly even her father couldn't complain. She wanted to suck in every square inch of scenery, truly a work of art, a work produced by nature. Mr. Marino put his hand across his forehead, shielding his vision, searching for animals. Even before they entered Yellowstone, elk grazed on the side of the road, as did mule deer. Sam's face was plastered to his window.

Once in the park, Mr. Marino sifted through the stack of maps and brochures that would guide them on their journey through the geological wonders. Kate didn't know who screamed louder when they spotted a herd of buffalo on the right side of the road. Sam and Mr. Marino both wanted to get out of the car and see how close they could get to what appeared to be docile creatures. Kate argued that it was too dangerous, waving the leaflet with the not-so-comical drawing of a man flying through the air as an angry bison gave him a head butt. Sam backed down, but Kate was surprised by her ever-so-cautious father's insistence on getting out of the car.

"You stay in the car, Sam. I'll take your camera and get you a close-up."

Kate was flabbergasted by his immature behavior but held her tongue, not wanting to scare Sam. She watched as the massive animal lifted its head and looked at Joseph Marino as he snickered and said, "Say cheese." The animal snorted in disgust and lowered its horns, ready to charge. Joseph ran for the protection of the car. Kate had had the foresight to keep the motor running.

There were many more stops along the way. The Marinos learned that a line of cars pulled off on the side of the road meant there was wildlife close by. After five elk sightings, a coyote running across a ravine, and several bison herds resting casually in the pines, Kate decided she had to be the party pooper.

"The dining room stops serving at eight at the lodge. If anybody wants dinner, we'll have to hurry. The wild kingdom will have to wait until morning."

"Ah, mom," Sam pouted, then rubbed his eyes, clearly exhausted.

"We have all day tomorrow and Sunday to explore the park. And how about that geyser! If we stop we'll miss seeing it before it gets dark."

"Your mother is right, Sam. You don't want to miss Old Faithful, and we certainly don't want to drive in the dark."

Kate was shocked that her father was actually agreeing with her, even though it was in a roundabout way. Safety, whatever, she was ready for a hot shower and a cold martini.

The Old Faithful Inn, with gigantic pine beams lining the walls and a towering stone fireplace snaking its way five stories up, was a sight to see. The lodge was crawling with tourists. They stood in line to check in, Kate with her designer suitcase in a sea of families with nothing but backpacks. She was glad she had decided to leave her fur vest at home.

"The geyser goes off next at seven twelve, plus or minus seventeen minutes," Sam read on the sign next to the reception desk.

"We should be in our room by then, and I requested a view

that looks right at Old Faithful. If we hurry we'll see it go off right from our window!" Kate felt a little guilty about the room situation for her father. He was stuck in a small single staring at an exterior wall of the hotel, and she and Sam were in a large suite. It wasn't like she'd purposely planned it that way; those were the only two rooms available for that night. She rationalized that they would all be together in a two-bedroom suite the next night in Mammoth Springs, and they had connecting rooms the last night at the Jackson Lake Lodge. It was just this first night she felt bad about. They received their room keys and agreed to meet in Kate's room to watch the geyser and then go down to dinner.

At twelve minutes after seven, Mr. Marino, Sam, and Kate watched Old Faithful, water bouncing up and down at first, then finally exploding, shooting like liquid fireworks three hundred feet up into the sky. Mr. Marino forgot to complain, Kate forgot about her martini, and Sam forgot how tired he was.

THE FOLLOWING DAYS WERE SPENT chasing down everything Yellowstone National Park had to offer. They saw waterfalls, boiling mud pots, petrified trees, and wildlife moving freely in their own habitat. Sam took so many pictures, he ran out of the ten rolls of film Kate had brought. Finally she gave him the camera without film, figuring he'd never know the difference.

Kate gave up washing her hair every morning. The brisk winds and intermittent rain made it impossible to keep it from frizzing. The ponytail was the updo of the weekend, and she wore the same pair of jeans three days in a row. Unpacking and repacking every day was too much of a pain. Sam didn't care about how she looked, and neither did her father. For Kate, that was a vacation in itself.

The Yellowstone Loop took the full weekend. By Sunday, Kate was almost sad that she had to take her father to the airport in the morning before she and Sam headed to the dude ranch. They had seen every animal in the park other than a wolf. And Joseph Marino had been kind and patient, two words Kate normally didn't associate with her father.

Their last night was spent at the Jackson Lake Lodge in Grand Teton National Park. Their adjoining rooms were nicely appointed with log furniture and spectacular views of the lake. At twilight, the three of them stood on Mr. Marino's balcony, waiting to see if they could spot a moose. They were told they migrated closer to the hotel in the evening to feed off the willows.

"Look!" Mr. Marino whispered and pointed as he handed Sam his binoculars. "Now, be very still or you'll scare the animal away."

Sam shook his head up and down and put the binoculars up to his eyes. He had learned much about wildlife and nature from his grandpa in the past three days. His eyes found what his grandfather had already seen: a large, long-legged creature ambling in the dark, gingerly nibbling willow branches as it moved toward them. Behind it followed a smaller version.

"It has a baby!" Sam whispered, handing the binoculars back to his grandfather.

"Must be a cow and its calf," Mr. Marino said, refocusing the lenses, finding the second moose. He offered the binoculars to his daughter.

Kate took them from him, inhaling the sage-scented air. At last, a vacation with her father she could fondly remember.

Jake

ALTHOUGH JAKE ENJOYED MEETING the various guests that visited the ranch, horses were his preference for company. Generally, he found them to be more honest and dependable than people, and usually smarter, too. A horse knew how to communicate when sometimes a person did not. Horses let you know just how they felt—scared, angry, hurt, or happy—by just a twitch of an ear. And Jake knew how to talk back and counter those feelings with a stroke of the hand and a soft or stern voice. When he rode, he became part of the horse, a relationship based on mutual respect, one that he didn't find among most people.

Most women found Jake attractive, very attractive indeed. He was handsome underneath his battered black cowboy hat, with surprisingly fair skin that burned easily in the summer sun. The ladies often commented on his tall, solid, muscular build. They imagined him racing up on his trusty steed and saving them from whatever scared them.

Jake woke at dawn, a good half hour before the other wranglers at the Prickly Pear Guest Ranch. Six of them slept in the large, dust-covered room located above the barn. There was another room adjacent to the bunk room that housed a big-screen TV, two ripped-up recliners, and a vinyl couch. The trash can in the middle of the floor overflowed with beer cans from the night before.

He fumbled in the dark room, trying to locate his can of chew. As soon as a dip was secured, he rolled out of bed, pulled on his jeans, and grabbed a clean shirt. He carried his muddy boots and spurs quietly downstairs, not wanting to wake the other hands. The tack room was at the bottom of the stairs. He made his way over to the long oak bench and sat down. Before he pulled on his boots he paused, inhaling deeply, loving the smell of leather, saddle soap, and musty horse blankets.

Outside, the first beams of sunlight bounced off the dew-coated trees, grass, and outbuildings that surrounded the ranch. It looked as though everything were coated in tiny drops of diamonds, as if nature were showing off. Other than dusk, this was Jake's favorite time of day, when all was quiet, before he and the other cowboys wrangled the horses and the speed of the day caught up with him. After he put on his chaps, he walked toward the main lodge. His spurs clanked and jingled as they came in contact with the wood plank walk. Out of the corner of his eye, he caught a rosy light glowing behind the drapes of one of the guest cabins. He thought it might be the pretty lady who had checked in with her son from St. Louis the day before. Jake had noticed how feminine she was, so sweet to look at. The way she moved was slow and deliberate, not chopped and rushed like the other women at the ranch.

"No way I have a chance with that," he muttered to himself.

She was fine, so beautiful, and looked smart, too. He imagined what it would be like to go out on a real date with someone like her. A moment of wistful longing shot through him. Then he laughed, knowing his place.

The main lodge was humming with conversation. Most of the

guests were already seated, plates piled high with eggs, pancakes, and breakfast meats. Jake walked over to the breakfast buffet, poured himself a cup of coffee, and grabbed a slice of bacon. He heard Vern, the ranch cook, humming behind the saloon-type doors that separated the dining room from the kitchen. Jake ducked behind the doors.

"Mornin'," Jake said, walking towards the griddle. A vintage radio, wedged in between the canned goods on the shelf above the old stove, was tuned in to a classic country-western music station.

"Mornin', Jake. How about some breakfast?" Vern flipped flapjacks and fried bacon faster than a short-order cook.

"No, thanks." Jake's stomach was always sour first thing in the morning. The only thing he could tolerate before ten o'clock was chew and coffee.

"Suit yourself. Looks like it's gonna be a fine day. News said it should reach almost eighty."

"Perfect ridin' weather!" Jake smiled, thinking it might just be the day to skip rolling up all those silly rain slickers. He hated taking them off the saddles, shaking them out, making sure they were dry from the day before, then refolding them, only to retie them on to the back of every guest's saddle.

Jake liked hanging out in the kitchen watching Vern go about his business. Vern made it look so easy, although Jake knew it was not. He had never warmed to the idea of cooking, not that he had had much of an opportunity to learn. There were times in his life when all he and his mother ate were peanut butter and crackers, both stolen from the neighbor's cupboard. That was when his mom drank pretty much all the time, when he was too young to work. But there wasn't much chance he'd go hungry now; there were always fresh-baked cookies cooling in the kitchen and mesquite-grilled steaks for dinner, courtesy of the Prickly Pear Ranch.

"I suppose I ought to head towards the corral. Old Earl will be lookin' for me."

"Sure as the sun rises, he will. Sure you don't want something to eat?" Vern didn't miss a beat, continuing flipping his flapjacks and stacking them on the plate at his side.

"No, thanks, pard."

Jake intended to go directly to the barn but instead did a U-turn right back into the dining room. On impulse, he grabbed another Styrofoam cup and filled it with coffee. He carefully placed a white plastic sip lid on top and headed to the front door of the main lodge. The screen door slammed behind him.

The pretty lady from St. Louis and her son were staying in cabin number three. The light was on, the sun just breaking through the trees on the hill behind it. Jake, hot coffee in hand, walked toward her porch, nervous as a young buck in rut. He had no idea what possessed him. He'd never done anything like this before. She was a paying guest, and it was not in his job description to deliver coffee to her cabin. The front door opened on the second round of knocks.

"Mornin'," he said. "Didn't see you two at breakfast. Thought you might like a cup of coffee." Jake held out the hot Styrofoam cup.

"You're a lifesaver! I didn't know the ranch offered room service!" She took the cup from him, clearly overjoyed with his simple gesture.

"Only for pretty ladies stranded with sleeping sons." Jake was relieved his tongue had untied itself long enough to speak.

"Well, it just so happens, ole sleepyhead just rolled out of bed."

Sam, still foggy from sleep, staggered into the room. He cautiously walked up behind Kate and poked his head around the back of her leg.

"Howdy, pardner!" Jake said with a smile as wide as Wyoming.

He'd always gotten on well with the little folk. "You gonna ride some wild broncs today?"

Sam inched toward Jake, then rewarded him with a grin and a nod yes.

Jake squatted down. "I'm Jake. Pleased to make your acquaintance."

"I'm Sam," he said meekly, sticking close to his mama, like a newborn lamb. His mother put her left arm around his slight shoulders and extended her other toward Jake.

"I'm Kate Marino."

"Well, howdy, Ms. Marino." Jake gently squeezed her soft, petite fingers.

"Please, call me Kate! And again, thank you so much for the coffee."

"It's my pleasure." Jake thought she looked so sexy, all soft and warm, in red long johns, her hair slightly tousled. As if reading his mind, Kate put her hand up to her chest, clearly embarrassed. Jake thought it made her look all the more attractive. "Are you planning on goin' on the morning ride?"

"I am. And Sam's going to join the other kids for their riding lessons." She giggled and looked back at Sam. "But I think we'd better put on something more appropriate, don't you think?"

"Oh, I don't know, I think you look pretty good to me!" Jake paused, then blurted out, "I could help you! No different than outfittin' a horse!"

Laughter poured out of Kate, bubbling like a creek in the spring. Jake thought he'd never heard anything so beautiful. Kate steered him toward the door.

"You need to go, and we need to get dressed. If we don't hurry, we're going to miss the ride!" She gently pulled the screen door closed after him.

Jake took his time walking to the barn; a tingle of excitement intermingled with fear tickled his center and sank into his soul. There was very little that scared Jake, and even less that excited him. He felt like he had done and seen it all. In fact, for excitement he defied fear. Every Saturday he'd rodeo, hoping he would pull one of the never-been-ridden bulls. Jake had begun riding bulls and broncs in his early teens, needing the quick but intense rush. He realized that was how it had felt when he was talking to Kate—pumped up, as if he were about to mount one of those unrideable bulls.

For a minute he thought about calling his mother. He had sent her that hundred dollars. It was all he could scrape together after he paid his last debts. Lately, she hadn't been drinking as much. Jake thought it was because she had a new boyfriend. She was always more settled when there was a man in the house. He was surprised this one was still around. His mom usually went through men like most people went through underwear. Jake decided not to call her after all, not wanting to ruin a perfectly good day.

Jake eyed Earl as he rounded the corner of the barn. Earl was the head wrangler. Jake got a kick out of him. Earl got his kicks out of teasing all the other wranglers. Jake mostly stood back and watched. The close quarters at the ranch created a sort of family atmosphere. And Earl had appropriately adopted the role of big brother, being a quarter of a century older than most of the hands.

"Already sniffin' up that gal's skirt?" Earl snickered, and spat a wad of thick brown mucus in the dirt.

"Oh, you just simmer down. I just brought her a cup of coffee," Jake said.

"Bet you'd like to bring her more than that!"

Jake walked toward Earl, shaking a lead rope as if it were a noose. "You better watch out there, pard, or you'll find yourself in that there horse trough." Jake smiled as Earl backed away. Earl was 145 pounds to Jake's 190, and his slight but strong five-foot-eight frame was no match for Jake's towering height of just over six-foot-three.

"Okay, okay, why don't you just head on over to that there corral and start saddling those horses. And while you're at it, why don't you get Vandi ready for your new friend."

Jake chuckled. It appeared Earl wasn't in the mood to get wet. It was just the shot of confidence Jake needed that morning.

He made his way over to the corral, unlatched the heavy metal gate, and peered over the sea of horses, looking for the delicate sorrel. Vandi was one of the ranch's better mounts, well bred, fine confirmation, and a sweet disposition. He spotted the mare huddled in the far corner against the big bay named Bodi. Once Vandi saw Jake, she moved slowly toward him, head lowered, ready for the bridle. She took the bit easily.

He thought about Kate. There was no doubt he was drawn to her. It made no sense. But then again, nothing in life made much sense to him. These days he was just doing his best to set himself straight, trying hard not to follow in his mother's footsteps, getting to know himself—his possibilities and his limitations.

The herd whined in chorus, letting the wranglers know they were ready for their morning grain. After saddling Vandi, Jake helped Tom gather and feed the rest of the horses. It was Tom's first summer working at the Prickly Pear too. They hadn't had the time to get to know one another, although Jake guessed by the end of the season they'd know each other quite well.

Cecil was Jake's best friend and probably only real friend.

They'd gone to grade school and high school together back in Washington. They had left Spokane a few months ago, and had driven to Wyoming together in Cecil's lime-green Monte Carlo. Cecil claimed he needed a change of scenery. Jake figured what he really needed was to get out of town. Jake didn't have any use for drugs, but evidently Cecil did. He was pretty certain Cecil was wrapped up in some seriously illegal transactions. At this point, Cecil was hiding out at the ski resort in Jackson, working on the trail maintenance crew, not sharing what Cecil called Jake's pursuit of the great cowboy dream.

Jake circled the corral, checking the cinch straps. He spied Kate gliding toward him, wearing a pair of faded Levi's, well-worn cowboy boots, a denim shirt, and a fancy Western belt. Her dark hair, tied loose at the neck, shimmered a burnished gold in the bright summer sun. He untied Vandi and led the mare to Kate, feeling oddly nervous.

"What a beautiful animal!" She slid her hand down the mare's neck and whispered, "You're a pretty girl, aren't you?"

"She's a looker, all right, just got her. One of the few horses here with papers," Jake said, trying to sound professional.

"We're going to be good friends, right, Vandi girl?" Kate cooed.

Jake watched her walk around the horse, squeezing her fingers between the girth and Vandi's belly, checking to make sure it was tight before she swung her leg up onto the saddle. He was impressed. Kate was no dude; she appeared to know her way around the ponies. Besides mounting correctly, he also noticed how she had rubbed the animal's rump as she walked around its rear end. Most folks didn't know a horse spooked because it had limited vision. All it took was a reassuring touch to let the animal know what was going on in the areas he could not see.

"You must ride a lot." Jake opened her saddlebag, making sure she had a sack lunch.

"Used to," Kate said as she slid her camera in the saddlebag. She then gave Vandi a light kick, expertly neck-reining the animal toward the group.

Every day, dudes snaked behind Jake as he led them along trails, through cathedral-like branches of lodgepole pines and out into the open meadows blushing with early summer flowers. Today, Earl had asked Jake to bring up the rear. Jake guessed Earl was trying to help him out. A wrangler in back could sort of take it easy, and if they wanted to, they could take that opportunity to start up a conversation with the guests. Jake caught up to the group. He was glad Kate had positioned herself at the end of the line.

"Is it okay that I hold her back? I hate doing the tail-to-nose thing," Kate said, not looking back.

"No problem. Some of the horses like being close, but I don't think Vandi will mind." Jake was enjoying the view, and it wasn't the Tetons in the distance.

"Can I trot?"

"We normally don't let guests do that. But you seem to know what you're doin'. Just don't let her run up the hills. They get pretty steep, and she'll get winded."

They rode awhile in silence, the rocking in the saddle having a hypnotic effect.

Jake had observed guests come and go, circling the summer season like a revolving door. Folks arrived at the Prickly Pear eager to experience ranch life. After a week, most left having enjoyed their vacation, but knowing it certainly wasn't their vocation. Stiff limbs, precarious weather, slow nights, and sleep interrupted by howling wolves wasn't their cup of tea.

Even some of the hired hands lasted only a few weeks. A job at the ranch entailed long hours in the saddle, a steady diet of fixing fences and clearing trails, and a cot in a dingy room, bunking with men you didn't really know. A good hand got room and board, seven hundred dollars a month, and a day off every two weeks—and that's if they were lucky. Jake had been lucky and got a day off last month, and he took the opportunity to go to Jackson Hole and see Cecil. He spent almost his entire paycheck that day, went to the Tack Shop and bought a bridle and a bit he'd been eyeing. Jake didn't own his own horse, but he was optimistic. The rest of his fun tokens were blown at the Cadillac Steak House and the Million Dollar Cowboy Bar, buying dinner for Cecil and rounds of drinks for people he didn't even know. But it made him feel good. And he did save that hundred dollars for his mother.

Kate broke the silence. "God, I miss this. My family has a farm back in Missouri. I grew up with horses, haven't ridden in years. My first horse was a little palomino named Goldie. In the summer I would ride down to the creek at our farm, bareback in my swimsuit . . ."

Jake didn't hear the rest of her sentence. His thoughts were too tied up in imagining her perfectly proportioned hourglass body nearly naked.

"Have you ever been swimming on a horse?" she interrupted.

"You bet. They paddle like dogs," he said, still trying to hold on to the vision of Kate in her bathing suit—or lack thereof.

"I think Goldie loved it as much as I did. I would just hold on to her mane and float right along with her."

Jake listened. Her words floated through the air like wind chimes. She spoke of her summers at the farm, the other horses her family shared: Tres, a petite quarter horse her mom had ridden; her sister's horse, Couchon (she told him that was French for "pig"); and a big, old American Saddlebred gelding called Jeff. It all sounded so perfect, right out of a storybook. Yet Jake sensed a sadness in Kate; he read it in her like he read it in a horse.

"I got Jeff when Goldie died. He was a horse for the mounted police, and his hooves had grown too soft to be ridden on the pavement. Boy, he hated men. When my dad opened his stall door, Jeff would back into the corner, ears flat back and snorting."

"Probably mistreated," Jake replied knowingly.

"He loved me, though. I was the only one that could ride him." She said it proudly, not as if she had taken pride in conquering the gelding, but proud that she had quieted him and gained his trust.

Kate talked to him on and off for the duration of the ride, never looking back, head forward as if she was scanning the open range for something long forgotten. Jake found out that her dad owned a car dealership, and from what he gathered, a very successful one. She had gone to private schools and traveled to places he'd only read about in magazines.

At noon they stopped for lunch, in a shady spot under the cottonwoods. Jake was kept busy hobbling the horses and making sure the guests had everything they needed. Kate walked around and took a few pictures before she settled on a rock next to the water to eat her sandwich. She chatted with a couple from California. They had a son the same age as Sam, in the kids' program at the ranch. After lunch, back in the saddle, Kate settled comfortably once again at the end of the line.

"So, tell me more about your farm. It sounds like a real nice place," Jake said as he rode up beside her.

"Well, it's very green in the spring and summer, a lot of trees and rolling hills. But I think fall is my favorite time of the year.

The leaves start changing colors, the temperature drops. Sweater weather, I always say."

"Fall is my favorite time of the year, too. We've got aspens back home, just like here in Wyoming. In early September their leaves turn yellow. When the wind blows it looks like the hillsides have been sprinkled with gold."

Kate did not comment. The pain he sensed earlier had returned, hanging heavily between them.

"You okay?" His hat sat just above his brow. He cocked his head so he could get a better look at her.

"Oh, I'm fine. I was just thinking about our farm. It's such a beautiful piece of property. It's a shame there's so much sadness and pain tied up in it."

Ordinarily this was where Jake would shut up or change the subject, not wanting to get involved in a stranger's private affairs. But Kate was different, and something inside him pushed forward.

"You feel like talking about it?" He spoke softly, as if trying to gentle a nervous horse.

"I had an older brother. His name was Anthony. He was killed in a minibike accident. It happened at our farm. I don't know much about how it happened. All I know is that he and my cousin were riding down the gravel road. Anthony was riding ahead, probably going too fast and not paying attention. He must have hit a pothole or something and was thrown off the bike. My cousin found him lying on the side of the road unconscious. He died on the way to the hospital."

"Gosh, I'm so sorry, Ms. Marino," Jake said, wishing he had something more comforting to say.

"Please, call me Kate. And it's okay; it was a long time ago. I was just a baby when it happened. I don't remember anything.

But the farm hasn't brought joy to our family since the accident. Even when we had the horses there, I could see how hard it was for my mom to drive me out there on the weekends for me to ride. When I went off to college, no one would go there to feed or water them. My dad finally found a caretaker."

"I take it your father doesn't like going there."

"It's really weird. He actually goes there all the time. We used to go there every weekend with him when we were kids. It's only a half an hour's drive from the dealership. There are days when he disappears for a few hours, no one knowing where he's gone. But I know. He's at the farm. I think the memories, good and bad, must keep Anthony alive for him."

And Sam keeps him alive, too. But Kate kept this thought to herself.

"So, what happened to your horses?" Jake asked.

"We finally sold them. It just wasn't fair for them to sit there most of the year while I was at school. Even though I stayed in St. Louis for my first three years, I suppose you could say I got distracted with my social life." She turned to Jake and smiled.

"Oh, I see, your interest in four-legged critters was replaced with the two-legged variety?" Jake laughed.

"I guess you could say that. But I used to test anybody I was thinking about dating by taking them to the farm. It was easy to tell if they liked the country. If they didn't, that was the end of that!"

"Sounds like a good test!"

"I thought so. And then, my senior year, I finally escaped from the city, and I fell in love with the mountains."

"Is that so?" Jake chuckled. "Where did you escape to?"

"Fort Collins, Colorado. I went to Colorado State for one glorious year." Kate's face lit up like a Christmas tree. "Enough about me. Where are you from?"

"I'm originally from Washington."

"DC?" Kate asked, clearly confused.

"No, no, the state of, the West Coast!" Jake cried, causing a few riders to turn around to see what was going on. He smiled, waved, then added, "I could never live in a big noisy city, especially one infested with a bunch of lyin', cheatin' politicians."

"Okay, so if you didn't grow up in DC, or a big city, where did you grow up?"

"I'm still not so sure I've grown up," Jake joked.

"Well, at least you're honest! And I'm beginning to think that most men don't. But really, tell me about where you're from."

Kate appeared to be interested, so Jake found himself rambling on and on, describing the countryside he grew up in.

"It's good country to cowboy in," he finally ended, thinking he'd talked too long and had probably made a total fool of himself.

"Have you always been a cowboy?" she asked, as if he were a god.

"Not always." Jake said it quietly. He remembered the days when he stayed home and took care of his mother. He shoved the thoughts aside, back in that space where he filed things best forgotten, and added, "I'd like to hire on to a real working outfit."

He felt himself relax as he thought of chasing cows, branding and calving, watching clouds float by like ghosts in a sky bound only by fence and horizon.

"I think that sounds wonderful," Kate said.

"Not a lot of money in cowboyin' for a living." Jake countered quickly.

"Who cares! Like my mom said, 'Do what you love for a living and never work another day in your life.'" Kate said.

"Something tells me I'd like your mom."

"I'm sure you would. She's pretty cool." Kate's voice drifted.

The ranch came into focus as the group headed down the steep embankment just north of the barn. The horses got jiggy, knowing that feed and open pasture were only a short trot or gallop away. The riders filed into the corral like soldiers, most dismounting with some difficulty. Kate didn't seem too much the worse for wear, dropping out of the saddle as if she were born to it. She gathered her things out of her saddlebag and ran off in the direction of the recreation center in search of Sam.

The wranglers all pitched in, eager to end their day as well. Horses were unsaddled, brushed down, and given buckets of grain. It was about an hour-long process, and Jake was one of the few that really enjoyed it, knowing that when they were finished, it would be time to wrangle. It was Jake's job to make sure the herd made it through the ranch, around the giant U-shaped yard to the gates on the far side of the property, across the two-lane highway, and into the fenced-in pasture. It was an impressive sight, fifty head of horses running and bucking, Jake in the saddle, rope swinging in the air, guiding them to their freedom. Guests would gather on their porches every night to catch the show.

When Jake got back, he went to the barn to make himself a drink before dinner. He allowed himself only one, for medicinal purposes. There was nothing like a little whiskey after a long day in the saddle fielding questions like, "What kind of flower is that?" Although today was not an ordinary day; his body needed to release a different sort of tension. He poured himself a double shot of Jack Daniels and made the trek to the main lodge to top it off with some lemonade. After he mixed his drink, he headed to the corral.

Jake hooked the right heel of his boot on the bottom rail of the fence, scanning the hillside, waiting for the moon to peek out above the feathery pines. A screen door slammed in the distance, causing Jake to jump and turn around.

"Hi there!" Kate called out and waved.

He quickly looked over his shoulder, making sure she was really waving at him. Not seeing anyone else in sight, he waved back and shouted, "Howdy!"

"You know, I've been so rude. I forgot to thank you for the wonderful ride!"

Jake bent at the waist, removed his hat, and swept it down in a grand gesture. He stood back up hatless, revealing perfectly chiseled features: a face that belonged on a gentleman, a man of breeding.

"It was my pleasure, ma'am." A circle of sweat plastered his cropped blond hair to his head.

"Well, how about a beer? It's the least I could do!" She held out a Bud Light.

"Oh, I already got me some firewater." His words were deliciously slow, like honey dripping from a spoon.

"Pardon me?"

"Lynchburg Lemonde. Jack Daniels and lemonade." He held up his plastic 7-Eleven cup. "Gotta disguise it. We're not supposed to be drinking on the property."

"I see," she said, and then added mischievously, "You're old enough to drink, aren't you?"

"Are you?" he removed his heel from the fence, standing tall in his cowboy boots.

"Flattery gets you everywhere, and yes, I am north of twenty-one." Kate paused. "So how old are you?"

"Old enough." He looked her square in the eye.

Kate stared right back.

Jake could have sworn he saw *I dare you* in those dark, gold-flecked eyes that seemed to hold so much.

First Rodeo

JAKE KEPT A CLOSE EYE ON SAM, who was riding Dancer, a gentle old gelding. Sam followed Kate, who was on her favorite horse, Vandi. Sam seemed comfortable, almost fearless. Most young riders were that way. Later, Jake would warn Sam that horses could change directions like the wind—something as silly as a piece of paper on the trail could spook a horse, and just like that you're off to the races. But he'd wait. Kate was tickled pink that Sam had learned enough that week to go out with the group ride. She turned around to look at Jake, a syrupy smile glued across her face.

He rode up next to her, untied the lariat from his saddle, and pulled at the loop on the end. Kate watched him as if in a trance. He began swinging the lasso in a continuous circle to his right. Finally his rope found the object of his intention, landing around a large bunch of balsamroot, bright yellow daisies that resembled sunflowers. Jake yanked on the rope, lifting the wildflowers from the soft brown earth, and pulled them to his hand. He then loosened the noose and carefully shook the clumps of dirt from the bottom. Kate almost fell out of her saddle when Jake gallantly removed his hat and presented her with the flowers.

Kate put the bouquet up to her nose, smelling the sweet scent of romance. As she exhaled, she watched Sam pull back Dancer almost to a stop, wait a minute, then kick the poor horse in the ribs, urging him into a trot to catch up with group.

"Attaboy!" Jake laughed and looked at Kate. "Where do you think he learned that?"

Before Kate could answer, Sam blurted out, "I watched you, Mom!"

"I'm thinking you like to ride," Kate said.

"I do! Can we ride when we get back home?"

"I'll see if I can make that happen." Kate pictured the empty barn at the farm and thought how wonderful it would be to have it filled with animals again. But she was smart enough to know that horses needed a big commitment, time-wise and financially. Once they got back home, there would be more lessons. Sam would have to stick with it and prove to her that he was really interested before she'd go horse shopping.

"Keep it to a walk for a minute!" Kate yelled out to Sam, who was trotting ahead again. She wanted to capture the moment on film.

"Okay," Sam said without looking back.

Kate gently tucked the stems of the flowers behind the saddle horn, then bent over and removed the Olympus from the saddlebag. After removing the lens cap, she checked the light meter. The sun was behind them. "Perfect," Kate said under her breath. She steered Vandi closer to Sam.

"Hey, Sam!" Kate called out.

Sam turned his head, and Kate started shooting. Adrenaline pumped through her body as she forwarded the film, keeping him in focus as he rode Dancer next to her. Sam wore an impish grin. He looked like a little boy right out of an old-time Western, his cowboy hat pushed back on his forehead, his dark hair peeking out from beneath it. Kate smiled, feeling the weight of the camera in her small hand. It felt good, so damn good, to be taking pictures again.

Jake rode ahead, now leading the group. Kate turned her attention to the riders that followed. Jake sat straight up in the saddle, their fearless leader, pointing ahead at the Tetons in the distance. The long line of riders, dressed in a rainbow of colors, looked like a Chinese dragon in a parade. Kate took picture after picture. Through the camera lens she saw nothing but beauty.

Once back at the corrals, Kate photographed close-ups of chaps, spurs, and boots. At the barn everything fascinated her, even the halters, combs, and fly spray. And something about the intricate tooled leather on the dusty Western saddles still drew her like a magnet. She was reminded once again of the photo that hung in her office.

Thank God for Paul Freeman, Kate said to herself. He was the brother of one of her dear friends in high school. Paul was a few years older, a college boy when she was a junior. Kate always liked him; he was creative when most young men thought it was "gay" to be artsy. But Paul didn't care. He studied photography and became a professional photographer. After Kate got her camera for Christmas, she asked him if she could follow him around to his photo shoots.

"The key is to go through as much film as you can. You can take three hundred shots and only a handful might turn out to be something really special," Paul said.

Kate always remembered that. Paul had also taken her into his darkroom and showed her where the real work began. There were so many tricks: dodging and blocking made things darker or lighter, using sepia tone gave the image an old-time feel—so many ways to manipulate the image even after the picture was taken.

"Kate, can Sam help us brush and feed the horses?" Jake broke her photography trance.

"Can I, Mom, please?" Sam begged.

"Sure, but you be careful, and don't walk behind any of the horses!" Kate said, feeling a happiness she had never known. Sam, in his tiny black cowboy boots, looked like a miniature cowboy. He was stuck to Jake like gum on a shoe.

"I'm going to run back to the cabin to get my postcards. I completely forgot to mail them. You be sure to listen to Jake!" she said as she put her camera back in its case.

Kate walked across the lawn thinking about Stella. She'd go wild when she saw how pretty Wyoming was. The postcard she had bought for her had a stunning shot of the Tetons backlit with a surreal pale-pink light. Stella was the only person she knew back home who would truly appreciate the photo's beauty. Kate counted at least five cameras when she helped Stella move into her new apartment before she left for Wyoming. Kate had a feeling Stella wouldn't last long in that apartment. There wasn't even a yard. Stella, like Kate, needed space to roam.

The postcards were right where she left them, in the bedroom on the bedside table. Kate grabbed the one for Stella and one she had written to Betty, her dear friend that lived in Denver. They had met through a mutual friend at a party in St. Louis. Betty was visiting and was the guest of honor. When Kate found out Betty was from Colorado, she immediately introduced herself. The two started talking and never stopped. They hadn't seen each other for awhile. Betty understood that Colorado wasn't exactly in Kate's travel plans now that she was steering clear of Ted. So they settled for phone calls, keeping the two of them close despite the miles between them. They frequently chatted into the wee hours about everything from men to meditation.

Kate looked outside and saw that Sam was still busy helping Jake, and decided she just might have enough time to write a few lines in her journal. The journal thing was a new ritual she practiced, at the instruction of a self-help book. It claimed that writing cleared the mind and calmed the emotions; it also taught that by putting your wants and wishes on paper it presented them to the universe. The universe would then bring those wishes—or affirmations, as they called them—into your life. The problem was, she didn't know what she wanted. What she did know was that she did not want to be a car dealer anymore, and that her father was a problem. At her father's direction she had already managed to marry a nice man, but the wrong man for her. She was also in a career that she pretty much hated, again her father's idea—he liked to sell and fix cars; she did not. And she was just beginning to figure out that she wasn't terribly content living in the city. Not that St. Louis was that bad, but it certainly wasn't Wyoming.

In the past, Kate had seen a therapist, with appointments as frequent as her every-other-week manicures, but they seemed to be of little help. After they worked through her family baggage, the therapist quizzed Kate about her goals and interests. It was then that Kate found herself at a loss for words, a very rare moment indeed.

Kate opened her cabin door, took the journal from her leather travel bag, and pulled a chair out onto the front porch. In that seemingly silly little spiral notebook, Kate started to hear a quiet little voice. She began to listen, letting her pencil wander freely across the page, reveling in what her heart whispered.

It was my hope to bring Sam to a place where he could learn about the things that have always been important to me—riding, hiking, the mountains, nature in general. I could not have done this alone in St. Louis. Today we rode together for the first time! I feel as though a new bond is forming. God, it's great not to have a TV on all the time!

Ranch life agrees with me. As always, the mountains around me and the simple life puts me at peace. Maybe I could work here for a month or so, see what it's like to live this life day in and day out. I often dreamed of owning a small guest ranch. I could cook, be outdoors, ride every day . . . I've been taking pictures again, of Sam, the landscape, saddles, spurs—I love everything Western! Maybe I could try to paint again, from the photographs? But could I make enough money?

And I met this tall handsome cowboy named Jake McComb. He treats me like a queen, nothing like Ted. Ted, what an asshole, it makes me sick to my stomach to think how much time I wasted with him . . .

Sam broke her reverie, running toward the cabin yelling, "Hey Mom, can I go to the rodeo with Nathan?"

"Well, I kind of thought we'd go together," she said.

"Mom!" Sam whined. "I see you all the time. It's my last night with Nathan!"

"You're right, you're right," Kate repeated, thinking it was his vacation, too. "How are you two planning on getting to the rodeo?"

"All the kids are riding in the van with the counselors."

"Okay, you can go with Nathan, but go wash up first and then we'll get some dinner before you go."

Sam bolted to the bathroom, stripped off his dirty clothes, and turned on the shower. Kate let out a sigh, half-disappointed, half-elated. Now she could accept Jake's invitation to go to the rodeo with him.

KATE WALKED FROM THE CONCESSION stand at the Jackson Hole Rodeo, a Coors Light in each hand, trying to look cool, as though she fit in. She'd never been to a rodeo, but she didn't want anybody to know it. Evidently it was a big deal. The locals and tourists were all decked out in their Western finest. Kate was glad she had worn the almost-too-tight Wranglers she had purchased at Best of the West, her coveted antique turquoise concho belt, and her custom-made, chocolate-brown, lizard-skin cowboy boots. The boots were a divorce gift from her old married self to her new single self. She scanned the sea of straw cowboy hats for Jake. Kate had been amazed when she found out that he was only twenty-three, thirteen years her junior. He certainly looked and acted older.

And now we are on a date, she said to herself, feeling as though she were living in some made-for-TV movie. Kate could not resist Jake's old-fashioned courting. The constant compliments and attention tugged at her heartstrings. Her morning coffee was now delivered in a thermos accompanied by muffins and a tiny bouquet of wildflowers. It wasn't every day that a lady got pursued by a young, handsome cowboy with a butt and abs of steel. She was afraid if she thought too much about it, she would tell herself she was crazy. Or was she?

Just enjoy, just enjoy, she told herself. It didn't really matter. She and Sam would be back home before she knew it, and life would return to normal. Why ruin the fantasy?

Jake, in his white hat, towered above the group standing near the bucking chutes. As Kate nudged her way through the crowd, she spotted Gale, a tough yet pretty wrangler who worked with Jake at the ranch, leaning close to him, as if she was telling him a secret. Gale's curvaceous figure was clad in a glitzy Western shirt and thigh-hugging, hot-pink jeans, topped off with a rodeo belt buckle the size of a dessert plate. Kate knew the buckle was a trophy. Still, it was a bad fashion statement. But she guessed Gale wanted to make sure everyone knew she was a champion barrel racer. Gale's black hat hid most of her twenty-something face. Kate tapped Jake's shoulder with the cold beer.

"Oh, thanks, hon." Jake put a possessive arm around Kate, gave her an adoring look, and then turned his back on Gale. He pressed his thigh against Kate. "Would you like to go sit down?"

Kate stood up on her tiptoes and gave Jake a quick, sweet kiss. She pulled away, surprised at her own actions. "I'm just fine, darlin'. We can stay here," Kate said, loud enough for Gale to hear. Gale slithered away, quietly fading into the crowd.

Jake guided Kate closer to an empty space along the rodeo ring. He hitched his boot on the bottom rail, then focused his attention on the action on the other side. He leaned forward and spoke almost reverently. "This is my favorite time of the day. Sun's goin' down, the day's coolin' off, the stock is all excited knowing what's to come."

To the west the sky exploded, and the wind pulled fluorescent sprays of clouds across the horizon like cotton candy. A cool breeze replaced the afternoon heat. Although there were hundreds of people around them, Jake felt as though it were the quietest place on earth.

"It just doesn't get any better than this," he said, squeezing Kate closer to his side.

He had this beautiful, sexy, smart woman wrapped in his arm, and felt like he had truly hung the moon. In some weird way, he felt as though it was his job to protect her. Jake needed to feel needed, and he'd bet his last dime that Kate really needed him. He kept that secret to himself.

Kate felt the weight of his arm on hers. As a rule, she didn't go for the possessive, protective type. But tonight she found she loved it. Jake made her feel wanted, and Kate hadn't felt wanted in a very long time. In fact, she couldn't remember the last time she felt so sexy or desirable. She didn't dare breathe, much less move a muscle. She closed her eyes. She was somewhere else. The national anthem blared from the speakers. Horses' hooves pounded the dirt. Kate leaned into Jake; an intense warmth radiated from him. Never had she felt so right, so natural, so perfectly safe. Safe from what, she did not know. All she knew was that she wanted to stay in this one moment, embraced in Jake's arms forever.

Jake grasped the rough wood fence, his face intent on the rider circling the arena with the American flag. His body, vibrating with longing and passion, was drawn forward, as if it were ready to jump the fence to be a part of the evening's events. A horse and rider blew by. He knew he belonged in that ring. What he didn't know was why he felt he was supposed to be with Kate. He could not believe that in one short week he had somehow managed to fall in love with her. He wondered if he had the guts to tell her.

They stood and watched the rodeo together, just like that, arms around each other, Jake teaching Kate what was etched in his soul. When the rodeo came to an end, they walked toward the bleachers looking for Sam. Kate saw a flash of red, and Sam in his tiny jet-black cowboy hat came running toward them.

"Hey, Mom! Can I spend the night in Nathan's cabin?" Sam gasped between breaths.

"Whoa, slow down. How did you like the rodeo?" Kate asked.

"Oh, it was great!" His eyes sparkled with excitement. "Can I spend the night with Nathan? His mom said it was okay."

"His mom probably has no idea what you two are scheming."

Kate spotted Catherine, Nathan's mother, heading their way, and waved. The wind had blown Catherine's waist-length hair into a mass of knots. Kate could tell she didn't really care what she looked like. Her slight frame was draped in a faded fleece, shorts, and well-worn Birkenstocks. She was a little too earthy for Kate, but her clear blue eyes were gentle and kind.

"I hear the boys have planned an overnight in our cabin," Catherine said, smiling.

"That's what Sam has told me. Is that okay with you?" Kate asked.

"Absolutely."

Catherine and Kate watched the boys kick dust at each other.

"Looks like they've struck up quite a friendship," Kate said.

"Yes, they have." Nathan's mom laughed. "We'll have to exchange addresses so they can keep in touch."

Kate interrupted the dust fight. "Are you guys riding back to the ranch in the van?"

"Yeah!" the boys chorused.

Kate gently pulled Sam aside. "Now, we're leaving in the morning, so come right over when you wake up so we can pack."

"Okay, Mom." Sam gave Kate a hug and ran back over to Nathan.

"I'll be sure they get some sleep. If there's any problem, I know where to find you." Their cabins were conveniently located next door to one another. "You two have fun." Catherine winked and said good-bye.

"Alone at last," Jake said, steering her to the exit.

"For the moment." Kate giggled.

JAKE SUGGESTED THEY TAKE THE SCENIC route back through Teton Park. Silver beams of the full moon danced on the ripples of the Snake River. The scent of pine and sage lightly tickled the air. Jake fiddled with the radio.

"Listen," Jake whispered as he rolled down the rental car's window. Kate slid closer to him. His lips brushed hers with a feathery kiss. "You like Beethoven?" he asked.

Moonlight Sonata floated from the radio, its melody blending perfectly with the sound of the distant rushing water.

"I love Beethoven." Kate was shocked. "This is one of my favorites. Do you like classical music?"

"I do. Bet that surprises you." He chuckled, enjoying Kate's reaction. "There is a lot you don't know about me, Kate Marino." He stopped laughing and took a few breaths before he continued. "That's why I love being with you. I love that you love this music, that you like to go out to fancy dinners, drink wine, and see plays. You're not like most girls around here. All they want to do is get married, have kids, and settle down."

"Don't you want to get married and have kids?"

"I don't think it would suit me. I want to work a big ranch, I want to travel; there is so much country I want to see. I want to train horses and rodeo . . ." His voice trailed off.

"Well, I think that's wonderful, Jake. But you're only twenty-three. Down the road, you might change your mind."

"I don't think so." Jake was sure he never wanted to be fenced in or tied down with kids. Maybe marriage would be okay, but never kids. His mother's pained face flashed before him. He let the rushing river drown out the unhappiness.

"Kate, I know you think I should be with someone closer to my own age."

Kate saw little point to this conversation. She was leaving in less than twelve hours and didn't want to ruin the moment. "Jake, let's not talk about it." She snuggled closer, finding herself wanting more than a kiss. Jake took her face in his hands and turned it so she could not miss the determination in his eyes.

"I got something to say to you."

"I'm listening." She looked into his soulful green eyes hooded by pale lashes. They told her he wasn't quite as tough as he seemed.

"I saw how you looked at Gale talking to me. I don't want to be with her, or any other woman, for that matter." He paused, picking his words carefully. "I want to be with you. You are the sexiest, prettiest, smartest woman I've ever known."

Kate kept silent and let his words sink in.

"I love you," Jake whispered.

A lump formed at the base of her throat, obstructing any speech, tears threatened. No one had ever said anything so sincere, so sweet, so totally raw and open. If she could pick a storybook romance, a perfect landscape with the perfect partner, she imagined it would be in Wyoming with Jake. But it was impossible. So why was it that every bone in her body wanted to walk right into the love Jake so clearly represented? She just didn't know how to get there. Jake grabbed her hand as if showing her the way.

"I really don't know what to say," Kate managed to choke out. "I'm flattered, of course. Jake, you are a wonderful, beautiful man." She could not deny that deep down she had developed some pretty strong feelings for him.

"I know this is kind of fast. I understand. I just needed to tell you before you left."

They sat there listening to the river and watching the moonlight bounce off the water for what seemed like an eternity. A sigh escaped from the depths of destiny.

Kate kept her seat next to him as they drove the dark park road back to the ranch. As they got closer, she felt a tug of war. His words were so strong they had broken a barrier in her heart, and now she wanted him so badly she ached for him. But her head screamed, *He lives in Wyoming, he's a cowboy, and he is thirteen years younger than you!*

Jake parked the car in front of Kate's cabin and walked around to open her door.

"I've been waiting a long time to do this." He bent over and kissed her. Kate was lost in the warmth of his circling tongue. Her body responded to his immediately. He stopped at just the right moment and glanced up at the star-studded sky.

"It's incredible, isn't it?" he said, rubbing her back. Then he gazed down with the love he could no longer hide.

"It is." Her heart raced. "Would you like to come in?"

"We don't have to do anything, you know." Jake said.

"I know. The problem is, I want to." She found his hand and led him up the stairs to the cabin.

"I was hopin' you'd say that." He smiled.

Kate fumbled for the light switch and looked for something, anything, to drink. "I'm a nervous wreck."

Jake pulled her to him, stood there, and held her, letting the tension melt from her limbs.

"Are you sure about this?"

Kate was so touched by his concern that it made her want him all the more. "I'm sure," she said, all nerves forgotten.

He picked her up, carried her to the bedroom, and undressed her as if she were a fragile doll. Jake took his time caressing her, wanting to explore every inch of her body. Kate floated, pushing away all the complex emotions that swirled in her head. Finally, once Kate felt Jake's body joined with hers, all doubts and fears disappeared. His masculinity blended with her femininity like the ingredients of the most divine recipe.

"I believe God has sent me an angel," Kate said, just before falling sleep. She had never known such fearless peace.

The two didn't sleep long, both wanting to make the most of the time they had left. In the early morning light, they shared more intimacies.

"I've had this dream for a very long time," Kate said as she rested her head on Jake's chest.

"What's that?"

"I have this painting of a cabin in the woods. It's surrounded by snow and tucked back in a grove of pine trees. I used to stare at it and say, 'This is all I want.'"

"What's wrong with that?"

"It's hard to explain. My father depends on me to take over the business. If I leave for good, he has no one."

"What about your brother? You told me he works there, too."

"He does, but my father doesn't trust him like he trusts me. James likes the ponies, too, only he'd rather bet on them than ride them. My dad will never hand over the business to him."

Jake did not understand all this talk of business and money. He had little use for it. "The way I see it, everybody has the right to be happy. I've learned things go the easiest when you follow your heart."

The truth in his words struck a chord in Kate.

"And besides, wasn't it your mom who said, 'find what you love to do and don't work another day in your life'?"

Kate held on to Jake as if he had wings.

"I want to see you again," Jake cooed in her ear.

"I want to see you again, too," Kate answered, feeling the power of possibility. She knew she had just received the rarest of gifts.

Blank Canvas

KATE DREAMED MORE OFTEN NOW, as if Wyoming were trying to tell her something. It was as though her rides in the wise old mountains had a direct link to her subconscious; most of the time she dreamt she was in school. The dream dictionary, another self-help tool she had picked up at the local bookstore, told her school was a symbol for life:

> Life is school; you are here only to learn and grow. You are taught by all people and all situations. Be enthusiastic; you are going to go through it anyway. Lessons never change until you learn them, so might as well get in there and work through them now. Each night you are out of body and learn in schools on higher levels. Each level is teaching you something about the nature of self.

When she returned to St. Louis, Jake called her every day, keeping the romance well kindled. When Michael took Sam to Florida to visit his parents, Kate hopped on a plane and headed right back to the Prickly Pear Ranch. And she decided that if this was school, she wanted to be a student forever. She loved being at the ranch and she loved being with Jake.

But figuring out her inner self, the seed to her soul—now, that was another story. All she knew was she had two voices yakking away in her head, one that told her what she *should* do, and the other that kept trying to tell her what she *could* do. The could-do side was told to shut up, smothered by the rationalizations of the should-do side—you should have a "real" job, you should be a good mother, you should live in the city where there are top-notch schools, soccer parks, lacrosse teams. At the ranch, things were different. It was so quiet. The only sound Kate heard was the wind rustling through the trees and the voice of her heart.

And now Kate dialed her parents' number from the very same pay phone at the Prickly Pear that Jake had used to call her. She stared at the magical view. The Buffalo River wound through the silence of the valley below, wisps of tangerine-colored clouds stuck on a turquoise horizon. The Grand Tetons, a sculpted purple masterpiece, sat ruling, like a king on a throne.

"Now, that is a painting," she said out loud, wiping the perspiration from her forehead with a bandana. Her mother answered on the third ring.

"Hi, Mom. It's me!"

"Kate, hello! I am so glad you called. I almost didn't answer the phone because I didn't recognize the number!"

"I figured you wouldn't. No cell service out here in the Wild West. You'll be seeing this number a lot—it's the pay phone at the recreation center." Kate was feeling a wee bit homesick. It felt good to hear her mother's voice.

"How is everything going?"

"Mom, they've nicknamed me 'perma-guest'! And I have a different cabin this time, a little bigger. It sits high up on a hill above the ranch. And I swear, I can see all the way to the Tetons! And they're letting me ride Vandi again. I love that horse. I ride her every day with Jake." Kate's thoughts drifted to Sam. She hoped he was having fun at the beach. She would call him next.

"Sounds like you're having a grand time. And it sounds like you're still smitten with this young cowboy," Jenny Marino said, with undertones of concern.

"I am. Mom, he is just so good to me. How's Dad?"

"Oh, you know, same old, same old. He still complains about how business is off, he's not making much money, Mr. Doom and Gloom."

"I guess me being out here doesn't help his mood much. Is he still mad at me for leaving again?" Kate felt as though she were a child being scolded, even though her father was over a thousand miles away.

"He'll get over it." Mrs. Marino paused nervously. "He did express his concern for your financial situation, now that you're not working. I mean, it is expensive to fly back and forth, isn't it?"

"It is. But do you remember James's friend Matt? The one that works for the airline?"

"Yes, I think I do remember James talking about him."

"Well, I've done him a few favors when he's come in for service, given him some good discounts and loaned him cars to drive while his car was being repaired. Now it's his turn to help me out."

"What do you mean?"

"Matt got me a buddy pass, which means you just pay the taxes for the airfare. It only cost me ninety-five dollars to fly here!"

"That's great. I am so relieved. Your father got me thinking. You know how he is. I started worrying about you spending all of your savings, and you've worked so hard." Jenny Marino remembered when she had tried to make it on her own and failed. It was too difficult for an older woman to carve out a living when so many young people were out looking for jobs. That had ended up being the biggest reason why she had gone back to Joseph after their separation. That, and . . . old habits die hard.

"Mom, I'm fine, really. I have plenty of money, and I have a load of frequent-flyer mileage that I need to use. Plus they've given me a discount at the ranch for being a repeat guest." Kate calculated this week was going to cost her somewhere around two thousand dollars, including the rental car. Her finances were fine now, but dating Jake was definitely not cheap.

"Well, you just relax and enjoy your time with Jake. And do not worry about your father."

"Thanks, Mom. I love you."

Kate hung up, surprised and relieved she had finally been able to say the words that were so hard for her to utter. She had been angry at her mother for a long time. But the pain of the past had miraculously subsided. Living with her father was no picnic. Her mother poured her whole life into raising Kate, James, and Grace while her father worked six days a week. It wasn't really a choice; it was her job. For some people, that job would have been okay, but not for Jenny Marino. Kate was beginning to understand her mother—why she left her marriage and maybe, more importantly, why and how she came back.

During her parents' separation, Jenny Marino went back to school to earn a nursing degree. Her father ranted and raved about how ridiculous it all was. He did his best to put his wife down and get Kate and whomever else would listen to agree with him.

"She needs to have her head examined!" he would say.

Deep down, Kate never really saw things his way. Sure, she was upset with her mother for leaving, but on the flip side, she was proud that she had gone back to school. Not many women had the guts to do that at forty, or at any age, for that matter. Even when her mother moved back home, Kate had never told her mother she was proud of her. She held it back like a cruel punishment.

The sun ducked behind a cloud. A shadow draped the Tetons. Kate sat with her thoughts, letting them take shape. Her mother had to become a whole person before she could live with her father as "the other half." That nursing degree was what gave her the strength and self-esteem to come back to the marriage. Kate let out a long, heavy sigh. When she got back home, she would sit down with her mother and have a long, very overdue talk.

THERE WAS LIGHTNESS TO THE DAYS that followed. Kate had taken to helping the wranglers unsaddle the horses at the end of the rides, though she refused to roll out of bed at dawn to help with the saddling. Jake would knock on her cabin door to wake her in the morning, after sneaking in and out of her place like a thief in the night. Earl pretended not to notice Jake's absence during the wee hours—cavorting with guests was a sure way to lose your job. Jake still brought Kate breakfast to her cabin, although playful kisses were now added to the menu. There was no doubt Jake's lips stirred Kate much more than the coffee. After much fondling, Kate would jump out of bed; splash water on her face; throw on jeans, a T-shirt, and her old cowboy boots; and run out to the corrals in time to hit the trail. Her face hadn't seen blush or lipstick for weeks.

After working with the horses, Kate would be covered from head to boot in dust, hair plastered to her head, smelling of horse sweat, and Jake would just stare at her. She would shift from side to side uncomfortably, and after many torturous moments he would say, "You are soooo pretty."

THAT SUMMER, MICHAEL'S MOTHER became ill. He had to go to Florida every few weeks to care for her. He and Kate decided that a two-weeks-on, two-weeks-off schedule would allow Sam to go with him. When Sam and Michael flew south, Kate headed west to Wyoming, burning through frequent-flier miles like matches. When the freebies ran out, Matt came to the rescue with more buddy passes. Instead of staying at the Prickly Pear, which was becoming more and more unaffordable, Kate rented a cabin a mile down the road from the ranch.

The cabin ended up being perfect, more of a temporary home for the couple, and certainly more private. Kate was still able to go on rides with Jake, yet she had plenty of time to write in her journal, hike, and enjoy her newfound freedom. At the end of the day, when Jake finished his duties at the ranch, he would come to the cabin. Sometimes they would just enjoy a simple meal Kate had prepared, watch the sun go down, and wallow in their new romance. Other nights they took turns planning some sort of adventure. Kate initiated trips into Jackson Hole for an evening of fine dining at the Snake River Grille, where she'd introduce Jake to gourmet delicacies like smoked salmon with crème fraîche and seared foie gras. Afterwards, she'd produce tickets to a performance at the Main Stage Theatre or lead Jake to listen to local musicians and sip cognac. Jake drank in the experiences, developing tastes for things he'd never known existed.

In turn, Jake delighted Kate with outings to the Million Dollar Cowboy Bar, where he schooled her in the art of two-stepping to country music. There were also overnight excursions. The most memorable for Kate was when Jake took her to Turpin Meadow for a fly-fishing lesson and campfire cookout.

It was on that campout that Kate really opened up to Jake. She held a secret, something heavy and dark. That night, under the cathedral of trees and stars, she confessed to Jake as if he were a priest.

They had just finished their steak dinner. It was a perfect night—cool, no wind, and the August sky was so clear you could see the Milky Way. Kate cuddled with Jake under an old wool blanket.

"Have you ever been in love? I mean, I know you've dated and been with other women, but have you ever been really in love, before me?" Kate asked.

"I was once."

Kate was not surprised. Jake told her about Erin, his high school sweetheart. He asked her to marry him their senior year. Her family was less than thrilled about the engagement, wanting Erin to wait, at least go to college first. After graduation, Jake had gotten a job running heavy equipment, trying like hell to make enough money to prove he would make a good husband.

"What happened?" Kate asked, truly impressed with his ability to commit at such a young age.

"Erin and her parents fought like cats and dogs. Her parents wouldn't budge. They were dead set on her going away to some fancy college. She didn't want to go. She was afraid I'd find someone else."

"And?"

"As it turns out, she was the one that found someone else."

The yellow-and-orange flames jumped up and down like clowns, and the dry wood popped and cracked.

"I'm so sorry," Kate said.

"Yeah." Jake sucked in the mountain air that seemed to give him so much strength. "She went to college and I gave up rodeo. I gave up on the notion I could work on a real cow outfit to boot. I did everything I thought she wanted me to do. I was willing to settle down . . ." He paused and continued in a much lighter voice, "But that was a long time ago, a whole other rodeo."

"Sometimes giving up on yourself isn't the answer." Kate's words rolled out so fast she couldn't even remember formulating the thought before, as if someone else were speaking through her. She leaned into him, wrapping the unzipped sleeping bag around them. Somehow he had captured her missing spirit. There was a connectedness she felt with no other.

"I need to tell you something. I was pregnant once before Sam." The statement hung between them. Jake said nothing, and Kate felt no judgment pass between them. She lowered her voice and went on.

"The guy was an asshole. He was unbelievable. It was like he had a sixth sense or something, like he knew when I was just getting over him, moving on. And then he'd call or show up or something."

Jake didn't respond. He just took a deep pull off his beer. Kate continued.

"I met him through a friend at Economy Plus Leasing in Denver. His name was Ted. He was quite a bit older. Anyway, the friend wasn't such a good friend. She forgot to mention he was married."

Kate remembered every last gory detail of the day Ted had dropped the bombshell. He had just picked her up from the Denver airport; she had flown in for a surprise visit, and they were on their way to their mutual friend's house for dinner. Ted told her he had good news and bad news. He asked which she wanted to hear first. She was busy putting on mascara in the review mirror when she answered, "I'll take the bad news first," always the optimist.

"The bad news is I'm married. The good news is I'm getting a divorce," Ted said.

Kate poked herself in the eyeball with her Maybelline Great Lash mascara wand. She never saw it coming. They had done the long-distance dance for six months. At a hair over twenty-one, she wasn't savvy enough to guess that his attentive calls from the office and his cell phone—and late-night chats from hotels when he was traveling—didn't mean he was madly in love. It meant he was hiding a wife. He never called from his house.

"Why didn't you tell me?" Kate had screamed at the "mutual friend."

"Ted really loves you. He knew if he told you up front, you'd never see him again. He was always going to leave his wife. She's horrible."

It was Kate who felt horrible, betrayed, and hopelessly in love. And Ted took full advantage of her feelings, smoothing over the situation as if it were a dream come true instead of a nightmare. He finally did file for a divorce, but that was when he started his disappearing act. He wouldn't answer the phone at home, and when she called the office his secretary always claimed he was in a meeting. He never returned the calls. Kate was heartbroken.

"He showed up in St. Louis about a year later, in town for one of his business meetings. He called, wanted to see me, told me that he realized he made a huge mistake. I met him at his hotel. That was my mistake. I drank too much and slept with him. I really don't know why I did it."

Kate fibbed. She knew exactly why she had done it. She wanted to sleep with him and feel nothing, prove to herself she didn't care.

"It turns out it was awful. I didn't trust him. I couldn't wait for him to get back on the plane."

"Let me guess." Jake said no more, roping in his anger so as not to scare Kate.

"Like my mom always says, it only takes once. I hadn't been dating anyone so I wasn't on any birth control."

Kate went on to tell Jake that when she found out she was pregnant, she called Ted to tell him the rabbit had died. He played stupid and asked if she was sure. When she said she had just gotten back from the doctor, he said he wanted to go to a more private phone and would call her right back.

"He never called back."

"I'll shoot the bastard if I ever see him," Jake said without missing a beat.

"He's not worth it."

Inside, Kate felt hard as stone. She had been so scared. Her father would have killed her. She would rather die than disappoint him. Kate thought about the unborn child often, sometimes counting out how old the baby would be had it been given life. To this day, when she saw a TV commercial or program showing or involving babies, she got so emotional she had to turn it off, change channels, or leave the room.

Jake brought her closer to him, hugging her, making an even tighter cocoon in the flannel sleeping bag. His emotions dug at hers, slowly pulling the sorrow to the surface. Finally, the tears she held back broke loose.

"I'm not sure I made the right choice. I didn't have anyone to talk to. I didn't know what to do," Kate choked out. "Ted finally called to apologize, years later. By then, I was married to Michael." The call was obviously too little, too late, although the fact that Ted acknowledged and took responsibility for his part in the horrible ordeal made her feel a little bit better. She felt a little less dirty, a little less ashamed, yet it couldn't erase the dull pain she carried. Kate wondered if it would ever go away.

Jake fought with her, for her, holding on to her shaking body.

"I love you." Jake's lips grazed her hair.

Kate could not believe he still loved her. It was the strangest sensation. The more Kate peeled away, the more loved Jake made her feel.

When her nerves calmed, she said, "I know it wasn't all his fault, and if I could do it all over again, I would never have slept with him. But I'm convinced there is a reason for everything, and if it weren't for him, I would have never married Michael, and then I wouldn't have had Sam." Kate paused to look up into Jake's loving green eyes. "And then I would have never met you. I love you, too."

THE PEACE KATE FOUND AT THE ranch was replaced by a restlessness when she returned to the city. She did not recognize it at first, because inspiration had not called on her for a very long time. There was a time when all she wanted to do was paint, make beautiful pictures, recreate what only her eyes could see. That was years ago, back when she was in art school.

And now her art was attempting to reclaim her. In her mind blazed the image of Jake willing himself into that rodeo arena. She wanted so much to capture that moment, that pure essence of him. Uncertainty loomed above her. She didn't know if she had the courage to face another canvas. It had been so long. Was it possible to create something of worth? Something people wouldn't laugh at? Or more importantly, could she recreate something as beautiful as Jake's passion for rodeo?

One rainy afternoon in early September, Kate found herself in an art supply store. Her fingers went directly to the tubes of paint, like a hand reaching out to a long-lost lover. She picked up a tube of alizarin crimson and unscrewed the top. The pungent odor of the oil brought tears to her eyes.

Immediately Kate began gathering paints, turpentine, linseed oil, and brushes, throwing them into her cart before she changed her mind. She hesitated when she stared at the empty canvases stacked on the shelves. Jake had erased the ugliness she felt inside, but it seemed almost inconceivable that she could cover a canvas with enough paint to hide all her inadequacies.

Kate stood before the abyss. She had no job, no husband, a child to support, and no idea what she was going to do for money.

Jump! It's not as far as you think! the could-do side of her brain yelled.

You shouldn't, you can't, you're not good enough! the other side volleyed back.

The bear within her roared, telling her she'd rather die trying than walk out that door without those supplies. It was time to reassess her world, a world she had the ability to recreate on her own blank canvas.

The Dance

J. P. BENTON WATCHED KATE SCOUTING the buffet like a general planning a major strategic attack. Her long, flowing, black velvet dress and finely tooled Larry Mahan cowboy boots showed off her form and flash like a prize-winning racehorse. J. P. had an eye for fine horseflesh and recognized Kate to be bred from a long line of blue-blood thoroughbreds. He butted into line right behind her and began to calculate how he would introduce himself to a woman of such obvious pedigree. He ran his finger down the faux gold chain shoulder strap of Kate's expensive designer purse.

"Is that real gold?" he asked, causing Kate to jump.

"It is," Kate lied, speaking without turning around. She wasn't much in the mood to speak to strangers. Jake had brought her to Bradley's wedding, a wrangler he had worked with at the Prickly Pear, and it was filled with rowdy, drunk cowboys.

"Well, you'd better be careful then, young lady. I might just snatch you up with that there purse!"

Lucky me, Kate thought, *I've got the most obnoxious drunk in the crowd hitting on me.* She turned and found herself looking up into the mustached face of the handsome groomsman she had spied at the chapel. He had stood at the altar, clad in a black cut-away jacket, black wranglers, and high-heeled Olathe cowboy boots. Despite Jake at her side at the service, Kate couldn't help but stare, even strain, to get a better look at the stranger. J. P.'s eyes locked with Kate's just for a minute, as his hand brushed against the soft fabric of her dress.

"If there was a hot tub around, you and me'd be in it," he leaned over and whispered in her ear. A split second later, another groomsman came up from behind and gave J. P. a friendly slap across the back.

"How goes it, J. P.? Aren't you gonna introduce me to your friend?" the man asked with a smirk.

"I was just fixin' to introduce myself, Josh," J. P. said, annoyed at the interruption. "I'm J. P. Benton, and this here is Josh Lucas."

"Nice to meet you," Kate replied, still a little shell-shocked.

"Sorry, but I'm gonna have to steal J. P. here away from you for a few minutes," Josh said. "We're getting ready to toast the bride and groom."

"Gotcha," J. P. said to Josh and then looked at Kate. "I'll be seein' *you* later." He tipped his hat and walked away.

J. P. Benton's fast and furious flirtation left Kate feeling like she was a victim of some sort of weird hit-and-run. She scanned the room for the safety of Jake. He was nowhere to be found. She headed toward the bar, lacking anything better to do.

Jake was on the opposite side of the room, hidden behind a pillar. He was feeling frisky; free drinks always put him in a good mood. The gal he'd met the week before at the Fireman's Ball had cornered him. He had been alone at the ball. Jake didn't think there was any harm in dancing a few dances with the tall blonde. But the whiskey somehow took over his brain, and later that night he had landed in her truck in a serious lip lock. That was all that had happened, some heavy petting and kissing. Still, he felt like he had betrayed Kate and hated himself for the slip.

Kate was a prize, and he knew it. No other woman had treated him so well. Sometimes he wondered why she loved him. He gave the blonde the polite brush-off, slipped into the crowd, and hoped Kate wasn't around to see the exchange.

Jake searched the sea of guests for Kate. He was really having a good time, shaking hands and talking to folks he hadn't seen for months. As he neared the bar, he finally spotted Kate. He joined her in line, still feeling somewhat guilty about the yellow-haired girl.

"Have I told you how pretty you look?" He grabbed Kate around the waist possessively, knowing she outclassed every woman in the room.

"Only a million times." She smiled warmly, relieved that she no longer had to stand alone. In the room filled with buckle bunnies and cowboys, she felt like a fish out of water. Jake bowed, the brim of his dark hat covering Kate's small face. His mouth found hers and devoured it. Kate was a little put off by the sudden public display of affection. After all, he had left her standing there alone for nearly half an hour. She heard the gentle tinkling of the dinner bell and pushed him away.

"Why, Jake McComb, I do believe you are making me blush," Kate said with a Southern accent.

"You are truly ravishing, and I sure as hell would like to ravish you."

His words were unmistakably slurred, and this bothered Kate. Normally she liked it when Jake was loose and feeling playful, but not tonight. Tonight he simply seemed sloppy. He tried to bring her back to him, but she stepped away.

"I've already checked out the buffet and it looks wonderful. I'm starved. Let's go eat!" she said, thinking perhaps food would sober him up.

"Ya know, that's probably not such a bad idea."

It was quite a spread, all of Jake's favorites—prime rib, salmon, potatoes, and breads. But Jake could only pick at his food; the booze had already soured his stomach. Instead he focused on talking to Cecil about his new job at the Bear Track Ranch. It sounded like an ideal job, caretaking a spread out in the middle of the Gros Ventre. He had heard the area was beautiful, but a little tricky in the wintertime. There was so much snow, you had to pack your gear and supplies in and out of the ranch via snowmobile. But that didn't bother him.

"Why don't you partner up with me?" Cecil asked.

"I don't know." Jake's brain was so fuzzy he had a hard time concentrating on what Cecil was saying. He took another pull off his beer.

"Well, huntin' season's almost finished at the Prickly Pear. Are you plannin' on winterin' there?"

"Earl hasn't exactly told me what the plan is." Now that Jake thought about it, Earl hadn't really committed to keeping Jake on for the winter. There wasn't a need to keep many hands on. The ranch pretty much shut down after November, except for a few cross-country skiers that came in from Jackson for the weekend. Jake had no plans to become a cross-country ski guide, that was for sure.

Kate studied the interesting centerpieces, tacky plastic flowers arranged in real leather cowboy boots. She was sure she had never seen anything like them before. Cecil and Jake's conversation seemed to be getting louder and louder, and she wished they'd turn down the volume. They were drinking beer, laughing and talking like two sailors on leave. Once again she felt invisible. She folded her napkin, placed it on the white tablecloth, and moved her hand to Jake's thigh.

"I'm going to go powder my nose." She stood up.

"Sure thing," Jake answered without looking at her.

In the small gray stall, she sat thinking about how uncomfortable she was with Jake's lack of composure. The wedding was the first big public event they'd attended. If this was how he acted at a party in Wyoming, how could she ever bring him to an event in St. Louis? She flushed the toilet, and Ted's warning words shot through her head: "Who are you kidding? He's a frigging uneducated cowboy, and he's way too young for you!"

"Just because he didn't go to college doesn't mean he's uneducated! And for your information, my father never went to college." Kate deeply regretted ever mentioning her relationship with Jake.

"Well, your father wasn't a cowboy with pie-in-the-sky dreams. He worked his ass off selling cars. I doubt Jake will ever be able to take care of you, Little Miss High Maintenance."

Kate wanted to throw the phone at the wall but held her Sicilian temper. Ted was a good client. He was driving his fourth Marino Motors Jeep.

"I might be high maintenance, but I maintain myself." Kate waited a beat, thinking there was no way Ted could argue with that.

"You can fool a lot of people, Marino, but not me, and not yourself. It'll never work out." And then Ted hung up.

Kate opened the door of the stall and cursed herself. Why did she let Ted get to her? He was obviously just jealous. She walked to the mirror, unzipped her purse, and took out her lipstick. While lining her lips she thought, *Maybe Jake's just kicking up his heels. He has been stuck out on that ranch for months.* She put the lipstick back in her purse and decided she needed to lighten up.

J. P. had been sitting on a barstool on the opposite side of the room, eyeing Jake and Kate's table like an eagle perched on a branch. He had met Jake a few times at the Jackson rodeo and thought it the perfect time to go say hello.

"Hey there, J. P.!" Jake extended his hand and grinned. He could not believe J. P. Benton had gone out of his way to shake his hand.

"Jake, how the hell are you?" J. P. gripped Jake's hand as if he were making a fist in his rigging.

"Good, J. P., real good." Right away Jake dove into talk about rodeo. J. P. was a champion bronc rider, one of the best Jake had ever seen. He guessed J. P. to be at least forty, yet he still rode every Saturday night. And he usually won.

Jake rambled on while J. P. watched Kate stand in line at the bar. "Is that who you're motherin' up to these days?" He pointed at Kate.

"Yeah," Jake said, wondering why J. P. stopped talking about rodeo.

"New blood in these parts, eh?" J. P. saw that Jake's beer was empty. "What do you say we go get us a real drink and you tell me all about her."

"That's a hell of an idea." Jake was so drunk by now he forgot all about waiting for Kate to come back from the bathroom. And he was so absorbed in talking to J. P. he completely missed seeing Kate at the bar.

Kate was busy making sure the vodka wasn't splashing out of the tiny martini glass as she made her way through the crowd of strangers. By the time she got back to their table, Jake had once again disappeared, and she wondered why he had even bothered bringing her to the party. Kate downed her martini in two gulps. It didn't help; it just made her feel more lonely. She thought about going back to the restroom and calling Stella. Stella had been fascinated with Kate's tales about Wyoming. It was certainly more entertaining than gossiping about the same old social scene back home. In fact, Kate had been trying to talk Stella into moving to Jackson. She looked at her watch. It was eleven o'clock, twelve in Missouri. Stella would probably be passed out on her couch, in a marijuana-induced sleep, snoring peacefully to the sounds of the TV.

Kate got up and moved toward the band, hearing a familiar Garth Brooks tune. She leaned against the wall and watched the dancers whirl around the dance floor like colorful tops. Kate loved to dance and was a little ticked off that Jake hadn't asked her all night. He was obviously too busy bobbing from one set of friends to another. Then she felt a tap on her shoulder.

"Would you like to dance?"

It was J. P. Benton.

Kate was shocked. She scanned the room for Jake, with no luck.

"I'd love to." Kate answered. The vodka had kicked in.

J. P. put his hand on the small of Kate's back, steering her to the rear corner of the dance floor. He didn't speak to her at first; they just swayed to the music, his shorter, muscular frame molding perfectly to hers. Kate didn't have much choice; her body seemed to respond to J. P.'s embrace whether she liked it or not. She felt all warm and tingly. She wondered if maybe she was a cowboy addict, then giggled into his shoulder.

"What's your name?" J. P. whispered into her ear.

"I'm Kate." She lifted her head and studied his profile. His face was angular, with sharp features and coal-black eyes. *He looks almost Native American* Kate thought.

Had she asked, she would have found out she was right. J. P. was more Indian than cowboy: his mother was a full-blooded

Shoshone. His senses were finely tuned, like a wild animal; his heart was married to the land. At times he could be as quiet and gentle as the deer that lay resting in the tall grass up in the Wind River Mountains. Yet at other times, he could be as tough and unforgiving as a blizzard whipping through the miles and miles of rock, sand, and sagebrush.

"Where you from?" he asked, spinning her slowly and gently under his arm.

"St. Louis," she said, trying desperately to keep up. Kate wasn't the two-stepper she aspired to be.

"I figured you weren't from around here." J. P. found his footing in the scent of competition, leading her through a complicated series of twists and turns.

"I'm sorry if I'm not a great partner."

"Oh, you're finer than a frog's hair." He laughed softly.

After a few more circles around the dance floor, J. P. felt Kate finally relax and found his rhythm. He let his hand slide down to explore lower territory. Her ass was perfectly sculpted, slightly round and firm. He wanted to feel more of her.

Kate normally would have reached around and yanked his hand away from the part of her body she deemed personal. But for reasons unknown to her, she let it rest there, liking the way it felt, strong and so goddamn sure of itself.

The music stopped, yet J. P. didn't move to untangle their arms. Instead, he stepped back and let the effect of her sink in. He had not felt so warm and good for a very long time. He felt the heat of Jake's gaze before he saw him, and ushered Kate off the floor.

Jake stood waiting, ears pricked forward like a horse, paying attention for the first time that evening. He had watched the two dancing, a little too close for his liking, a sobering scene. Jake willed his brain to clear as they moved toward him.

"How long you in town?" J. P. asked before he got within earshot of Jake.

"A few more days."

"Maybe I'll see ya around," J. P. said quickly. He didn't give a rat's ass about what Jake thought, but starting lovers' quarrels wasn't his style.

"I'd like that," Kate said, surprising herself.

"I'm in the book. Only J. P. Benton in it," he said under his breath, smiling at Jake as he handed Kate over to him. "Your girlfriend here looked a little lost, so I thought I'd help you out by asking her for a dance. I didn't think you'd mind."

Jake was so drunk and tired he didn't know whether to be offended or flattered. "That's real nice of you, J. P." Jake pushed out his chest, hoping his wobbly legs would support him. He put his arm around Kate.

"Darlin', I think it's time this cowboy went home."

"I think you're right. Let's head back to the hotel." Kate watched J. P. shake Jake's hand and slip back into the crowd, this time quietly, like a winter sunset.

BACK AT THE HOTEL, KATE WATCHED the snow build up on the windowsill while Jake fell apart. In his drunken stupor, he told Kate about his mother, and how his father had left them when he was only a child. He was worried Kate would leave him too. He couldn't handle that. Then, Jake showed her just how desperate he was. He begged her to let him move to St. Louis.

Kate didn't respond right away. His evening performance had been less than stellar, that was for sure, but the deep love she felt for him softened her. She needed him as much as he needed her, yet the responsibility of it all overwhelmed her. Kate shut her eyes and tried to picture Jake in the city, cloaked in his Carhartt

jacket, cowboy hat, and muddy boots. She saw him lost in traffic on some highway, horns blaring, confused and scared as a child. It just wouldn't work, and in the end it would kill the miracle that had happened between them. As much as she dreaded their separation, she knew a move to the city wasn't the answer. And then there was her divorce decree. It said while she was single, she agreed to not have a man stay overnight while she had Sam at her house. That was half of the week.

Jake cried. Kate, not sure how to handle the situation, held him and rocked him like a baby. The longer she held him, the harder he bawled. She had helped female friends through hard times, but never a man. Not like this, ever. A single snowflake captured her attention. Its rare brilliance sparkled in the moonlight. She could only think of one thing: to comfort him. The next words she uttered were a promise. She promised she would never leave him.

Car Jack

THE AUTOMATIC TIMER ON THE Mr. Coffee machine kicked in at 5:45 a.m., and J. P.'s alarm went off at six. The hot, brown liquid splashed into the glass carafe, sending the aroma down the hall to his bedroom. Boots, saddle blankets, jeans, and a small weight set cluttered the bedroom of the tiny two-room cabin he rented from his aunt. J. P.'s family had lost their ranch years ago due to skyrocketing taxes. It was now too expensive to buy anything within a sixty-mile radius of Jackson Hole. The billionaires had succeeded in pushing out the millionaires, driving prices on scarce private land up and the locals out.

"Now I know how my brothers felt. These rich white bastards have stolen all our land, and then the sons-o-bitches got the nerve to come back during huntin' seasons and kill all our animals!" he said repeatedly to anyone who would listen. If you weren't born in Wyoming, you didn't belong in Wyoming. That was the long and short of it, according to J. P. Benton.

J. P. rolled out of bed, scratched his fairly firm, forty-year-old belly, and headed to the toilet to relieve himself. His manhood was on the small side, something J. P. had a hard time dealing with. He shook his nub of an appendage and walked down the

92

dimly lit hallway, passing the ironing board that served as a hanging rack for his rainbow of perfectly pressed shirts.

Once in the kitchen, J. P. turned on the *Wyoming Agricultural Report*. He poured a mug of coffee, listened for a few minutes, sipping, waiting for the effects of the caffeine to kick in. He then put the elk meat he had smoked the night before in Ziploc bags, sat down, turned on the TV, and switched the station to the hunting channel. This morning they were bow hunting deer. J. P. watched, detached. He wasn't much of a talker in the morning, although he did call to check on his mother just before he left for work.

The Car Corral, home for the nearly new or rarely used cars and trucks, was home to J. P. Monday through Saturday, 8 a.m. until 5 p.m. He seldom took a day off, except for the days he rodeoed. He would have preferred working at a ranch, but it was nearly impossible to carve out a living, unless you were lucky enough to snag a job as a foreman to oversee one of the rich out-of-towner's ranches. And most of those jobs required a college degree, which he didn't have. Anyway, they were all bastards, too, using once-historic ranches as modern tax shelters. The Car Corral was more honest for J. P., keeping his pockets full for entry fees and his calendar flexible to chase hard-to-ride stock on the rodeo circuit. He'd do anything to get to Vegas for the National Finals, even sell cars instead of rounding up cattle.

J. P. rinsed out his thirty-six-ounce, heavily stained thermal mug and poured the remaining coffee into it. He moved to the bedroom, pulled on his jeans and boots, selected a bright-red shirt from the ironing board, and then grabbed his dusty brown, beaver-belly cowboy hat from the elk antler hat rack. He opened the front door, called his dog, Alice, and walked out to his truck.

"Load up," he said, pointing to the three-quarter-ton pickup parked in the narrow gravel driveway.

Alice, a stout Australian blue heeler, ran at the open tailgate and leaped into the air. Her rather portly midsection barely cleared the cold blue steel, causing her stubby hind legs to claw at the edge of the tailgate. J. P. gave her rear end a shove and closed the tailgate. Alice's stump of a tail wagged excitedly.

KATE WAS HAVING A HARD TIME getting Jake out of bed. "Jake, honey, the kitchen stops serving breakfast at nine o'clock and it's almost eight thirty," she said, thinking if food wouldn't move him, nothing would. He groaned and mumbled something about needing more sleep and to go ahead without him. Kate decided it wasn't worth a fight, even though her feelings were hurt. It was their last day together; she had to leave the next morning. She put on workout pants, a black turtleneck, and tennis shoes, grabbed her fleece vest, and slipped out of the hotel room.

The cold morning air hit her face like a splash of ice water. But as she moved down the walking path, from the shade to the sun, she unzipped her fleece, feeling the heat. The sun set off the shimmering gold leaves of the aspens and the soft beiges of the tall grasses planted around the ponds. Spring Creek Ranch was definitely a slice of heaven, just what the doctor had ordered. The room oozed romance, with a private deck, stone fireplace, and a king-sized bed swathed in a down comforter. She had been lucky enough to reserve one of the rooms that had a view of the Tetons. Their first night had been ruined by that god-awful wedding, but after that, things had returned to normal. The next evening, they had sat outside sipping a smooth pinot noir, talking and watching the sunset, followed by a quiet dinner alone. Kate was relieved, to say the least.

She took a right, walking toward The Granary restaurant, rationalizing that all was well. Jake's behavior at the wedding was less than acceptable, but he also had the right to sow a few oats and have a good time with his buddies. It was her fault she didn't know anybody at the party, not his. And that next morning he had woken up in a good mood, ordered room service, and made love to her as if nothing had happened. Kate thought maybe he had been so drunk he had forgotten about the whole thing. She decided she would forget about it, too. She stopped before she went into the restaurant and took off her fleece. It was definitely warming up; it promised to be a perfect September day.

"A table for one?" the hostess asked.

"Yes." Kate replied, not shy about eating alone.

"Inside or out?"

"I think it might be warm enough to sit outside, don't you think?" Kate looked at the inviting tables topped with umbrellas on the pine deck.

"Absolutely. It's gorgeous outside," the hostess said. She led Kate outside, placed a menu in front of her, and asked, "Would you like to start off with a cappuccino or perhaps some fresh orange juice?"

"I'd love a cappuccino."

Kate sat back and breathed in the crisp mountain air, watching the clouds float across the cobalt sky like ghosts. She reflected on how happy she was, even just sitting there alone.

A few minutes later, the waitress placed her drink in front of her, along with a copy of the *Jackson Hole News and Guide*. Kate licked the delicate white froth and opened the paper to the real estate section.

If only I could afford to buy a house, she thought.

For a moment she wished she were Stella. No responsibilities, no rules. Free as a bird, Stella could live and work wherever she wanted. The last time Kate had spoken to Stella, they had been shopping at Plaza Frontenac and stopped for lunch at The Zodiac restaurant in Neiman Marcus, or "Needless Markup" as they so fondly called it.

"Neiman's and Saks have the *best* shoe sales. I don't know why anyone would ever pay full price. All you have to do is have a little patience and wait for them to mark everything down 75 percent. I mean, you can buy like four pairs of shoes for the price of one!" Stella said with wide eyes, sipping her iced tea. The muted tones, comfy booths, and fresh flowers on the tables made for the best girlie lunches.

"Just wait until you get to Jackson Hole. You'll die. The Bootlegger has the coolest cowboy boots, and you have to go to Wyoming Outfitters. They carry Double D Ranchwear. I know you've seen the ads in *Cowboys and Indians* magazine!" Kate had fallen in love with the fact she could wear cowboy boots and jeans anywhere in Wyoming and not only look fashionable, but be considered very well dressed.

"Shit, I wish I could go right now. This heat and humidity sucks! I hate it here in the summer." Stella's face was framed by beautiful, thick brown hair and a striking white blaze that ran down the right side of her cheek. In her designer jeans and Chanel jacket, she looked like a well-heeled skunk.

"God, me too, I can't wait to go back to Wyoming." Kate started in on her sales pitch about how wonderful the weather was in Wyoming, with zero humidity, warm days, and nights so cool there was no need for air conditioning. She added that besides the great shopping and unlimited photo opportunities, there were so many other things to do.

"It would be awesome to go fly-fishing on the Snake, don't you think?"

"I fished with Jake several times. It's so peaceful, standing there in the cool water, the sun shining, just casting your fly rod back and forth. There is something almost meditative about it," Kate said as she took a bite of her almond chicken salad. She and Stella shared so many passions—clothes, food, and wine being at the top of the list. But what was interesting was they both truly loved nature. Both of their fathers had hunted and fished. Kate and Stella, at very early ages, were taught the magic and excitement of the great outdoors.

"You know," Kate lowered her voice, "the ratio of men to women is ten to one in the state of Wyoming." She said it as if it were a huge secret.

"Are you kidding me?" Stella was stunned. She pulled off a piece of her popover, slathered it with strawberry butter, and added, "Well, at least with those odds I might have better luck getting a date."

"No kidding. And the guys out there are so manly!"

"Nothing like a cowboy in boots and a tight pair of jeans . . ."

"Ah, yes, and Jake has one of the best asses I've ever seen," Kate gushed. "But remember, be careful—the odds are good, but sometimes the goods are odd!"

Stella nearly spit out a mouthful of soup, she laughed so hard. "Where in the hell did you hear that?"

"I'm not sure, out there somewhere. Seriously, there are a lot of good-looking cowboys but geez, there are some real characters, too."

"As in all places!" Stella chirped, her mind spinning so fast she could barely keep up with her thoughts. "This is totally changing the subject, but I keep forgetting to ask you; how is your painting coming along?"

"There are good days and bad. I have a hard time painting when I'm in the city." Kate thought about the studio she had set up in her spare bedroom at home. The double bed had to be shoved against the wall to make room for her easel. She was working on a painting of Jake leading a trail ride, the Tetons in the distance, copying from a photograph she had taken when she was at the Prickly Pear. The light in the room was okay, but when she looked out the window she was faced with a view of the blacktopped street, cars parked on the side, and rows of houses. This scenery wasn't exactly inspiring.

"I'm sure. It's pretty tough getting the old creative juices going in this bullshit town. Everybody is so goddamn conservative." Stella lit up as if someone had just plugged her into an electrical socket. "Maybe you should try smoking a little Roy Green!" Stella was always afraid someone would find out she occasionally smoked a little pot, so she had come up with the code phrase "Roy Green" so she could talk freely about it in public. She was so paranoid she even used the code when she was talking on the phone.

"You never know when someone is tapping your phone!" she had warned Kate.

By the time the girls had finished their long, long lunch, they agreed Stella should skip visiting Wyoming and just go ahead and move.

"What the hell, if you want to move there, I'm sure I'll love it. Besides, since my asshole of a father sold me out of a job, I appear to be gainfully unemployed. Think I can find a Roy connection?"

Stella's father had sold his interest in his law firm to his partner but had not made any provisions for Stella. She had worked there since graduating from college.

"I'm sure Cecil, Jake's buddy, can help you out." Kate was thrilled. It had been so easy to talk Stella into moving.

"Here's your spinach and bacon omelet." The waitress at Spring Creek Ranch interrupted Kate's reverie. Jake appeared, hair still wet from the shower. He gave her a sweet kiss and then planted himself in the chair beside her.

"Is it too late to order?" he asked. "I'd kill for some biscuits and gravy." He grinned boyishly at the young waitress who stood attentively at the table.

"I'll see what I can do. Anything to drink?" she asked, smiling back.

"Just coffee."

The waitress kept her glued-on smile and went back inside. Jake fixed his attention on Kate.

"What would you like to do today?"

"Well, I thought I might go look at trucks." Kate tried to concentrate on the automotive section of the paper, but the look Jake gave that waitress bothered her. Insecurity reared its ugly head. *You are thirteen years older than he is; he should be with someone younger, like that waitress*, it said.

"Looks like there's some sort of sale at the Car Corral," Kate said, trying to push the thought right out of her mind.

"Kate, I thought I told you that you don't need to buy a vehicle."

"I know we talked about it, but if I can find something cheap, it will be easier for me and you."

They'd had the car conversation several times in the past month. Kate knew there was a good chance Jake would be losing his job at the Prickly Pear by the end of the month. If that happened, he'd be needing transportation. Kate was willing to buy an old beater. When she wasn't in town, Jake could use it.

"I don't know . . ." Jake was having a hard time swallowing the idea. It was one thing letting her pay for dinner, but it was another story if she bought a truck.

"Well, it's costing me almost four hundred dollars to rent that Blazer this trip. I bet I've spent over two thousand dollars renting cars this past summer. I could have bought a car for that!"

The smiling waitress had returned and poured Jake a cup of coffee. "Thank you, hon," he said, putting the cup to his mouth. He looked at Kate. The last thing he wanted was their relationship to become a financial burden.

"Kate, are you sure you're okay? I mean, it is expensive, you doing all this traveling. Maybe I can move to St. Louis for awhile after things wind down at the ranch."

"Jake, we've talked about this. St. Louis is a big, crowded city. And I've got Sam half the time. I told you about my divorce decree. We'd end up having to rent you an apartment. You'd hate it."

Actually, she was the one who would hate it. She wasn't ready to bring him into that part of her world and was beginning to wonder if she ever would.

"You're right." He hung his head low, as if he were a sick animal.

"Maybe a visit sometime," Kate said gently.

"We could go to a baseball game." Jake kept his eyes on his coffee cup.

"In the spring! That would be perfect! I'll get tickets to a Cardinals' game. We can take Sam!" Kate reached across the table, put her hand on his, and squeezed it. She knew she had just dodged a bullet. "Honey, listen, I love coming here to see you. I really do. I wouldn't be doing all of this if I didn't want to. It's not like someone is holding a gun to my head."

Jake thought it strange that Kate had chosen those words, because that was exactly how he was beginning to feel. He could never keep up with Kate financially, and she was right about his not liking St. Louis. He'd feel like a caged animal.

"Well, if you think buying a truck is going to save you money, it's probably a good idea," he said, trying to perk up. "And I suppose it wouldn't be any good if the vehicle just sat there in the cold for a month. Probably needs to be driven a little."

"That's the spirit! Trust me, Jake, I'm in the car business. I'll only buy something if it's a good deal; otherwise, I'll keep renting."

J. P. PULLED INTO THE CAR CORRAL at ten minutes to nine. Mondays were always filled with surprises. He hoped the two car deals he had written that Saturday had gone through. Both had mouthwatering commissions. He walked through the double-glass doors, passed the dead elk, deer, bears, and mountain lions mounted on the wood-paneled walls, and then ambled down the hall to Clyde's office.

"Mornin'." J. P. stood just outside the door, gauging Clyde's mood.

"Fuck you! Why in the hell is there always so much hair on your deals?" Clyde's face swelled like a big red balloon.

Clyde was the Car Corral's finance manager, a good ole boy who drank too much caffeine, ate fast food two out of three meals, and smoked one cigarette after another. J. P. decided to try a little humor. "Hell, I don't know, Clyde, I reckon I have a big ole sign painted across my forehead advertisin' 'don't mind those bumps and bruises on your credit, come on in and buy a rig from me!'"

Clyde smirked and took a swig of his cold coffee that sat on the only corner of his desk that wasn't strewn with files and loose papers. He wasn't the most organized guy in the business, but he'd been around forever. He knew what bank would finance who and could get just about anybody bought. He was worth his weight in gold.

"Well, your guy that wanted to buy that Dodge Ram seems to be a little behind, and when the bank called to verify employment, his boss said he quit almost a month ago."

"Shit. Why the hell do these assholes waste my time? Don't they know what a credit check means?"

In reality, J. P. hadn't known what a credit check was until he started working at the Car Corral. He, like most of the cowboys in town, thought if you came up with a good, believable story, you could just drive off the lot in a brand-new truck, easy as writing a bad check. They didn't hold a master's degree in business; they were masters of bullshit. So when J. P. started working at the Car Corral, it was only natural that he put his talents to use. He learned the sometimes dishonest tools of the trade, earning the nickname "Car Jack." J. P. hated using his given name of Jack, and wasn't so sure he liked being called Car Jack. Whether he liked it or not was immaterial; the name stuck.

"I'll see if he's got a wife, or a brother. Maybe we can put it in somebody else's name." He cursed under his breath, wishing the dumb-shit customer had told him the real score up front.

KATE STROLLED UNDER THE STRINGS of flapping neon-yellow flags that hung over the acre of cars and trucks at the Car Corral. In need of still more caffeine, she had stopped at Shades for another cappuccino after she dropped Jake off at Cecil's. Having Jake along wouldn't be of much help. She was more than happy to let the boys have some bonding time while she did her business. Besides, if Jake hung out with Cecil today, perhaps Kate would get him all to herself again tonight.

Parked in the third row, a white '72 Chevy pickup caught her eye, a big lime-green "$2,999" printed across the windshield. The truck was a flatbed and a dually, Jake's dream truck. The funny thing was, deep down, Kate had always wanted a pickup too. She stood on her tiptoes and peered into the window. It was in immaculate condition. The turquoise vinyl interior wasn't even scarred from the wear and tear the truck had surely endured. She tried the door, found it unlocked, hopped into the driver's seat, and let out a "Yee-haw!"

Her father would have a cow if he knew what she was doing. He had never let her drive a pickup; it wasn't a practical car for city driving, he had argued. But Kate guessed the real reason he didn't let her drive a truck was because he didn't want everyone in town to know his debutante daughter was a redneck at heart.

"Well, I'll be! If it ain't the little filly in the black dress!" a booming voice yelled, making Kate nearly jump out of her seat.

"Oh my gosh, I didn't hear you walk up. You just about gave me a heart attack!" she said, trying to catch her breath. It took her a minute to realize she was staring directly into the face of none other than J. P. Benton.

J. P. leaned on the truck's door, reached his hand through the window, and extended his hand. "I'm sorry. Didn't mean to scare you."

"You work here?" Her stomach did a flip-flop.

"Best salesman they got!"

"Well, isn't it a small world." Kate tried to collect herself. She willed her mind to focus on why she was sitting in a used flatbed staring at one of the most handsome and irritating men she had ever met, now her friendly used-car salesman. "I don't suppose this is a one-owner?" She thought the one-owner thing would impress him and let him know that she knew a thing or two about what she was talking about.

"Sure as hell is! One of the big outfits right here in Jackson used her, infrequently, as you can tell, kept her clean as a whistle, never used her to haul anything heavier than hay," he said, crossing his arms.

Kate wasn't sure if she believed him or not. She climbed out of the truck and walked around the vehicle. Kate could see that the twenty-five-year-old truck was well maintained, but it was becoming increasingly difficult to concentrate.

"How much you asking?" she asked.

"That would be twenty-nine ninety-nine, just like the sign says."

The cocky grin on his face was enough to snap Kate's attention away from J. P.'s tight ass back to the truck.

"I know what the sign says, but it's a little bit out of my price range." Kate decided to play coy. She didn't feel a need to do the test-drive routine, knowing that even if the truck ran well now, it would be only a matter of time before it would need work. Jake was a good enough mechanic to repair whatever needed to be taken care of.

"Well, she sure is a beauty, runs like a top, too. What do you say you and me take her out for some exercise? Maybe we could stop for a little lunch." J. P. wondered where Jake was.

"You are too kind, Mr. Benton."

"Call me J. P.!" He removed his hat and gave her a charming smile. His nearly black eyes were impossible to read.

"All right, J. P." Kate smiled back, completely caught off guard. "I appreciate the offers but I'm in a bit of a hurry." Kate's pulse raced, and she could feel the color rising to her face. *Oh my God, I actually want to go with him*, she thought.

"Well, then, why don't we walk inside and I'll have me a talk with my manager and see what we can do about getting that price down a little ways." J. P. couldn't believe his lips were moving and saying what was coming out. He never came off a price, at least not right away. Dropping the price was a last-ditch effort to close a deal, not start a deal. Not to mention he was cutting his commission right from the get-go.

Kate followed J. P. inside. She was used to her father's hunting and fishing trophies back home, yet nothing prepared her for the showroom at the Car Corral. The moose's eyes followed her first, then the elk, then the rest of wild kingdom. She felt like Little Red Riding Hood being stalked for the kill. She finally settled into a chair in front of J. P.'s cream-colored metal desk.

"I'll go track down my sales manager. If I can't buy you lunch, how about a cup of coffee?" he said with so much politeness it scared him.

Kate held up her paper cup and said, "Had plenty, but thanks for asking."

The last thing I need is more caffeine, she thought. It was probably the reason she felt faint. Kate still couldn't figure out why J. P. had switched from wildcat to pussycat but didn't really care. She watched him through the glass partition. He was talking to a man that looked like he had swallowed a sofa. Smoke curled from his nose as he swiveled back and forth in his chair. J. P. turned and walked back to his desk.

"My sales manager is out to lunch, so I had to check with our finance manager. I can sell you that rig for twenty-seven ninety-nine."

"Is that the best you can do?" Kate knew she had exactly two thousand dollars in her checkbook for this extravagance.

"Ah, lady, don't go beatin' me up like an unwanted stepchild." J. P. whined, thankfully making him look much less attractive.

"First of all, my name is Kate, not lady. Second of all, I've worked in this business and I know all about this little show. I don't want to sit here all day 'beatin' you up.' I just want to buy a truck."

"Hey there, I wasn't trying to piss you off. I was trying to lighten things up. It was a joke. A bad joke, I guess."

The sincerity in J. P.'s voice was so genuine, Kate had no other choice than to back down. "I know that you know what you have in that truck. I'm not sure about your manager, but you seem like a fair man. I just want a fair deal."

J. P. paused and said, "That sounds reasonable." He hadn't heard the word "fair," especially in reference to himself, in a very long time.

Kate leaned forward in her chair, batted her long black lashes, and showed her Victoria's Secret push-up bra cleavage. "I'm going to be honest with you. I have exactly two thousand dollars I can spend on this truck, not a dollar more."

J. P. was normally immune to the charms of beautiful women, but with Kate he felt as helpless as a newly castrated bull. He knew exactly what they had in that truck, eighteen hundred dollars. If he sold it for two thousand, the insignificant profit would go to the house.

"Let me go back and talk to Clyde," J. P. said.

"HAVE YOU LOST YOUR MIND?" Clyde choked out between bites of taco. A big blob of orange grease dripped out of the corner of his mouth and hit the center of his baby-blue polyester shirt.

J. P. waited for Clyde to chew, hoping he wouldn't get indigestion, making this painful transaction even more unpleasant. After a minute he went on. "I'm just tryin' to help the little lady out."

Clyde looked at J. P. as if he had grown three heads. "I don't get it. You never give away the house. Are you sweet on her or what?" He said it loud enough for all of Jackson Hole to hear.

J. P. jumped out of the cheap steel chair, accidentally knocking papers off Clyde's filthy desk. He didn't bother to pick them up. "You just never mind what I'm doing or why I'm doing it," he said, trying hard to keep his temper in check.

It was apparent to Clyde that this deal was fairly important to Car Jack. In any other situation he would have made Car Jack go back to the rich-looking lady with the fancy city purse and ask for a few more bucks. He was sure she had it, and he wasn't one to leave money on the table, not for anybody. But the way Car Jack was prancing and snorting genuinely concerned Clyde. He'd never seen Car Jack so upset, and he certainly didn't have a death wish. Car Jack could take him with one hand tied behind his back, maybe both.

"I'm gonna do you a favor. Go ahead and dump the heap. It's been on the lot for over ninety days," Clyde said.

"I appreciate that," J. P. said. He heard Clyde whisper, "You owe me one," as he walked out of the office.

Kate watched J. P.'s smile flip over to a frown when she told him how to title the truck.

"You wanna put it in *whose* name?"

"It needs to be titled to Jake McComb, PO Box one-one-five-two, Jackson Hole, Wyoming." Kate could see that J. P. was hotter than a hickory fire in mid-July. She quickly added, "The truck is for me, really. But when I'm gone, Jake will be driving it, like to pick me up from the airport and stuff. He doesn't have the best driving record. If it's in my name, I'll have to insure it. If it's in his name, I won't have to worry."

Kate prayed her explanation made sense to him. J. P. had worked hard for her, and she was sure she had gotten a really good deal. Plus he was easy on the eyes, to say the least. If she weren't so in love with Jake, she'd be tempted. Hell, she was tempted anyway.

J. P. pondered Kate's story about the whole insurance business as he filled out the papers. He couldn't really argue with her, yet somehow he felt like he'd just been fucked over, and even though it was by a pretty brunette, it didn't feel good. He kicked himself thinking that he, of all people, had just been Car Jacked.

The Bear Track Boys and the Red Dress

A HARVEST MOON PEEKED OVER THE hill beyond the French doors. It was warm for a fall evening, nearly sixty degrees. The temperature didn't warrant a fire, but Kate built one anyway. She sat on the corner of her couch, curled up like a cat with a snifter of cognac. Sam was the only reason she dragged herself back to the city. St. Louis left her feeling depressed, stuck, as if her feet were weighted by blocks of cement. She stared at the flames, missing Wyoming, and Jake, and the miles of silver-green sagebrush she had grown to love so much.

Stella had moved to Jackson Hole. She had found a cabin on a big ranch to rent temporarily, and the landlord just happened to be a fortyish eligible bachelor. Stella was already baking him her famous whiskey-apple pie. "The quickest way into a man's pants is through the stomach," Stella had said.

Kate was honestly happy for Stella, but at the same time jealousy bit at her heels. Stella had begged Kate to move with her, and Kate wanted to in the worst way. But she could never leave Sam, and her ex, Michael, wouldn't ever consider letting Sam move with her. She then thought about renting Stella's guest room anyway. Jake had ended up taking the job with Cecil at the very secluded and evidently hard-to-get-to Bear Track Ranch. A place

109

in Jackson Hole would certainly come in handy. Kate poured over her finances; so far she hadn't had to dip into her savings.

But her father was losing patience. By now he was well aware that Kate was seriously dating some cowboy thirteen years her junior. He was less than pleased. His retaliation was to hit Kate where he thought it would hurt her most. He declared her sabbatical officially over, stopped paying her, and told her if she wanted to keep her job, she'd better get her head out of the clouds and back to work—pronto. Kate didn't have much choice. She did the math again, and even with a full paycheck, there was no way she could handle travel expenses and rent for Stella's cabin in addition to her mortgage.

"My dad is being such an asshole. I just hope the Bear Track turns out to be nice," Kate told Stella.

"I wouldn't count on that." Stella said. "The place is in the middle of fucking nowhere. Hell, it's past the Goosewing."

The Goosewing Ranch was in the Gros Ventre, and it was a haul. It took forty-five minutes from Jackson Hole just to the get to the parking area at Slide Lake. From there, guests had to board a four-wheel-drive shuttle and ride another thirty minutes through some rugged country—but beautiful rugged country, Kate was told. And this was just the summer commute. She couldn't imagine what the trip entailed during January, nor did she want to.

"Well, we'll just have to see, won't we?" Kate was determined not to be discouraged.

"Why don't you come out for Thanksgiving? I'll even cook dinner: turkey, stuffing, all the trimmings. It'll be fun. Maybe Jake can come down from the Bear Track."

After Kate and Jake had hashed out the impossibility of his moving to St. Louis, Jake decided to join Cecil out at the Bear Track Ranch. Once his decision was made, all of his anxieties were replaced with the excitement of being out on his own and managing a ranch.

"It'll be just like the old days! Just me and Cecil and thirty head o' horses!"

Kate was enormously relieved, certain that the job was perfect for Jake.

Stella took Kate's silence as indecisiveness. "I'll even invite Cecil!" Cecil was a little rough around the edges, but the fact that he had some very good hooch smoothed things out.

"That might just work. It's Michael's year to have Sam for the holiday, and I have Friday off."

It was October. Kate wondered how in the hell she would endure the next few months.

KATE DOVE BACK INTO THE BUSINESS of selling cars like an Olympic athlete. This time she was fueled by the almighty dollar, not for what it could put on her back but for how it could feed her soul. She saved for her trips out West. Again, she thanked God for Sam, a welcome companion who greeted her with hugs at the end of the day. He rarely whined or complained. "Negative attention-getters," Kate called them, like most five-year-olds she knew. Kate imagined Sam got plenty of love: from her, Michael, and their babysitter, Jennifer. They were a team, and the goal was to keep Sam happy and content without spoiling him.

Jennifer had been with them since Sam's birth. She was there for Kate when she came home from the hospital after having a C-section. When Sam had colic, Jennifer stayed late, walking poor, screaming Sam around the neighborhood so Kate could at least cook dinner in peace. Later, when Kate and Michael got divorced, Jennifer was the shoulder they both leaned on to make sure Sam was okay. Jennifer never took sides. Sam was her charge, and she loved him as if he were her own son.

When Sam started full-time kindergarten, Jennifer enrolled in the local junior college. Even though she carried a full load, fifteen credit hours, she still had plenty of energy and enthusiasm left over for Sam. She picked him up from school for Michael, and for Kate if she had a late meeting. Jennifer went with Sam back and forth between Kate's and Michael's houses. There was consistency. Jennifer was studying for her teaching degree, so she was big on after-school projects and trips to the zoo, museums, and the park. Often, Kate would come home to the smell of fresh-baked chocolate chip cookies. Jennifer liked to cook. They were *so* lucky. Both Michael and Kate knew it.

"You know, Jennifer would be the perfect wife for you," Kate later joked with Michael.

"You're right. But she'd have to drop a few pounds first," he joked back. Jennifer was probably twenty pounds overweight and had long, mousy brown hair. But what she lacked in the looks department, she more than made up for in personality.

"Who cares? She's great with Sam, and she would love to be a stay-at-home mom."

"Kate, she's twenty years younger than me!"

"Age is just a number," Kate automatically replied.

Now, after dating Jake, she wasn't so sure.

Halloween came, and Sam dressed up as a ninja. He seemed content and often asked when he would see Jake again. Kate promised when it got warm she would take him back to Wyoming, and he could ride horses with Jake until he rolled off his saddle with exhaustion.

Then November finally yawned, the trees dropping their dead leaves in preparation for winter.

KATE STOOD IN THE LONG SECURITY line at Lambert International Airport with the rest of the people crazy enough to travel on the busiest day of the year. She brought out her cell phone and punched in Stella's number.

"Have you heard from Jake yet?"

"No, but I'm sure he's on his way to civilization at this point, right on schedule to pick you up at the airport," Stella said. "It'd be nice if he got himself a cell phone, don't you think?"

"Well, first of all, he can't afford one, and even if he had one, I doubt he'd get cell service up there."

"Good point. Well, good thing you got him that truck. Geez, that would have been a real bummer if he didn't have wheels."

"I know, and now I don't have to rent a car!"

"Well, I can't wait to see you. Is the flight on time?" Stella put down her wine glass, then reached for a joint she had in the ashtray.

"So far, so good. I'll call you when I land to see if you need us to pick anything up."

"I think I'm set. I already got you a bottle of Titos vodka. Maybe get some ice. I don't have an ice maker, and I always seem to run out of ice."

"No problem. How about I get some wine? It's the least I could do." Kate was so grateful for Stella hosting what promised to be a real feast minus the Marino family drama. For once she was looking forward to a holiday meal.

"Perfect. I just uncorked my last bottle of red."

THANKSGIVING DINNER AT STELLA'S SHOULD HAVE been an evening to remember, but the martini kickoff, followed by copious amounts of wine with dinner and several pours of port, caused some serious holes in Kate's memory. She woke up in Stella's nicely appointed guest room, which could have been her room had she been able to afford it. Her eyes were heavy and dry, as was her mouth, and her stomach felt hollow. Silently she scolded herself. She had not followed her "one cocktail in the evening followed by one glass of wine with dinner, two if the wine is really, really, good" rule. And anything sweet, like port, or even dessert, was a no-no late at night. The sugar was an unwelcome wake-up call at 3 a.m. Just then, Kate had a sobering thought: *Why is it that I drink so much more when I'm with Jake?*

It's because you're on vacation and are just relaxing! the-girls-just-wanna-have-fun side of Kate shot back.

She rolled over and moved her hand from beneath the pillow and rested it on Jake. The slow, steady rise and fall of his chest told her he was still in a deep sleep. Sometimes, after these big nights out, Kate felt as though all her senses were dead. Now, that wasn't fun. Not fun at all.

Jake jumped like a horse who had been spooked. "Kate?" He sounded oddly scared.

"It's okay, sweetie, I'm right here," she said, wrapping herself around him, feeling the onset of a bursting headache.

"Oh, sorry, for a minute I didn't know where I was."

"We drank enough last night for us to forget who we are, much less *where* we are. I need Advil and I hate to say it, but I'm going to have to have a Bloody Mary eye-opener." For Kate, the combination of the two was the only sure-fire cure for a severe hangover. "God, I hope we didn't drink all the vodka."

Jake jumped out of bed, and chased down a bottle of ibuprofen and a bottle of water. He got back into bed and watched Kate as she downed three Advil and drained the bottle.

"Honey, you are the best, if not the very best. You are soooo beautiful. You are so good to me. I still can't believe you bought that truck!"

Kate laid her head back on the pillow, willing her head to stop pounding.

"I had a feeling Prickly Pear wasn't going to work out. I couldn't leave you out at the Bear Track all winter without any wheels." The white flatbed brought a flash of J. P.'s face in his brown hat, tight jeans, and boots. She never told Jake she bought the truck from him. Every time she mentioned J. P.'s name, it brought out a foul mood in Jake.

"Ah, honey, I got me a crotch rocket now!" Jake laughed.

Kate punched him in the arm, hating the slang term. "And you were planning on pulling up at the airport on your hot little snowmobile?"

"I don't see why not. I could just strap you on the back and ..."

Kate silenced him with her lips and jumped on top of him. Her headache had all but disappeared.

An hour later they emerged from the bedroom looking for tomato juice, the bottle of Tito's, and breakfast. Stella was still asleep in her bedroom with her dog, Franklin. Cecil was passed out on the leather couch. He looked like a papoose rolled up in Stella's bright Indian print blanket. Jake kicked him with the heel of his boot.

"Burnin' daylight, pard. If you want to ride back to Slide Lake with us, you'd better get your butt in gear."

Cecil turned over and moaned. A pipe, a bag of weed, beer cans, and several empty wine bottles littered the large coffee table.

"Hey, you play, you pay. Now get your ass moving." This time Jake shook Cecil's shoulder and pulled off the heavy wool blanket.

"All right, all right." Cecil grumbled. He sat up, ran his hand through his curly red hair, and belched. His face was drawn and had lost the softness of youth. Even though he was the same age as Jake, his broad, hunched shoulders and slow moves suggested a much older man.

"By golly, that Stella knows how to party."

"She's a trained professional. Don't even try to keep up with her," Kate said. She could hang with Stella as far as the drinking went, but that was about it. She had never liked to smoke pot; it made her too paranoid.

Kate ended up leaving Stella a note on the kitchen table thanking her for the incredible dinner. She also told her they were going to town to continue the holiday pig-out at Lee Jay's. It was sure to be crowded, so they'd be there for at least a couple of hours. Kate knew Stella wouldn't stir until well after twelve, but thought the invitation would make her feel good. Kate said if she missed her at Lee Jay's, she'd be sure to see her on Sunday before she left for the airport.

Lee Jay's was packed. Kate was thankful she had had the foresight to make herself a Bloody Mary before she left Stella's. She was just starting to feel human when they finally got seated in one of the back booths. The boys ordered the traditional biscuits and gravy. She ordered toast, sausage, and eggs over easy. Eating toast dipped in the runny yolks seemed also to help with the hangover-recovery process. So did hot sauce on the eggs.

Cecil and Jake didn't talk too much as they shoveled food in their mouths like starving animals. Kate took her time, scribbling a shopping list on a paper napkin in between bites. If she was going to rough it, she'd do it with good food and wine. The waitress placed the check on the table. Kate picked it up.

The three of them squeezed back into the Chevy, made a pit stop at the grocery store, and headed to the parking lot at Slide Lake. The dirt parking area was empty. Cecil grabbed his gear and was on his snow machine in a flash. Before he took off he yelled, "I'll ride out ahead and go start that stove! You two have fun now, ya hear!"

Jake waved, then transferred the provisions from the truck to the back of the snowmobile, using bungee cords to secure them to the rear end of the machine. Kate swallowed hard as she looked at the stark white landscape.

"Are you sure that lake is solid?" she asked, with much more apprehension than she cared to show. She imagined them sailing across the frozen water at about fifty miles an hour, hitting a thin spot, and breaking through the invisible ice. Drowning in sub-zero water was not her idea of a peaceful death.

"It's solid, all right. Are you sure about this?"

"Absolutely. At least we're on a snowmobile instead of a covered wagon!" She put on her helmet, tightened the chin strap, climbed on the back of the snow machine, and tried not to think about how petrified she was. Was she "man enough" to handle the old ranch? It was in the middle of nowhere, with no running water or electricity, much less a phone or fax machine. Her father's voice rang inside her head: "I know you and your expensive tastes! You won't last a minute out there. You'll be looking for a Ritz-Carlton faster than you can ride that snowmobile back!"

"Here we go!" Jake gunned the engine.

The wind bit into the only exposed piece of flesh, which happened to be her face. If she turned her head to the side, Jake's body acted as shield, but then she couldn't absorb the frosted beauty of the Gros Ventre. It was as if Old Man Winter had taken a deep breath and then blown it all out in one explosive gust. Everything from the pine trees to each and every blade of grass was covered in a fine layer of sparkling white dust.

They made their way down the path to the lake, and Jake

opened the throttle, leaving a spray of snow behind them. Once on the immense sheet of ice, the snow machine seemed to float over the fine white powder that hid the frozen lake beneath them. Kate tightened her grip. The arctic wind penetrated her gloved fingers. She thought about putting one hand under her rear end to warm it, but she was too afraid to let go.

"How fast are we going?" Kate screamed into Jake's ear.

"Almost seventy!" He laughed, clearly enjoying the speed.

Kate was so stunned that she forgot her fear. In the moments that followed, all she felt was a sense of freedom. She smiled as the wind whipped at her burning face. The world flew by in a dazzling white blur.

Kate was amazed at the way Jake managed to miss most of the big ruts once they reached the old road to the ranch. Suddenly he swerved to miss a puddle that had grown into a small pond, threatening to throw Kate and all their supplies off the back of the sled.

"Jake!" Kate yelled, her exhilaration now replaced with irritation. She could not fathom why Jake had insisted on adding the bulky Western saddle to the load. Jake slowed down so she could turn around and rebalance it. As Kate rearranged the load, she wondered if Jake's attraction to adventure was a complicated disguise for a lack of common sense.

Afternoon turned to dusk and the blinding sun ducked beneath the mountains in a yellow burst, casting muted shadows of lavender and blues on the hillsides. Kate wiggled her toes to make sure they were still there. Tears rolled down the sides of her cheeks from the cold, and her chest ached as she thought about kissing Sam good-bye the night before she left.

"It's only five days, sweet pea." She had held him in a bear hug before she boarded the plane. He had grown accustomed to her comings and goings. Sam knew she was seeing Jake, but still wanted her to stay close. He wanted to go with her, and she had to explain that it was a little too rugged at the Bear Ranch in the winter. Again, she promised to take him with her in the spring.

Jake opened the throttle one more time as they rounded the last bend. Kate held on to Jake's waist with her left hand and clutched her Jackson Hole survival bags and saddle horn with the other. She had been careful to select items that could be prepared on the grill or wood-burning stove—thick, nicely marbled steaks for the boys, a tuna steak for herself, potatoes, and asparagus. Who said roughing it had to be unpleasant? She would be a pioneer making dinner for her man out in the wilderness! For backup she always had her friend Jack Daniels—if things got ugly, she could always get drunk. In the distance she spied an old sign swinging precariously in the wind. Jake steered them toward it.

The crudely carved sign read "Bear Track Ranch." Kate's visions of a romantic ranch began to fade as they drove through gates that looked as though they would drop from their hinges with the slightest breeze, much less the heavy nor'easter sure to blow all winter.

She scanned the uninviting main house. The once well-oiled lodgepole pine was dry and weathered. Windows were covered by sheets of plywood. It looked sad and lonely, as if no one had cared for it for a very long time.

Across the road sat three smaller cabins in even worse shape. Someone had taken the time to board up the windows but had neglected everything else. Snow was falling through the caved-in roofs, and the once-charming porches were rotted. The place looked and felt like a ghost town.

Jake pulled up to the side door of the main house and killed the engine. He read the disappointment on Kate's face, gave her a quick reassuring kiss, and tended to the business of unloading the sled. He was oblivious to his surroundings, having lived in worse conditions back in Washington. Kate tried to follow him, struggling not to sink in the knee-deep drifts by carefully placing her boots in each one of Jake's footprints. Jake looked back over his shoulder.

"Cecil is real sensitive about his cooking. I reckon he'll try to help you with dinner, but you just stand your ground, make a big deal about giving the cook a night off or something. Now, breakfast will be another story. You just steer clear and let him do his thing. His cooking isn't that bad, just go ahead and eat it. Pretend you like it even if you don't."

At this point, Kate wasn't worried about Cecil and his culinary skills or lack thereof. She was more concerned about making her way to the door without getting buried alive in the snow. She managed to lift her arm, heavy with bags, in a makeshift wave as Cecil came to the door. He stepped off the sinking porch, carefully navigating his way through the drifts. He took the groceries from her hands and gave her a hug.

"What took you so long! I guess Jake took it slow, seein' he had all that precious cargo aboard."

Kate noticed that Cecil had taken off his snowsuit. He looked heavier and older in his grease-stained coveralls. Kate hooked onto his forearm and followed Jake into the house.

A once magnificent great room was walled off by a series of blankets and quilts hung on a clothesline. To the right sat the remainders of the kitchen, a long row of white metal cabinets, and a sink. The counters were littered with empty cans of soup and vegetables. Salt, pepper, and flour formed a thin layer of dust. Bulging trash bags were stacked against the wall.

Cecil had, as promised, a well-stoked cast-iron stove kicking out enough warmth to heat the two-hundred-square-foot area. Twin mattresses were placed closest to the heat source. A petrified-wood cocktail table was crammed in the opposite corner, flanked by two large logs standing on end, serving as chairs. Stacks of backdated *Hustler* magazines rested on another log, and a single oil lamp glowed on the windowsill. Kate rummaged through the groceries for the bottle of Jack. She was going to have to get drunk—very, very drunk.

Cecil grabbed the oil lamp, parted the blankets, and disappeared into the dark space beyond. Jake went outside to light the grill. Kate found a coffee-stained mug, walked outside, and rubbed it clean with fresh snow. She poured herself two fingers and added a log to the fire, leaving the heavy metal door open. The flames seemed to cheer up the filthy, rank room. The whiskey slid down her throat and warmed the parts of her that had grown so cold. She wondered how in the hell Jake could live like this. Jake burst back inside, a big smile plastered across his face.

"I see you've cracked open the whiskey. How about pouring me a drink?"

"It would be my pleasure, sir." Kate said and moved toward the sink. "So how does one do dishes around here?" she asked, trying to make light conversation.

"We don't!" Cecil answered as he emerged from the shadows behind the blankets.

Both of them laughed. Cecil eyed the Jack Daniels.

"So, I see you brought some whiskey. Mind if I have me a taste?"

"You find a glass and I'll be happy to pour," Kate chirped with fake enthusiasm. She was beginning to feel nervous, but didn't understand why. Jake was there with her. She should feel safe as a clam.

Kate forced herself to focus on Jake and how handsome he looked, even in his Carhartt coveralls. Then she looked over at the mattress setup and wondered if she was expected to sleep between the two men or what. Again, she thought about her attraction to Jake's love of adventure, and she knew this was one adventure she could have lived without. Her father's voice echoed in her head. Kate had reasoned that the Bear Track was extreme rustic living conditions on a ranch, and that Jake would surely take care of the sleeping arrangements.

"I'm guessing the bathroom facilities are limited?" Kate laughed.

"Oh, we got the finest technology in plumbing here at the Bear Track Ranch!" Cecil cackled.

"Oh, Cecil, you shut up." Jake broke in and drew Kate to his side. "Honey, there is an outhouse out back," he said, with a sincere smile.

Kate stared at him. Jake laughed and kissed her, melting all her doubts. She joined in the laughter, finally relaxing into the absurdity of the situation. Indeed it was an adventure she would not relive, but she was knee-deep into it now.

"You guys are a hoot! An outhouse! Well, I guess it beats squatting in butt-deep snow!"

"And I recommend you doing your business before too long." Cecil spat a wad of tobacco on the plank floor. "It can get mighty Western out there in the dark."

Kate drained her Jack Daniels and poured another.

DINNER TURNED OUT TO BE SURPRISINGLY tasty. The steaks were done to perfection, as was Kate's tuna. Jake had even managed to find a few glasses for the red wine.

Cecil and Jake talked about a mysterious red dress all through the meal.

"I'm gonna bring that red dress to the rodeo come this summer. And, by cracky, if a woman puts it on, then by the end of the night she'll be a-ridin' me after I ride my bull!" Cecil slurred.

It was Jake who had found the bundle of red silk and black lace beneath the shotguns and kerosene in the living room closet when they first moved to the ranch. When he shook it out he was surprised to find it was an old dance-hall-girl dress, in reasonably good condition. There were two cigarette burns along the hemline, but other than that, all it needed was a good press.

In the back of her mind, Kate tried to visualize the red dress. It appealed to her romantic notions of the West. In her drunken stupor, she imagined herself much like the woman that had once worn it, living in less-than-ideal conditions with a couple of wild cowboys.

"So, where is the dress?"

"Oh, it's hidden," Jake replied.

"How come?"

"Because it is special."

"What do you mean?" Kate said, miffed.

"Well, like Cecil said, it's gonna be the rodeo dress, sort of like our good-luck piece."

"Yeah," Cecil chimed in.

"You gotta be kidding me." Kate laughed.

"Nope."

"Well, now I want to see it, especially since it's a good-luck thing. I could use a little luck right about now!"

Jake and Cecil stuck to their seats like wads of chewing gum.

"Ah, come on!" Kate was intent on winning this charade.

No movement.

"Okay, aren't you the least bit curious to see what it looks like on?"

"Well, you've got a point." Jake's face brightened.

"You promise you won't take it?" Cecil said with uncertainty. He was very attached to the dress.

Kate laughed harder, hiding her diminishing patience. "Now, why in the world would I want to do that?"

Cecil believed her. He got up from the petrified-wood table and went back behind the curtain of quilts. He came back and placed the dress on the mattress next to the stove.

Kate stood up and approached it slowly, as if it were alive and would scare easily. She gently caressed the crimson silk, running her index finger down the thin straps, feeling the intricate black cording that embroidered the circumference of the bodice. She smoothed out the wrinkles and found delight in the puffiness of the skirt.

Kate lifted the skirt, feeling like a Peeping Tom. The skirt hid several layers of petticoats: the first a white Irish lace; the second a bold, sexy black; and the third an unusual white field scattered with tiny pink hearts. In a trancelike state, Kate slipped the dress over her head. Even with a thin turtleneck on, the dress fit perfectly. The zipper followed the trail from her waist up her back as if it were custom-tailored for her. Jake and Cecil let out whistles of appreciation as Kate twirled around the room.

Kate noticed the hungry look in Jake's eyes and wished they had access to some privacy. She danced a playful jig, then planted herself on his lap.

"Ah, hon, did you happen to bring any of that massage oil with you?" Jake whispered in her ear.

"But of course," Kate answered, slightly seductively. The red dress definitely had her under its spell.

"You know how much I love your back rubs . . ."

Kate could feel him getting hard.

"I can hear you two!" Cecil sang out.

"Now, you just simmer down," Jake replied.

"Cecil, if you behave, I'll give you a back rub, too." Kate didn't know why she had promised such a thing. The words slipped out before she knew what she was saying.

"Okay!" Cecil said with more enthusiasm than Kate was comfortable with.

Jake pulled her off his lap, took off his shirt, and lay down on the mattress closest to the fire. She dug out her sage-scented oil and straddled his back. Before she began, Kate hiked the skirt over her midthigh, making sure it would not get soiled. She then put her sensitive, strong hands to work, using her fingers, elbows, and knuckles to release the tension knotted in Jake's back. Cecil lay quietly on his belly on the other bed waiting his turn. Kate massaged Jake a full half hour before moving to Cecil. She sat next to him, began rubbing his spine, pushing all sexuality aside, thinking only of the healing her hands released. When she was finished, she let out a sigh. The soreness from the rodeo-like ride on the snowmobile had caught up with her. She was ready for Jake to reciprocate.

"Okay, now it's my turn."

Jake moaned, not happy from being awakened from his massage- and alcohol-induced nap.

"Hey there, I gave both of you one!" Kate's eyes bore down on Jake.

"All right," Jake said, his voice sounding like gravel hitting tires on a road. He sat up and made room for Kate. "But you're gonna have to take that dress off and your shirt for me to do you any good."

Kate waited for Cecil to leave them alone, or at the very least to move back over to the *Hustler* library in the other corner, but he didn't.

"Ah, honey, Cecil's seen breasts before," Jake said, as if reading her mind.

Kate shot Jake a look that should have made him back down, but it didn't. It was as if the whole room had gone slightly insane. At that moment, Kate wasn't sure about anything. Her mind was foggy, thick with booze and the uncertainty of love. She unzipped the neck of her turtleneck, shimmied her arms out, and pulled it off without having to remove the dress. Then, with the grace of a dancer, she twirled around, quickly unzipped the dress, let the straps slide off her shoulders, and plopped facedown next to Jake. There, she thought with relief, it wasn't so bad, and she was pretty sure Cecil hadn't seen a thing.

Jake began to caress her slender back. He gently pulled her long, wavy hair from the nape of her neck and kneaded her shoulders. It didn't take long for him to bend over and start kissing and nibbling on her ears playfully, skillfully. Kate melted into his hands, forgetting Cecil's presence in the room. Just as she completely relaxed, she sensed something move at the foot of the bed. An extra set of hands slowly rubbed the bottom of her feet, while Jake continued to run his hands up and down her back. Pleasure and panic rushed over her at once as yet another sensation assaulted her. A foreign, wet warmth began lapping and sucking her toes. Her breath caught in her chest—she couldn't breathe. How could Jake be at two places at one time? In a split second it registered what was happening.

"You get your ass outside, and you get it out now!" Kate hissed. She refused to turn over until Cecil left the room.

"I got nowhere to go," Cecil said, not the least bit ashamed.

"Go outside!" Kate's voice grew loud.

"Yeah, maybe you better step outside for a minute," Jake agreed.

"How could you! How could you let another man touch me like that?" Kate cried.

"Honey, I knew what he was doin'. I wasn't gonna let it go any further. I was right there!" he said.

"If you really loved me, you wouldn't want another man to do those things."

"We were just playin'. I thought you might enjoy it," he said, with his head held low as if he was trying to hide.

"Are you crazy? Do you think my idea of fun is showing a strange man my breasts and then letting him lick me like a dog?"

"Kate, honestly, I would never have done it if I knew how upset you'd be. And by cracky, if Cecil would have tried anything, I would have killed him—I swear it!"

"God, I want to believe you." And Lord knows Kate did. She wasn't ready to lose the sweetness of love that had grown between them. Her emotions felt as if they had been run through a blender.

"I guess this isn't all your fault," she said, looking at the pool of blood-colored silk.

Jake reached for Kate's turtleneck and helped her pull it over her head. He kissed her, then with the softest of kisses said, "I am so sorry."

Kate was far away as he ever so gently moved her back on the mattress. Something was not right, and in Jake's urgent passion, he never noticed. Kate closed her eyes, wanting to feel something, even anger or disgust. But she felt nothing, nothing at all.

A tap at the door sounded just as Jake rolled off Kate. She pulled a dirty wool blanket over her semiclothed body and turned her back to Jake, who had already passed out. The fire was still burning in the belly of the stove, but it did not warm her.

The next morning, after choking down eggless pancakes mixed with a few stray horse hairs, Kate had the opportunity to witness Jake and Cecil's new horse-training techniques.

Jake roped a young unbroken horse and wrapped the other end of the lariat around a post for leverage. He then pulled at the rope. The animal's eyes bulged as he bucked and twisted his neck in panic. Jake pulled the rope tighter, until the horse finally gave up and dropped to its knees. Kate stood on the perimeter of the fence watching the horrific scene. She couldn't take it any longer.

"Jake!" Kate yelled out.

Jake turned and let the filly go.

"Be right there!" He watched the horse get up and trot away. He smiled at Kate as he walked toward her.

"I think I had better go." As she said the words, an old memory tugged at her heart. The last time she watched Jake throw a rope, he had thrown it around the stems of a beautiful bunch of wildflowers. He had then handed her the bouquet.

Cry Wolf

JAKE TRIED TO MAKE THINGS RIGHT between him and Kate before they parted ways that November at Slide Lake.

"We don't have enough money to feed the herd," Jake confided as he transferred Kate's gear from the snowmobile to the truck.

"I don't understand." This was news to Kate.

"The feed store here in Jackson won't let us charge any more grain—evidently the boss man doesn't like to pay his bills."

It only took Kate a minute to figure out the rest of the story. "And let me guess, he hasn't paid you and Cecil either?"

"Not this month."

"Son of a bitch." Kate hissed. "What kind of person lets animals *and* humans starve?"

Jake didn't respond.

Kate wanted to scream. Just when she thought things couldn't get any worse, they did. Once again she wondered if this was all her fault. Maybe she should have let Jake come to St. Louis. Maybe she could have talked Michael into letting Jake live with her while she had Sam with her. The fact was, she never came close to broaching the subject.

Kate climbed in the truck, fished in her backpack, and found the soft ostrich-skin wallet. There wouldn't be a lot of cash. She used credit cards whenever she could to earn more airline miles. She counted one hundred and fifty dollars, kept twenty, and handed Jake the rest.

"It's not much, but maybe it will help."

Jake didn't bite and made no move to take the bills. When he reached over to close the door of the truck, Kate tucked the stack of greenbacks over her visor. He'd see them and use them in due time.

"I have a few friends in St. Louis that are attorneys. How about I ask them to write that asshole a nasty letter?" Kate couldn't believe something like this could happen in this day and age.

Jake shook his head. "I'm not so sure that's a good idea."

"Why?"

"You don't know how these outfits operate. It might just piss him off and make matters worse."

"So quit."

"I can't leave those horses." His face was drawn. He looked like he'd aged twenty-five years.

"What about Cecil? He's the one that got you into this mess!" Kate's dislike for Cecil was growing stronger by the minute. But in her heart she knew there was no way in hell Jake would leave Cecil and those horses alone to starve in the mountains.

"Kate, I appreciate your help, really. But it's not your problem. You don't need to get involved. I can take care of this myself."

They rode the rest of the way to Stella's in silence.

KATE FLEW BACK TO ST. LOUIS with a sour taste in her mouth. The whole Bear Track incident had her emotions tied in knots. In addition to the awful conditions at the ranch, Jake had treated her with a total lack of respect, and he had obviously lost respect for himself. She was having a difficult time getting past that. Was it his reaction to living in such a shit hole, or was what she saw really a part of Jake? She didn't want to believe the latter.

Once again, work provided a refuge for Kate. She put all her energy into selling cars and preparing for the holidays. Marino Motors needed lights, wreaths, pine roping, and a Christmas tree, and so did her house. Kate pushed aside her gloomy mood and took Sam out to their farm where she chopped down two Scotch pines. They delivered the tallest one to the dealership.

"Would you help me put on the lights?" Joseph Marino asked his grandson.

"Can I?" Sam jumped up and down.

James sat on the other side of the showroom floor, watching, arms crossed, and scowling. He looked like the Grinch, and Kate wondered if he would try to steal Christmas.

Two weeks flew by, and Kate did not hear a word from Jake. She knew his pride had been bruised, so she waited for him to contact her. Stella kept tabs on him through the Jackson Hole grapevine. She told Kate that the owner of the Bear Track had finally coughed up enough money for the horses, but only after someone reported him to the Humane Society. Stella did not know if Cecil and Jake had been paid.

As Kate addressed Christmas cards, she thought about sending Jake one. But a card would require saying something, and at this point she didn't know what to say. Instead, she sent him a beautiful Pendleton wool blanket, something to keep him warm during the bitter cold nights.

Sam's presence was Kate's best present. He made the holiday season fun and festive. They took a carriage ride through Tilles Park's Winter Wonderland to view the incredible display of lights. Kate's mom and dad got them tickets to the *Nutcracker* at the Fox Theatre. They drank hot chocolate and watched the Sugar Plum Fairy float across the stage. And Sam updated his Christmas list every other day.

"Mom, what do you want for Christmas?" Sam asked.

Kate felt like saying, "A new family and a new job," but didn't. The doom-and-gloom team at Marino Motors were becoming more and more unbearable. The day before had been particularly painful.

"Dad, I've got a great new idea for the newspaper ad!" Kate had said, in a desperate attempt to do something new and creative.

"Don't try and tell me what sells cars—price sells cars!" Mr. Marino yelled as he grabbed the *St. Louis Post-Dispatch* and walked into Kate's office. After paging to the automotive section, he continued his lecture.

"See? 'Year-End Blowout,' 'Clearance,' 'Everything Must Go!' Now, that's what gets people's attention!" He hit the paper repeatedly with his fist in the center of their competitor's full-page spread.

"Dad, I know price sells cars, but don't you think people want good service, someone that they can trust?" Kate replied evenly. She noticed that he wore the camel-hair sweater she had given to him for his birthday.

"People will drive thirty minutes down the road to save fifty bucks. They don't give a damn about service."

"Well, how about us being family-owned and operated? I think it means something to the consumer that we've been around for nearly fifty years," she said, in a last-ditch effort. Then James walked in and sat down in the chair next to her.

"So, I see you saw Riverfront Chrysler's ad. I told you we should have been more aggressive in our ad!" he said in his favorite condescending tone.

"God damn it! Get me an invoice on the cheapest vehicle we've got on the lot. I'll beat their price and then some!" Mr. Marino boomed.

James jumped like a soldier called to attention and ran to the sales office. He promptly returned with the big blue binder holding copies of all the invoices in inventory. Kate thought about leaving and letting the doom-and-gloom team make up yet another obnoxious ad filled with half-truths, but changed her mind. It would only give James another chance to attack her and say how she didn't really care about the business.

"Okay, give me absolute cost!" Mr. Marino said as James took out his i-phone and tapped the calculator app.

"Eleven thousand, eight ninety-seven, and forty-two cents!"

"Now, take a thousand off of that, and that's our loss leader."

"Brilliant!" James sucked up.

"Let Riverfront beat that price!" Mr. Marino sat back in Kate's chair and beamed.

All Kate heard was *blah, blah, blah* as she retreated into her own quiet world, where scenes like these slipped by like clouds on a breezy day. But she could only stay so long. Facing reality wasn't pretty. If she continued to work at Marino Motors much longer, she'd shrivel up and die. Without Jake there was no balance, no connection to Wyoming, those wide open spaces that seemed to hold limitless possibilities.

The voice of reason, the one that said, *Stay safe, work for your father,* was only a whisper now. Intuition nudged her, telling her she should jump into unknown parts of herself. As the days passed, it became more and more clear that she was going to have to leave Marino Motors once again—like the prodigal daughter, only backwards.

Kate wondered if she was losing her mind or finding it. At

this point it was common knowledge that she was dating a cow-boy from Wyoming who was barely old enough to order a drink in a bar. When people found out she wanted to go live in the mountains and paint for a living, they'd really think she'd gone off the deep end. Oh well, she thought, maybe it was a crazy plan, but it was her plan. She was never one to worry about what other people thought.

But there was one person she did need on her side to make her paint-in-the-mountains scheme work. Kate called him first.

"I know you are going to think I am crazy, but I want to paint full-time, and I want to find someplace in the mountains to set up a studio."

Michael waited a moment, then simply asked, "Where?"

"I don't know yet." Her voice faltered. She was nervous, but tried her best to hide it. "The important thing is that Sam is happy and stable. I will need chunks of time, maybe go away and paint for a couple of weeks, then come back to St. Louis for a few weeks to be with Sam."

"You do what you need to do," Michael answered, with a little more edge to his words than Kate was comfortable with.

"I can't do this without your support. Maybe we could go back to the summer schedule, like when you had to visit your mom in Florida?" Her throat constricted as she fought to hold back the tears. She was so tired of crying. If it was such a healthy release, why did she feel like she was a hundred years old?

"Kate, Sam is going to be just fine. He's already used to you traveling a few weeks at a time. It won't be much different," he said, "and I love doing the dad thing, cooking dinner, going to his games, all that stuff. So I'll be fine, too."

Kate knew Michael was being sincere. He loved being with Sam and was probably happy to have his son all to himself.

Somehow this made her feel even more guilty than she already felt. Then she did start to cry. She couldn't help it.

"Please don't cry. You know I hate it when you cry. Everything is going to be all right. And we've got Jennifer to help out."

"I know, but I still worry. If he even begins to show signs that he's suffering . . ." She wiped her nose with a tissue and cleared her throat. "Well, I'll just have to figure something else out."

"He's going to be fine. Like I said, you've traveled since he was a baby. A lot of women travel as a part of their job. Look at it that way."

His words gave her courage and made her feel strong. Michael was a good man, and she was a lucky woman. This lifestyle change was a big move for her, and she could not do it without his blessing. And now that she had it, it was time to move forward.

THE OPPORTUNITY CAME MORE quickly than she thought.

A few days later, Kate received a phone call from an old friend in Colorado, Grant Milton. Grant owned an enormous ranch between Dillon and Steamboat. It was a little remote, but absolutely beautiful.

"So, I hear you're looking to find a place to try out mountain living!" Grant said.

"How in the hell did you know that?" Kate was stunned. She hadn't talked to Grant in months. Then it dawned on her.

"You've been talking to Matt!" Matt was their mutual friend who worked for the airline.

Grant chuckled. "Yeah, I needed his help with a trip to Chicago. He took care of me, and I got him two tickets to the Nuggets game next Saturday."

Now they both laughed. Matt was a sports fanatic and worked on the airline barter system. It was great for all parties involved.

"He is the man! He's saved me a fortune in airfare this past year."

"I know. He told me about your new cowboy, and that you were looking for a place to paint for the winter."

"I am. I've had it with the car business and all the family bullshit that goes with it." Kate knew Grant would understand. A few years back he had been in a similar situation, working for his father in the steel business in Chicago. Kate didn't know the details, but she knew he left the business with enough money in his pocket to buy his ranch.

"Well, it just so happens I'm looking for a short-term renter at Willow Creek. With winter coming on, I don't need a hand until spring, so I could rent you the place for a few months."

"How long?" Kate could barely contain her excitement.

"I don't know for sure, probably until March, possibly April."

It was perfect. She could leave right after the holidays, when Sam went back to school. Three months would be enough time to find out if she could really paint.

"How much?"

"Well, let's see . . ."

Kate could hear the smile in his voice.

"Seeing how you're helping me with this short-term renter thing—how does six hundred a month sound?"

Kate just about fell out of her chair. The house at Willow Creek was every bit as nice as her place in St. Louis, only it had a magnificent view of the New York Mountain Range. There was also a lovely new kitchen and a master bedroom suite with a huge steam shower.

"Does that include utilities?" Kate held her breath, not wanting to push her luck, but she had no idea how she was even going to come up with six hundred for rent. She would be completely unemployed and would still have a mortgage to pay, plus she'd have to figure out how she was going to get back and forth to Colorado. Matt would help, for sure, but she didn't want to wear out her welcome.

"Sure, I'll throw in utilities; they're not much anyway. The furnace is wood burning, and there are two smaller stoves: one in the family room, the other one in the hall. I can cut you some wood, but you'll have to haul and stack it."

"You've got yourself a renter!" Kate was thrilled. This was her big chance and she grabbed on to it like a life preserver thrown to a drowning woman.

THE NEXT MORNING, KATE FOLLOWED her father into his dark, mahogany-paneled office. Kate took a seat in one of the sixties-vintage, orange crushed-velvet barrel chairs. It took her eyes a few minutes to adjust to the dim light, her palms moistened with a faint film of sweat.

"Dad, I've got something to talk to you about."

"What is it?"

Kate hated knowing she was about to disappoint him. Her hands were now drenched with sweat, and her mouth felt like a sheet of sandpaper. She decided the faster she said it, the faster it would be over with.

"I'm leaving the dealership again. I'm not coming back after Christmas, at least not for awhile."

Living dead silence.

"Did you hear me?" She wiped her hands across her flannel trousers.

Mr. Marino sat oddly expressionless, then finally said, "So what do you plan on doing for money?"

Money. It always came down to that. She hated how it

controlled and crippled her family. Kate was coming to realize it wasn't what money bought that made her happy. It never would be. All the money in the world couldn't buy what she really wanted most.

"I still have my savings." Her voiced sounded so small in front of her larger-than-life father.

"Kate, I think you are dreaming. And I guess that's okay. Your mother tells me you want to paint."

So that's why he hasn't blown a gasket, Kate thought. Her mother had prepared him.

"That's right."

"You're not going to make it peddling paintings. The best artist is a dead artist." He put on his reading glasses and picked an envelope from the stack of morning mail. This was his way of dismissing her.

And then Kate surprised even herself. She stood up and surveyed the room, walking by his wildlife paintings and bronzes, studying each and every one like the curator of a fine-art museum. After a few minutes ticked by, she finally said, "Well, when I die then, they'll find a bunch of beautiful paintings in my closet and Sam will be a very wealthy man."

Mr. Marino kept his head down, falsely absorbed in a letter, and said, "I'm not going to argue with you, but I think you're kidding yourself."

Let the joke be on him, Kate thought.

KATE PACKED HER JEEP AND LEFT for Willow Creek on New Year's Day. She brought books, pictures, her two favorite Navajo rugs, a down comforter, warm clothing, and boots, in addition to her painting supplies. The house was equipped with everything else.

What Kate wasn't prepared for was the solitude. The isolation and quiet passing of the hours was deafening. It was the first time she had spent large chunks of time completely alone. There was no television service, newspapers, or neighbors within shouting range. The radio had poor reception, picking up only one country-western station. There was no static from other people telling her what to do or how to act. Her sole companion was her own mind, and she still wasn't sure if she'd lost or found it. It was a difficult transition. Her imagination ran free, but its partners were doubt and fear. Being alone was one of Kate's biggest challenges; she loved and hated it.

The business of self-sufficiency came easier. Kate kept the wood stoves stoked during the cold nights and let the solar heat from the huge windows warm the house during the day. Twice a week, she'd navigate the sometimes-plowed, sometimes-not snow-covered roads into town to get groceries, painting supplies, and a few movies. In the evening, she took great pleasure in preparing a meal just for herself: pasta or an elk steak Grant had given her. Afterwards, she'd sit with a glass of wine next to the fire in the family room, listening to the coyotes and wolves howl. The animals didn't scare her. It was her own untamed thoughts, other old ghosts that continued to haunt her.

You don't have the talent to be an artist. People are going to laugh at you and your work! the invisible voice said.

Kate had only taken a few college-level art classes before her father pushed her into switching to the school of business. Other than that, her only training was at the high school level, which wasn't much—a few pottery and drawing courses. She started painting with acrylics on her own for fun. In the midseventies, there was a popular music store that decorated its walls with gigantic copies of album covers. Kate loved the idea. She took

Fleetwood Mac's *Rumors* cover, her favorite album at the time, and did the same thing, only smaller—a twenty-four-by-thirty-six inch version. Her girlfriends saw it hanging in her bedroom, then started spreading the news of what she was doing. All of a sudden, all kinds of people were asking if she would do a piece for them. It became a nice little hobby; copying was easy, and she made fifty bucks a canvas.

But this wasn't high school, and this wasn't copying other people's work. It was a stretch, this reaching for something she wanted so badly. And she had nothing but faith to hold on to.

When the chips were down, Kate picked up a book. She dove into philosophy, Native American culture and spirituality, Western history, Western fiction, and books written about the creative process. Kate soaked up the information. The words on the pages were like water on a sapling, nourishing, providing deep roots, helping her inner artist grow sure and strong.

Betty, her friend in Denver, had sent her *The Artist's Way* by Julia Cameron, and it was now her bible. As instructed by the author, each week Kate read a chapter, which was followed by mind-expanding homework or exercises. A few of the assignments seemed rather strange, so she called Betty for support.

"Okay, so I'm supposed to look at my wardrobe and see what colors I wear most. Then I'm supposed to go shopping and find something in a color I would normally not wear?" Kate whined.

"It's all about breaking out of the box, right?" Betty said.

"Yes." Kate paused, looking outside at the gray-blue clouds building to the west. A winter storm was moving in. "But I need to shop like I need a hole in my head."

"You don't have to spend a bunch of money. You know the outlet malls are in Dillon . . ."

Kate took a minute and thought about what Betty suggested.

She was right. Dillon was only about an hour's drive if the weather was good. It was a resort town and offered all the conveniences a big city boasted.

"I know. But I still don't see what a few new sweaters in different colors are going to do for me."

"You'll see," Betty said.

Kate drove to Dillon a few days later. She scouted the J.Crew outlet with the practiced eye of an artist, searching for just the right shade of clothing. A table of sweaters in a rainbow of pastel colors caught her attention. Her usual uniform—black and brown—was nowhere in sight. Somehow the cardigans seemed so feminine, and that, surprisingly, appealed to Kate. She rifled through the stack of pale-blue cotton and located her size, and then searched through the pile of lavender. At the register, the two items totaled just under thirty dollars. Betty was certainly right about the money issue, Kate thought as she drove back to Willow Creek, proud of her choices.

There were times when the days at Willow Creek dripped like Chinese torture. To break the monotony, Kate would strap on her snowshoes and trudge out into the softness of the snow. The repetitive movement of the traipsing motion matched with the muted gray tones and stark-white meadows created a blankness in her mind. In the silence, built-up fears and distractions were erased so she could find the broad strokes she sought to fill her canvases.

Kate had secured a few commissions. Michael had accepted the new schedule with Sam with one condition; Kate would paint a picture for him to hang over the mantel in his new house. It was a huge canvas, three by four feet, and he was paying her seven hundred and fifty dollars. Kate was only too happy to oblige. Michael had torn out a golf photo from a magazine and wanted her to basically copy it, just as she used to do with all those album covers back in high school. She started on the canvas right after she returned from her shopping excursion to Dillon.

The painting was coming along nicely; she felt her work was strong. It was the fact that she had not seen another human for almost a week that made her feel like she was going to jump out of her skin.

The bustling town of Parshall, with its combination post office/convenience store/sporting goods store and the Parshall Inn, was only twenty minutes down the road. The PI was a popular spot with the local ranchers—it was the only bar and grill within a forty-mile radius. Kate decided a drink, a little comfort food, and some friendly conversation was just what the doctor ordered. Before leaving, Kate went to her bedroom. She opened the closet, pulled off her black fleece, and replaced it with her new lavender sweater. A smile crossed her face when she looked at her reflection in the mirror.

"Not bad, not bad at all!" she said out loud, giggling. Somehow the simple little sweater made her feel different—lighter, almost playful.

The Parshall Inn was peppered with men clothed in camouflage and Carhartt, the dress-for-success attire in the West. A group was huddled at the end of the bar, deep in a heated discussion about their beloved Denver Broncos. Kate took a seat at the opposite end. She scanned the menu, then waved down the bartender.

"What can I get you?" One look at the attractive brunette in the soft sweater and clean Wranglers told the bartender that Kate had to be Grant Milton's new renter at Willow Creek.

"I'll have a cheeseburger and fries, please."

"Anything to drink?" he asked, then thought, *I bet she doesn't know the difference between a hammer and a hatchet, but who the hell cares. I wonder if Grant is doing her.*

Kate hated the fact that she'd never developed the taste for beer. "I guess I'll have a tequila, neat. And a water on the side." She rationalized it would dilute the strength of the booze.

The bartender raised his eyebrow, then reached for the bottle behind the bar. He poured a healthy two fingers and put it in front of Kate. She sipped it slowly, and listened to the men's conversation, content to hear the hum of human voices.

It didn't take long for one of the men to notice Kate. He made his way over to her and introduced himself.

"You must be Kate, Grant's new renter at Willow Creek!" he said, and proceeded to tell the bartender to refill Kate's glass. "My name is Virgil. Mind if I join you?"

"That would be nice." Kate remembered Grant mentioning Virgil's name several times in passing. He worked on his family's ranch, and the local ladies considered him to be quite a catch.

Virgil—big, blond, and handsome—kept Kate entertained while she ate. He told her she had just missed his big thirtieth birthday bash at the PI.

"I sure wish Grant had reminded me you were here. I would have invited you, and you could have met the whole gang."

"Oh, that's sweet. Sorry I missed it." Kate wasn't sure who the gang was but was pretty sure she wouldn't have much in common with them.

Virgil offered to buy Kate another drink. She accepted, but ordered a club soda. She thought it was smart to keep a clear head in this land of hunters. As the night wore on, Virgil took to rubbing her tired, sore neck. He offered her more coverage back at her place, and begged Kate to take him home with her. At that point, Kate knew it was time to make a move toward the door, and she delicately announced it was time to head back to the Willow Creek—alone.

"You got to be lonely out there all by yourself. Sure you don't want a little company?"

Kate had to admit she was lonely, but one night with Virgil wasn't the answer. Jake was still finely etched in her heart and was not going to be so easily forgotten. Kate slid off the chrome barstool, put on her down parka, and then said to Virgil, "You know, you seem very nice, but I'm in love with someone else." She gave Virgil a sisterly kiss on the cheek and walked out the door.

The day before she left St. Louis, Jake had finally called Kate to thank her for the blanket. He didn't sound great, but didn't sound bad either. They didn't talk about the past; Kate was too excited about the future. She told him about Willow Creek, and he had seemed genuinely happy for her. There were no "I love you's" uttered when they said good-bye, although it seemed to hang unspoken between them.

But they had not talked since. Not having a phone at the Bear Track was a big part of the lack of communication, and as hard as it was for Kate, it was also a relief. She still wasn't sure how she felt. She needed this time alone to sort out her own life. Did she want to live in the mountains because of Jake? Was it his soul or her own that drove her to this new life? Could she really make a living being an artist? She had to know. These were big questions, big steps. Kate had to answer them on her own, without distraction, and take the leaps of faith without Jake as her safety net.

The telephone rang. Fresh mouse droppings crunched underneath her bare feet as she ran from the bedroom out to the kitchen.

"Shit! I mean, hello!" she said, dripping wet from the steam shower and out of breath.

"Hello to you, too!" It was Betty.

"God, I'm sorry. I just jumped out of the shower."

Lately, it was as if Betty had an inner tracking device. Every time Kate was in conflict, Betty would ring her up. It was eerie.

"So, how is the artist formerly known as Kate?"

Kate forgot all about her chilled body as Betty's positive energy brought warmth to her heart. She wrapped her fleece robe around herself, sat down at the kitchen table, and prepared herself for a healing dose of the world according to Betty. Betty listened to Kate vent her doubts—how she thought maybe it was all a big mistake, setting up the studio and staying in Colorado.

"And Ted called."

"How the hell did he find you out there?"

"Oh, I'm sure he gave Janet, the receptionist at the dealership, some bullshit line about how he needed to buy another car and would only buy it from me."

"What a pathetic loser."

"Well, he's the one that made me feel like the loser. He went on and on about how crazy I was to give up a multimillion-dollar dealership to paint."

"Kate, stop it. First of all, you need to ignore Ted. Close your eyes and make him disappear. What he says is not important."

"Oh, I'm not finished. He started in on my relationship with my 'boy toy,' Jake!"

"I thought you and Jake had split up? And besides, it's none of his business!" Betty was finding it difficult to keep her temper in check.

"I know. He just loves to tell me, 'I told you so!' What I didn't tell him was that I just started getting letters from Jake."

"You have?" Betty had never met Jake, but she liked what he had done for Kate. When she met him, she was a caterpillar, and now she was a butterfly.

"Two and three letters at a time! They are all very apologetic." Kate paused, inhaled deeply, then let the next words rush out with her breath. "He says he still loves me."

Kate had not written back. Now she was ashamed at her own lack of awareness and sensitivity. She had been so busy fighting her own battles, she had lost sight of his feelings and what he must have been going through at that hellhole of a ranch.

"So write him back."

"I'm not sure what to say, or where to start."

"Just speak from your heart. Jake loves you. It'll be okay."

The challenge of the inner battle, the constant questioning and doubt with her emerging creativity, was a little more involved. Betty wasn't an artist, but she did know how to use the subconscious to solve psychological warfare and unravel the strings of doubt that so often tangle the brain.

"I've talked to you about meditation numerous times; have you ever tried it?"

"Yeah, but I can never do it. There's too much stuff that goes on. I just end up thinking about all the things I should be doing. And then what I shouldn't be doing."

"Okay, here's what you do. Do you have a candle?"

"Of course! And oil lamps, and wood-burning stoves, and ..."

"All right, all right, I forgot about your fire fetish!"

Kate loved anything that had flames. They both laughed.

"Now seriously, go to a quiet spot, light a candle, put it at eye level or in a place where it's comfortable for your eyes to focus on it, and then sit and focus on the flame."

"Really?"

"Really. If you have something to focus on, it will help. And then, if any thoughts interrupt, thank them, and just let them float in and float out, like clouds."

"Does it really work?"

"It'll take practice, like anything else. You may only relax into it for a few minutes at first."

"I'd be happy with even that."

"Well, after awhile, you'll be able to quiet yourself for as long as thirty minutes. It's like taking a nap, but you wake up feeling completely clear, as well as rested."

After Kate hung up with Betty, she looked across the room at Michael's painting. The finished piece was a field of bright green with a golfer chipping out of a sand trap. The sand was a wild splash of orange and yellow; the background, a tall grassy area, was brushed with narrow, delicate strokes of red, pink, yellow, and lavender. The scene was the same as the photo, but it was most definitely not a copy of the picture. Kate wanted to see how Michael would react to her bold interpretation of the sport. She was proud of her work and hoped he liked it, too.

What to paint next? Ideas flew in and out of her head like a flock of birds.

Her gaze shifted left to the untouched canvas that balanced on her easel. She had screamed at that canvas this morning, as if it could yell right back at her and tell her what to paint. Betty had given her the tools to cope with her doubts and frustration about painting, but she needed more. At first she had prayed for direction, but now she asked for a sign. Was she doing the right thing? Giving up her job, not seeing Sam for three weeks, painting? She worried again that she was losing her mind.

Kate went outside and strapped on her snowshoes. She looked down the long, winding road, bordered with bare branches and snowdrifts as high as walls, and asked the higher power to give her some sort of sign if she was still on the right path. Kate wanted something concrete, something she couldn't rationalize. She needed reinforcement from the universe.

After a mile-long trek around the ranch that left her cheeks rosy and her fingers half-frozen, she returned to the house. She set up a small candle on a footstool in her bedroom and lit it. The time was only eleven o'clock. Her peak productive painting time was from eleven in the morning until three in the afternoon, but she still had no idea what to paint. On her walk, she kept thinking about a wolf. She sat down on the floor and crossed her legs like a pretzel. The flame jumped in the drafty room as Kate squinted her eyes and concentrated on the movement from left to right, as if the candle were a primitive dancer. When she shut her eyes, colors—yellow, blue, and red—in the shape of teardrops burned on her closed lids. A thought floated by. *Wouldn't it be incredible if I could paint a wolf with eyes like that!* She thanked the thought and let it float by.

Half an hour later, she was dipping her palette knife in cadmium yellow, alizarin crimson, and cobalt blue, at the direction of an energy completely unfamiliar to her. She felt as though her whole body were charged with electricity, as if a white light were shining over her head and she was plugged directly into it. There was no sketching. The eyes came first, just like the image she saw in her meditation, and then the head of a wolf, staring right at her, the windows of its soul boring directly into hers.

Miraculously, after only two hours, the painting was about three-quarters finished. Kate stopped, interrupted by the phone again. She wandered over to it, still wired with energy, absorbed in what she was creating.

On the other end of the line was Patrick, calling from his home in Florida. Her sister had introduced him to Kate when she visited Grace and her husband in Naples last spring. Patrick owned a very successful commercial real estate company. Kate had spent quite a bit of time with him. Even though they enjoyed each other's company, they never clicked romantically.

"Happy holidays!" Patrick chuckled.

"Hey, better late than never." Kate said. It was good to hear from him, but she wondered why he was calling at such an odd time. "Did you have a good Christmas?"

"I did. But you know, I'm kind of glad it's over. You know how much fun my family can be." He changed the subject. "Speaking of family, I saw Grace at a benefit last night. She told me about your big move out West."

"She did, did she?" Kate prayed Grace wasn't trying to play matchmaker again.

"You know, I want one of your paintings."

"Oh, Patrick, you don't need to do that!" Kate was blown away by his kindness.

"No, I really do want one of your paintings. Now, I can't afford a three-thousand-dollar job . . ."

Kate cracked up. "Oh, honey, they're going a lot cheaper than that!" She was flattered.

"Okay, how much are we talking?"

"Well, depends on what size you want," she answered, thinking that another commission might just give her the jump-start she needed.

"Oh, I don't know, just a regular size."

"Well, an eighteen by twenty-four would go for about seven hundred and fifty dollars." Kate had given Michael a deal for obvious reasons.

"Sounds reasonable." High-strung Patrick sounded unusually mellow.

"So, what do you want the subject to be?" Kate crossed her fingers and prayed the subject would be something she could do.

"You know what I really want?" he said dreamily.

"What?"

"A wolf."

Her heart pounded. *Holy shit!* she thought. She struggled to contain her excitement as she stared at the painting she was about to complete.

"I just happen to be in the middle of painting one."

"A wolf?"

"Yeah, a wolf." She spoke softly, her voice barely a whisper.

"I'll take it."

"You haven't even seen it!" Kate was stunned.

"If you like it, I'll like it."

Kate stood back and stared at the painting. She liked it. She liked it very much.

"Well, I have to tell you, it's not even an ordinary wolf. Its fur is yellow, blue, and red, but his eyes are amazing; they follow you around the room." Betty's call, the meditation, the painting, and now this—it was all too coincidental to be a coincidence.

"You know how fascinated I am with wolves," he said.

And he was—Kate remembered that about him.

"I'll hang it in my bedroom."

"It's a wolf of another color."

"Perfect, because so am I."

They said their good-byes, and after she placed the phone on the receiver, she looked up and said, "Okay, okay, I hear you loud and clear!"

That night, the first full moon of the year was so bright Kate had to shut her normally open shades before she went to bed. She fell into an exhausted sleep. Somewhere after midnight, she dreamt there was a man on the deck right outside her window, sitting in a chair. His back was to her, but the back of his hand signaled for her to get out of bed. It was more like a vision than a dream because Kate was conscious that she was dreaming. In her half-awake state, she wondered if she should grab the bear spray she had hidden in her dresser drawer, in case the stranger wasn't friendly. Then the sound of a dog's claws clicking as it walked across the cedar deck fully woke her. She sat upright in bed and strained to hear if there really was a dog on her deck. All was quiet, except that in the not-too-far distance, she heard the clear pitch of a lone wolf howling.

First-Time Heifer

JAKE'S EMOTIONS RAN WITH HIM, on the verge of being out of control, as he sat on the big, high-powered stud. It was the most horse he'd ever been on, and he made the Bar Lazy J Guest Ranch in a record forty-five minutes, a six-mile trek. He could have taken one of the snowmobiles from the Bear Track, but the road was packed solid and he was desperate for the peace a long, hard ride brought.

In his saddlebag he carried three more letters to Kate, all penned in the faint glow of a crystal oil lamp. Jake had finally got the generator fired up at the Bear Track, but was careful to use it only when necessary. The propane tank was already almost empty. And judging from his boss's track record, it wasn't likely to be filled again, at least not while he was wintering there. It was cold, dark, and depressing. He made do with the wood stove for heat and oil lamps for light.

But there was no substitute for Kate. Jake missed her so badly his heart ached. He felt empty without her. He was so sorry he had hurt her, sorry that he had destroyed her trust in him. He spent many sleepless nights thinking about that night at the Bear Track, and Kate in the red dress. She was so beautiful, perfection. And he was a coward. It was that simple. He was convinced Kate would eventually leave him, so he took the opportunity to push her away. Now Kate was on a ranch somewhere in Colorado. Stella told Cecil that Kate was "very disappointed." Jake figured she was more than likely mad as hell to boot. The anger Jake could handle, but not the disappointment, and not talking to her was driving him crazy.

The Bar Lazy J was the closest ranch with winter residents. Ned, the caretaker, went to Jackson Hole on a regular basis and was willing to take and pick up Jake's mail at the post office. But Jake had to do the pony express to the Bar Lazy J to retrieve the parcels. It was only Thursday, yet it was Jake's second trip. He hoped these additional letters would bring Kate around, give him another chance, let him prove how much she meant to him, how desperately he loved her. The thought of losing her coiled around him like a boa constrictor, squeezing tighter with each passing day.

Jake tied his horse to the hitching post, his boots echoing a repetitive, hollow thud as he started to climb the plank stairs to the front door. Ned walked out to greet him.

"How goes it, top hand?"

"Oh, all right, I suppose." Jake was out of chew, which made him even more tense and anxious.

"Got a little something for you." Ned reached into his down jacket and produced a can of Copenhagen.

"Well, I'll be!"

Jake ran his thumbnail around the lid, shaking like an alcoholic who needs a drink. He popped off the top, pinched out a large wad, and stuffed it between his lower lip and gum. The nicotine relaxed him almost instantly.

"Got anything else?"

"Nope."

Jake's face fell. He couldn't believe there was no word from Kate. Their last morning together stood frozen in his mind. Her stinging comment about his wanting her just for sex had hurt. Kate was his best friend. He loved trying to make her feel like the prettiest, sexiest woman in the whole world and touching her body was one of the only ways he knew to convey that. He had to explain it to her, make her understand.

"But that girlfriend of yours called and left a message for you with her number. You're supposed to call her back," Ned said, grinning.

Relief pumped through Jake's body. At least she was willing to talk to him. He wasn't exactly a religious man, but he prayed she wasn't delivering him his walking papers.

"Ya reckon I could use your phone?"

"I'm way ahead of you." Ned opened the screen door and pointed down the entry hall to a phone on a table.

Jake took the remaining steps to the lodge two at a time but then stopped short of the door. He didn't have a dime with him and wasn't about to call Kate collect.

"Uh, Ned, could I bring you a few dollars for the call when I come back next time?"

Ned gave him a toothless smile and put his hand on Jake's shoulder. "No problem, pard. You just make that call, and we'll settle up later."

Kate sat in deep meditation, no longer in need of a candle for focus. She sat in front of the plateglass window, where she could feel the power of the mountains. She tried to meditate daily now, following the quiet time with a few yoga stretches.

The phone shrilled in the silence, causing Kate to jump. Her leg knocked over the stack of books that sat at the foot of her chair. She ran frantically around the room in search of the portable phone she could hear but not see. It would be Jake. She knew it like she knew the sun would set in the west at 5 p.m. Her heart pounded as she threw back the white drop cloth below her easel revealing the black handset.

"Kate?" Jake's low, gravelly voice was so faint, Kate could barely hear him.

"Jake!" Her eyes welled up. She struggled to keep her composure.

"How are you?" he asked.

"Better now that I'm talking to you." Tears rolled down Kate's pink cheeks, but this time they were tears of pure joy. She thought of the poem by E. E. Cummings that Jake had mailed to her only a few days ago. Kate read and reread it every night.

> *i carry your heart with me(i carry it in*
> *my heart)i am never without it(anywhere*
> *i go you go,my dear;and whatever is done*
> *by only me is your doing,my darling)*
> > *i fear*
> *no fate(for you are my fate,my sweet)i want*
> *no world(for beautiful you are my world,my true)*
> *and it's you are whatever a moon has always meant*
> *and whatever a sun will always sing is you*
>
> *here is the deepest secret nobody knows*
> *(here is the root of the root and the bud of the bud*
> *and the sky of the sky of a tree called life;which grows*
> *higher than soul can hope or mind can hide)*
> *and this is the wonder that's keeping the stars apart*
>
> *i carry your heart(i carry it in my heart)*

The poem was a beautiful expression of love, but what ripped Kate's heart wide open was what followed—Jake's own words, strung together so exquisitely: "After you become you and I become me, we will be together, every night, naked in each other's arms, and we will talk and talk for hours, because that is what I miss the most, the sharing. I miss sharing my life with you, Kate."

After reading his letter, Kate had sobbed for hours. The walls she had built around her heart came tumbling down. Never in her life had any person expressed such vulnerability, such honest and raw need. The should's and should-not's of traditional society screamed at her, and she yelled right back. It was okay for a man to date or marry a much younger woman, and nobody seemed to care if that woman had a "real job" or not. Kate decided what was good for the goose was good for the gander. Jake truly loved her, down to the depths of his soul, and to turn her back on him now would be a sin. She would be lying to herself for the rest of her life. Deep down, Kate loved Jake just as much as he loved her. It was time to take another chance.

BY MID-FEBRUARY, KATE HAD ARRANGED for Jake to be Grant's new hired hand at Willow Creek Ranch. Grant needed help with maintenance around the ranch and come March, there would be plenty of work with calving. There wasn't any horse training to be done, but Jake would have access to a few head of horses to ride for pleasure. Jake, however, was apprehensive about leaving Cecil alone at the Bear Track.

"Oh, hell, Jake, I can handle this outfit on my own, for Christ's sake!" Cecil said when Jake told him the news. "I was planning on wintering here alone to begin with, remember?"

"I remember all right. I also remember us having to dig

through two feet of snow so those nags out there could get to some grass to eat."

"Well, the snow's a-melting and spring is right around the corner. Come April I'm out of here. You go ahead and take that job in Colorado." Cecil smiled, revealing a missing tooth smack in the middle of his mouth, a memento from attempts to gentle a two-year-old. A horse whisperer he was not.

"Besides, I'm tired of seeing you mope around here like a lovesick pup."

AS JAKE'S MOVE-IN DAY APPROACHED, Kate started feeling buyer's remorse. It was an annoying and confusing emotion. She and Jake had talked about owning a ranch together so many times, she should be feeling like it was a dream come true. This was a gift, an opportunity for a dress rehearsal before the real production. She forced herself to dig deep, and finally she unearthed what was really bothering her.

The transition from mother in St. Louis to artist in the mountains was difficult, and it required the utmost discipline. Kate feared she would lose both, knowing that Jake could consume her to the point of complete distraction. There had to be balance. She had to have her own space to paint.

It was Grant who came up with a possible solution. There was an old trailer that sat on the property right below the house where Kate was staying.

"It could use a good cleaning, but it's fine. Heck, my last hand, Shane, lived there all last year. The wood stove works, and it's got a couple of beds."

"Really?" Kate had taken little notice of the trailer. It looked like it had seen better days.

"Well, the bathroom is questionable. Plumbing is probably all messed up."

"Oh, he can use mine!" Kate thought it would be perfect. Jake could have his own place to hang his hat during the day, and they could be together at night.

"I should think so—he's your boyfriend! He'll probably love that steam shower," Grant ribbed.

"That's enough," Kate said, embarrassed that he verbalized what she had just thought.

When Kate told Jake about the trailer, he was excited. Kate had made clear the seriousness of her painting, and he respected her need for space. Jake knew all about freedom and space. They were the two reasons he cowboyed for a living.

Kate waited until the morning Jake was to arrive to walk the fifty feet from the deck of her house to the trailer. The door was so warped she had to kick it with the heel of her boot. It sprung open to a ménage of filth. The bathroom might not be working, but the mice had seen to it that the entire place had been used as a toilet. It wasn't fit for a dog, much less a man. Grant probably hadn't stepped into the rusty old eyesore for years. He told her what she wanted to hear, and she chose to believe him. She thought about giving it a quick cleaning but knew "quick" wouldn't do the job. What the dump needed was a stick of dynamite and a match.

It was sunset when Jake pulled into Willow Creek. The white Chevy flatbed was pillowed with snow. Kate ran outside to great him. Jake jumped out of the truck so fast he nearly forgot to engage the emergency brake. They didn't kiss; they just held on tight, wrapped in each other's arms, not wanting to lose each other again. Neither felt the icy sting of the snow and the wind whipping around them.

Kate felt Jake lift his head as he peered over her shoulder at the oversize tin can that was supposed to be his new home. "Why don't you put your stuff inside the house for now," she said in a small voice. Kate kept her gaze down, too ashamed to look him in the eyes.

"'Kay," was Jake's reply.

He walked to the back of the flatbed, his shoulders rounded from the ten-hour drive from Jackson Hole. Kate followed him. They untied the dark-green tarp, peeled it back, and began gathering his meager possessions.

Kate led the way up the stairs to the deck, thinking that at least she had been smart enough to shovel a path. She opened the sliding glass door to the house. A fire blazed in the stove, and the welcoming scent of a good hot meal hung in the air.

"I have a few elk enchiladas warming in the oven. You hungry?" Kate said, trying to sound light.

"Sure. Sounds good."

Jake put down his duffel and saddle, then took off his hat, boots, and coat. He went around the corner to the kitchen. He stood and watched, letting the moment soak in. She was washing her hands, getting ready to serve him dinner. He was so happy he almost cried. He didn't care if he had to sleep in his truck or shovel shit for the rest of his life. Where he slept was not important. Whom he slept with was. He promised himself he would make this new job and his relationship with Kate work.

Kate turned around, and Jake moved toward her. With one swift move, he put his arms around her, lifted her onto the kitchen counter, and kissed her with the hunger he desperately wanted to satisfy. At first Kate's lips were tight with shame, but Jake's tender mouth worked to soften them. Finally Kate's mind shut off, and her body took over. Her hands slid up and down his back. He felt so solid and good. Kate wrapped her legs around his waist.

"Think we should move to someplace more comfortable?"

"Hell, no." Jake stepped back, smiled seductively, and started to unbutton his shirt.

Dinner was very, very late that night.

FOR THE NEXT FEW WEEKS, KATE attempted to balance her art and her heart. During the day, when Jake was out doing chores, Kate immersed herself in painting, experimenting with new techniques, using palette knives, sponges, and even her fingers. She desperately wanted to create something that reflected her vision of the world on the huge rough canvases. In the evening, she concentrated on Jake. She'd cook dinner for him, and afterwards they'd curl up by the fire and watch a movie. Sometimes, when they felt like being more social, they'd head into Parshall for a burger and a few games of pool. The two found that the quiet, simple existence suited them both. It worked well until Kate made her two-week pilgrimage back to St. Louis.

Once in the city, days started and ended with Sam. She dropped him off at school, went to the gym to work out, visited with her mom, ran a few errands, and then ran back to pick him up. After school there were soccer games, piano lessons, and playdates. It was all-consuming, and Kate wouldn't have it any other way. She cherished this one-on-one time with Sam.

When Kate returned to Willow Creek, the transition back to artist and lover wasn't so easy. Jake was up to his elbows in first-time heifers and newborn calves. Every three or four hours he'd hop in his truck, do slow circles in the muddy field, and check the herd. It was a round-the-clock job that was usually shared by two. But Grant thought Jake could handle the thirty four-legged mamas all on his own. So Jake popped in and out of Kate's bed like a jack-in-the box.

"Sorry to wake you, hon," he would say every time Kate opened her eyes when he got back into bed.

"I feel like I just got back to sleep. How long were you out there?" Kate asked, her voice showing a hint of annoyance.

"Not long, maybe half an hour. Nothing going on out there tonight."

Jake spooned Kate and fell into an exhausted sleep. Kate lay there wide awake wondering what in the hell she had gotten them into.

Kate tried to get back into her meditation and yoga routine, but the desired calming effect was lost when she was repeatedly greeted with surprise visits from Jake. In between calving chores, Jake brought Kate flowers, bursts of color that had managed to bloom through the melting snow, or stories of bovine births. Kate answered him with waning enthusiasm. He'd then go back to bed, snores echoing from the bedroom so loudly that Kate couldn't hear herself think. The interruptions were becoming a huge problem. Kate decided she had to do something.

"Why don't we go clean out that trailer so you have some-place to hang out?" Kate said, mustering up as much excitement as she humanly could.

"I was thinking the same thing myself. I was supposed to stay there anyway."

"I know, but after you got here I realized how much I missed you, and I really wanted you to be with me all of the time," Kate said, feeling guilty.

"And I wanted to stay with you, too. But you're not getting any sleep. It's not fair to you." Jake hated that he had somehow become an intruder in her creative process and now her bed. He quickly told himself Kate loved him, and that she had been there for him through thick and thin. Now it was time he stood by her, even though it meant standing farther and farther away.

The next day they put on masks and gloves, like two bank robbers, and got to the job of cleaning up the rodents' mess. They threw out all the old furniture and scrubbed every exposed surface with bleach and Lysol. Grant brought over an old couch, chair, and lamp from his main ranch. The project took all weekend, but when they finished at least the trailer was clean.

"It's not much, but it suits me just fine!" Jake smiled proudly as he hung a picture of himself and Cecil on the wall. He also hung a picture of Kate, smiling at the camera with a straw cowboy hat on. He carried these two possessions with him wherever he went.

"It's not half bad," Kate said softly, knowing there was still no way in hell she'd ever sleep there, much less sit down.

Jake took his move seriously, napping in the trailer during the day and steering clear of Kate as much as he could, even at night. He wanted to make sure Kate had plenty of solitude, which should have kept her happy.

But it didn't.

After about two days, Kate got upset. She couldn't believe it, but her feelings were hurt that Jake stayed away too long. She felt like a selfish, spoiled child who didn't really know what she wanted. Kate tried desperately to settle her roller-coaster emotions, yet most of the time she paced the family room, not knowing what to do from one minute to the next. Her painting time was becoming nothing but painful frustration. She didn't know real pain until she got "the call."

"Michael? What's going on? Is everything okay?" Kate said in a panic. Michael never called her at the ranch. She always called him to check on Sam.

"Sam is fine, everything is fine. Well, sort of."

"What do you mean, sort of?"

"It's Jennifer. She gave her notice. She's accepted a job as a teacher's assistant," Michael said.

"Oh my God." Kate plopped down on the hard kitchen floor not bothering to find a chair.

"I know this is going to be hard for all of us, but this is a really good opportunity for her."

"Of course it is." Kate cursed under her breath, dreading the answer to her next question. "When does she leave?"

"We have her through Friday."

"What?" Kate screamed. Friday was only four days away.

"I know this is last-minute, but Jennifer couldn't help it. They need her to start next week. I can handle it through the weekend but I leave for New York for our quarterly meetings on Monday."

Kate knew Jennifer. She didn't plan all of this on purpose. Kate mentally went through what needed to be done before her departure and told Michael she would be back by Sunday.

Kate stared at the phone long after she hung up. Jennifer was the only reason she felt comfortable going back and forth between Missouri and Colorado. Finding a replacement was going to be difficult, if not impossible. The reality of the situation made her stomach turn. This would be her last week at Willow Creek. Out of the corner of her eye, she saw Jake's truck heading in from the south pasture. She walked outside.

The sun threw off a blinding light. Kate put one hand up to her brow to shade her vision and waved the other in wide sweeps, hoping to get his attention. He finally looked in her direction, took off his hat, then waved it back and forth in acknowledgment. Kate's heart went out to him. She had Sam; he had nothing. A few minutes later, they were face to face. Kate broke the news as gently as she could. Jake took it as though he was expecting it.

SATURDAY HUNG BEFORE THEM LIKE a death sentence. Kate asked Jake to move back into the house. Instead of complaining about his crazy calving schedule, Kate rode with him, not wanting to miss any of the time they had left together. The hours flew by, and Friday night came all too quickly.

It was one of those nights when the moon burned so bright in the western sky it threatened to outshine every star in the heavens. Kate was busy preparing their "last supper." Jake rushed into the kitchen. A blast of cold air followed him.

"I got a mama in trouble. I need some help!" he yelled.

Kate turned off the oven and grabbed her coat and gloves. They ran out the door and headed to the barn behind the house.

The old cedar barn was small. Two stalls lined each wall, and a hay loft loomed above. A single sixty-watt bulb hung on a wire from the ceiling, not giving off nearly enough light. The heifer stood in the far stall, breathing very heavily, clearly in distress.

"The calf is turned inside her," Jake explained, as he hung a Coleman lantern from a nail. He then took a set of steel-gray chains and walked toward the heifer. Her sad brown eyes said she was ready to give up.

Jake opened the door to the stall, put his hand around her halter, and led her out.

"Okay, now you hold on to the halter while I tie the lead rope to this here pole."

Kate did as she was told. She knew nothing of calving procedures and had certainly never witnessed a birth.

"Now, hold on tight and don't let go until I say so."

Kate kept a firm grip. The arctic air sliced through her Gore-Tex gloves. Jake moved to the rear of the cow.

"Easy, ole girl." Jake's arm disappeared all the way up to his shoulder blade. The chains followed. He wrapped them around the calf's slippery, soft hooves, still buried in the heifer's womb. Jake poked his head around from its hindquarters.

"The baby will probably be stillborn, but I'm hopin' we can save the mama." Kate was too dumbfounded to speak and just shook her head.

Jake could see the cow was clearly exhausted. She had nothing left to make her want to push, too tired to fight the cowboy with his arm and chains halfway inside her.

"Okay, Kate, I'm gonna start pulling. You just hang on to that rope until I say to let go."

Jake pulled with everything he had. First the spindle legs appeared and then the bloody sack. It dropped to the cold, dirt floor with a hollow thud. The heifer turned her head to look at the dead calf. She and Kate stared at the small ball of wet fur.

"Are you sure it's dead?" Kate prayed that at any minute the newborn would lift its head and stand up on wobbly legs, and the mother would lick it affectionately, just like in all the movies.

But it did not happen. There was no movement from the small calf. Jake told Kate to let go of the rope. He unwrapped the lead rope from the pole and led the heifer back into the confines of the stall.

The heifer was now a cow; she had given birth. It did not matter that her calf had been born dead. She began to moo for the baby she knew she had delivered. Kate had never heard such a lonely, sorrowful sound.

THE NEXT MORNING, KATE SNEAKED out of bed as quietly as she could. She knew she was being a coward, but she did not want to wake Jake. The night before had been depressing enough. The mere thought of another emotionally draining scene wiped her out. It was a long drive back to St. Louis.

Jake heard Kate's Jeep start and launched out of bed like a rocket. He did not bother with clothes or boots. Outside he stood naked, barefoot in the snow, oblivious to his surroundings, as he watched Kate pull away.

Kate felt Jake's gaze but could not bring herself to turn around. Five miles later, when she turned on the county road, Kate allowed her pain to surface. She gripped the steering wheel, closed her eyes, and let out a loud, deep, throaty sound, inhuman and haunting, as if she were that heifer and had just lost her child.

Farson

WHEN HE FINISHED CALVING, JAKE HAD more freedom and more time to think. And he had two things on his mind—Kate, and the horses he didn't have to ride. Every time he moved, he was promised horses to ride or train. Each time, the promises turned out to be lies. Grant did have three horses. Two of them were nothing but worn-out, barn-sour nags. The third was a buckskin mare, a quarter horse, who must have been a real looker back in her earlier days. Jake watched the mare's arthritis, and when the weather was just right, he took her out. Jake could tell the buckskin appreciated the attention as much as he appreciated the ride. The horse gave him what she could, but it wasn't enough. Even though he talked to Kate every day, he felt empty and alone inside.

Jake started drinking again, and he didn't like to drink alone. The only company he could find was at the Parshall Inn. It was there he met Angus, an oilman from Rock Springs, Wyoming.

"I used to live near Jackson Hole," Jake said as he downed his second Lord Calvert and Coke. It was Friday night, and he did not have to fix fences again until Monday.

"Well, I'll be! Have you ever heard of Farson?" Angus asked.

"Yeah, I think I have. Isn't it just south of Jackson?" Jake vaguely remembered passing through the small town on his way to Willow Creek. It was flat country, with miles and miles of hay.

"It is, about a hundred and forty miles from Jackson, a hundred miles from Riverton. I have a nice ranch out there. That's where I pasture my horses." Angus watched Jake prick up his ears like a race horse at the starting gate.

"No kidding. I worked at a dude ranch last summer and wintered at an outfit called the Bear Track. It was a little rough, but a beautiful place. I sure miss Wyoming."

Angus threw back his chest and pulled out his wallet.

"Bartender! Another round for me and my new friend!" Angus put his arm around Jake. "Ever watch a chariot race?"

As it turned out, Angus raised some of the finest horseflesh in Wyoming. Jake told him about his dream to be a real cowboy. By the end of the night, the two had bonded.

"Why don't you come to Wyoming and work for me?" Angus offered.

"I don't want to be driving no tractor for a living. I want to train horses," Jake slurred.

Angus grinned. "You might have to help me put up a little hay during the summer, but trust me, you'll clock more hours in the saddle than you ever dreamed of."

Jake was just sober enough to say he'd have to think about it.

"Well, don't think too long. I'll need help by the end of the month. Here's my card with my cell number." Angus held out a black card with red lettering: Miller Farms—Breeding, Training and Sales.

"Yes, sir. I'll call you Monday. I'll have to talk to my boss at Willow Creek."

Jake really didn't care about Grant, but he did want to talk to Kate. It was almost midnight when he got to the house. He reasoned Kate would be so excited to hear his news she wouldn't mind the late-night call.

"Jake? Is everything okay?" Kate said in a sleepy voice.

"Everything is just perfect!"

"Really—you call me at one o'clock in the morning to tell me things are just perfect?" Kate laughed.

"I met a man at the Parshall Inn tonight. And he's offered me a job training horses in Wyoming!"

"What? Are you serious? Jake, are you drunk?" Kate said, a little miffed. Jake just laughed, a sound she hadn't heard from him in a long while.

"Honey, I have indeed been overserved, but I assure you I am telling you the God's honest truth."

"Tell me everything."

Kate listened to Jake's story. It sounded like the perfect opportunity, and she encouraged him to take the job.

"You've got nothing to lose and everything to gain," Kate reasoned.

"But what happens if I make a mistake?"

"You of all people should know: we don't make mistakes; we make choices. That's how we learn." And Lord knows Kate had made more wild choices in the past year than most people made in a lifetime.

"But these are really expensive thoroughbreds, not just dude horses," Jake whispered.

Kate spoke to him softly, like a parent speaking to a child. "Jake, you'll do fine. You were made to train horses."

ON APRIL 30, JAKE MCCOMB PACKED his things in black plastic garbage bags, climbed in the white Chevy flatbed, and headed for Farson, Wyoming. He was so excited, he could have fueled his tank with enthusiasm instead of gas.

Jake figured the drive would take him only about eight hours, a perfect day trip across some of the prettiest roads he had ever traveled. The gentle rolling hills in the Yampa Valley, just outside Steamboat Springs, Colorado, relaxed him. But when he hit the Wyoming state line, right at Interstate 80, his adrenaline started pumping all over again. As he drove through the wide-open range dotted with antelope and cows, he silently thanked God for Angus Miller bringing him back where he belonged.

Three hours later, he hit the big town of Rock Springs. He pulled into the Kum & Go. Dirt and dust circled the parking lot like small tornadoes, but Jake didn't notice. He went inside, grabbed a cup of coffee and a can of chew, and walked back to his truck. Sixty minutes later, he found himself staring at a yellow blinking light at the lone intersection of Highway 191 and 28, the epicenter of Farson, Wyoming. The town hosted a general store and the OT Café and Bar on one corner, and a Texaco mini-mart on the other. If you blinked, you'd miss it.

Jake opened the glove compartment and located the directions Angus had read to him over the phone the day before. He turned right at the light and continued two miles until he saw County Road Number 6 just past the red barn. The dirt road was long and straight. A few homes and trailers spotted the otherwise desolate road. After three miles, he turned again, on County Road Number 10. Jake started looking for Miller Farms signs on the left, as instructed. There were no signs, but an old metal gate with "Miller" painted across the top rail caught Jake's eye. The gate swung back and forth, vacillating in the wind. Jake wondered if it was meant to welcome visitors or keep them out. He didn't really care one way or the other. The trailer that rested just behind it was to be his first real home in Wyoming.

The trailer looked well maintained. Jake could see that it had just been hit with a fresh coat of paint. A note was nailed to the sun-bleached wood door. Jake removed it and tried the door. It was unlocked. The kitchen took up about half of the dark and confining ten-by-twenty-five-foot room. To the left of the kitchen was a tiny hall. Jake walked a few steps, finding a small bathroom on the right, and beyond, a bedroom with two sets of bunk beds. It wasn't much, but it was all his. He smiled, sat down at the chrome dining table, and unfolded the note. It was from Angus, and he apologized for not being there to greet him. In his place he had left a bottle of whiskey on the counter and some cold cuts and bread in the refrigerator. Angus instructed him to make a grocery list, and he'd be by in the morning to pick it up.

Jake looked around. A brown velour couch lined the opposite wall. Across from it was an old Zenith TV. Jake reached over without moving and punched the power switch. A wrestling match blared from the screen. His gaze shifted to the counter, where Jack Daniels held court. He stood up, crossed the room, took a coffee cup from the cupboard, and poured himself a generous drink.

Outside it was still light, even though it was nearly nine. Jake decided a good hot meal and some local company were more appealing than a cold sandwich.

IT DIDN'T TAKE MUCH TIME BEFORE Jake was all settled in. His proudest achievement was the entertainment center he had created—the DVD on top of the TV, the boom box on top of the DVD, and his new prized purchase, a Sony PlayStation 3, on the floor beneath it all.

"It's real nice. I think you're gonna like it," Jake told Kate. The wind howled and shook the thin glass doors on the phone booth at the Texaco gas station.

"I'm so glad you're happy!" Kate answered. "When are they going to hook up your phone?"

"Oh, Angus promised to have it done just as soon as he could."

Kate replied a hollow, "Oh." She thought, *maybe now is the time to get him a cell phone*, but then quickly decided there probably wasn't any cell service.

Jake was quick to detect the hesitation in Kate's voice. "Honey, Angus asked what kind of food I wanted and gave the list to his wife, and then she went to the store in Rock Springs and brought a whole box of groceries to my door! They treat me real good. I've never had an outfit treat me so good." He paused to catch his breath. "And honey, you can see the Wind Rivers. You can ride for hundreds of miles."

"I'm really glad things are working out. Have you ridden any of those colts yet?"

"Not yet. But I went to the chariot races and saw Angus's team run. Boy, he sure has some nice stock. I'm sure I'll be breaking some colts real soon." Jake did not want to admit he was a little disappointed about the fact that his ass had been planted to a baler and had yet to sit on a green horse. Every time he asked Angus when he would start training the ponies, Angus just said, "In due time." Jake became restless.

"I miss you." Jake felt like they had been apart for three years instead of three months.

"I miss you, too," Kate whispered back.

There was a thick pause, and it was Jake that broke the silence. "You still want to marry me, don't you?" They had lightly skimmed the subject before Kate left Willow Creek.

"Why do you ask?" Kate said, chuckling.

Jake knew Kate laughed when she was nervous and coughed when she lied.

"Because I told my mom."

"You did *what*?" Kate shouted.

"Well, I just kind of told my mom we talked about it. That's all. Don't get all excited."

"I'm not." Kate's voice became gentle and sweet. "I thought we decided we would wait at least a year or two."

"Yeah, I know." Jake could hear Kate's every thought as if he were plugged into her. He had the one-year employment contract with Angus and needed to put a few dollars in his pocket. It wasn't fair having Kate carry all the financial burden of their relationship. And then there was her ridiculous preoccupation with their age difference. He told her he'd love her even if she were 108 years old. She backed down after that one, but then shot back the issue of children.

"By the time you're ready to have children, I'll be too old to have them!" She had tried to push him away with that excuse a million times.

"I swear to God, I do not want to have kids!" Jake volleyed back.

"I felt that way, too, when I was your age."

"If God wants me to have a child, we can adopt one. There are plenty of children out there who could use a good home."

There was no way she could argue that one. Before he could continue the discussion, Kate expertly rerouted the conversation.

"Hey, I'm going to be there next weekend! We can talk more then. You still want to see me?"

"Wild horses couldn't keep me away!" Jake knew it was highly unlikely he'd have to choose between an equine and spending the weekend with his girlfriend.

KATE STEERED FOR THE CORNER parking lot in front of the OT Bar. Potholes hid like land mines, no match even for the "Trail Rated" four-wheel-drive Jeep Kate had driven all the way from Missouri. One of the deeper ditches, cleverly disguised with murky water, gave the Jeep a big jerk as the front tires hit it dead on.

"Shit!" Kate hissed. It had been a long day on the road, Denver to Farson in eight hours, with only one stop for gas. The last thing she needed was a flat tire. She wondered how in the hell she would change it, seeing as she had never changed a tire in her life. This was one of the rare times Kate missed Marino Motors.

She stepped out of the SUV, realizing there wasn't much help in sight. Evidently everyone was either out in the fields or inside the tavern. Kate bet that the majority of the thirty-seven people who lived in Farson were inside the OT Bar. Hunting and drinking seemed to be their favorite sports. Today, her highway hero would most likely be a cowboy or farmer, passing by on his way to anywhere but here. Farson appeared to be a shit hole of a town. After careful inspection of the brand-new, heavy-duty, all-terrain tires, she ascertained that there was miraculously no damage. She locked up the Jeep and headed for the bar.

Although the OT Bar looked about as inviting as a strip club in St. Louis's east side, Kate opened the glass doors and walked in. The bar was dark as night, even though the sun still hung high in the late-afternoon sky. The beer-bellied farmers were glued to the baseball game on TV. "All My Exes Live in Texas" blared from the jukebox in the corner behind the pool table. Kate slid onto one of the empty barstools, thinking that she could do a different rendition of that same song. She'd call it, "All My Exes Live in the West," thinking of Ted in Denver. She thanked her lucky stars she was finally over him, really over him. No doubt she had Jake to thank for that.

She waved to the bartender and ordered an ice water.

"Is that it?" The female bartender looked annoyed.

Kate decided the bartender was looking for a tip. Kate would have tipped her whether she was drinking water or champagne. Not that champagne was an option; it wasn't, and neither was wine, vodka, or tea. The only beverages served in the OT were cheap whiskey, bad bourbon, tequila, beer and day-old, strong black coffee. The kind that kept you awake for days. And soda, but Kate never touched soda.

"I'll have a tequila, too, up, no ice, please," Kate finally said, thinking she should make an effort to fit in.

The bartender poured a tiny shot of Jose Cuervo, eyeing Kate.

"You from around here?" she asked, knowing full well she wasn't. The French-manicured nails and diamond stud earrings were a dead giveaway.

"No, just visiting. My boyfriend, Jake McComb, lives here."

"Not sure I know him," the bartender said as she passed Kate the half-full shot glass and a tall plastic cup of water.

"He just moved here."

"Just in time for hay season!" The bartender laughed and turned around.

Kate decided it was a good thing she ordered the drink. She took a sip. The alcohol burned her throat, stinging, just like the lies that seemed to flow from the mouth of Angus Miller. Jake put on a good show, but she could tell everything wasn't as picture-perfect as he let on. Kate wasn't a rocket scientist, but it didn't take much to figure out that Jake had been dragged to this god-forsaken dust bowl of a town under false pretenses. There were more tractors circling the fields than thoroughbreds. She shifted uncomfortably on the barstool and wondered how in the hell she was going to deal with this new pain in her ass, Angus Miller.

At half past seven, Jake was already more than an hour late. They had planned to meet at the OT at six so Jake could lead her down the back roads to his place. The drive from Betty's house in Denver to Farson wasn't too bad, but the eleven-hour haul from St. Louis to Denver the day before was pretty brutal. She wished Betty was with her now. She had a feeling she was going to need some female support, and Betty's talent for reading people would certainly come in handy. When Kate had introduced Betty to Ted, she wasn't impressed. "He's a blowhard," she had said. And that was even before Betty watched Ted play the longest game of catch-and-release with Kate she had ever seen. Betty often told Kate, in her gentle motherly way, that she was really better off without him. Kate had promised Betty she would call when she got to Farson. "No service" blinked from her cell phone. "I knew it! Perfect, just perfect." Kate said under her breath.

She sat up, threw her shoulders back, and arched like a cat. She wondered how much longer Jake would be out there on that damn tractor. It was bad enough that Angus had Jake haying his fields, but now he had Jake subbed out to other farmers as well. Kate's stomach, knotted in anger, gave a low growl, reminding her she hadn't eaten anything since breakfast at Betty's.

The bar served two unappealing choices, frozen pizza or chips. The café that adjoined the bar offered fried chicken, chicken fried steak, fried shrimp, fried burgers, and french fries. Kate watched her weight like a hawk; fried food wasn't part of her diet. She sipped the last of her tequila, willing it to ward off her hunger.

Kate stared at the baseball game on the TV screen, bored out of her mind, realizing she wasn't into any sort of game playing, athletically or in life in general. The only competitive sports she liked were Sam's Little League games. She ordered another water and quietly thanked God, again, that she had Sam to hold on to when she was back in the city. Lately, in Farson, all Jake had was the smooth, round edges of a hot metal steering wheel.

"This one's on me." The bartender brought Kate another tequila with her water, only this time the tiny shot glass was full. The glass hit the bar with a hollow thud.

"Why, thank you." Kate was pleasantly surprised by the random act of kindness. She took the drink in her left hand and extended her right.

"I don't think we've met. I'm Kate Marino."

"Candi Johnson. I just moved here a little over a month ago." She was becoming more and more interested in Kate and her boyfriend, Jake.

"How do you like it?" Kate asked.

"I've lived in worse places." Candi began rinsing glasses at the bar sink. A tight cotton T-shirt with the word REAL stretched across her ample breasts, and a barbed-wire tattoo circled her arm.

"Yeah, Jake moved here in April, but with all the haying he's been doing, I don't think he has a chance to get out much." Kate would have added, "Like there's someplace worth going to," but she didn't know if Candi would share her opinion.

"Busy time of the year, I suppose. Who's he working for?" Candi's nose twitched like a rabbit's as she thought, *This Jake character must be one hell of a stud to get this gal to come to Farson.*

"Angus Miller," Kate said.

"Oh, sure, I know Angus! He's here all the time!"

That made perfect sense to Kate. Angus was sitting in the air-conditioned bar guzzling beer, flirting with the easy-on-the-eyes bartender, while all his hired hands were sweating their asses off out in the fields.

Hunger finally got the better of Kate. Her watch read eight o'clock. Apparently, Jake wasn't going to get a break and meet her for dinner. She was glad she had had the good sense to insist on getting directions to the Miller place. Jake was probably out in the field just finishing up.

"You gonna stick around for the pool tournament?" Candi flipped her copper-colored mane behind her shoulder.

"No, I'm pretty tired. Thanks anyway. I think I'll just grab some dinner for me and Jake at the café and surprise him at his place." Kate paid the tab, left a healthy tip, and headed for the café.

The cook, a curvaceous woman named Rose who also doubled as a waitress when they were shorthanded, noticed Kate walk in and head for the counter. Rose took her time finishing up her work at the grease-spitting deep fryer. She then glided out to the café, water pitcher in hand, topped off all the glasses, and made sure all the customers were happy. All the customers just so happened to be of the male variety. Then and only then did she turn her attention to Kate.

"What can I get you?"

Kate looked around the room and said, "Oh, I'm sorry, are you talking to me?"

"Ah, yeah," Rose answered impatiently.

"Oh, I thought maybe you were speaking to the man behind me, or in front of me, or right across from me." Kate smiled innocently.

Rose squinted her eyes and answered, "No, sweetheart, I'm talking to you."

Kate turned sideways in her chair and crossed her legs, revealing her custom-crafted lizard skin boots. She answered very slowly. "I'd like a cheeseburger to go, please."

"Chips or fries?" Rose snapped her gum and posed her pencil in midair as if it were a wand.

"Fries." Kate read her name tag while Rose scribbled the order.

"Anything else?" she barked rudely.

Kate could tell Rose wasn't feeling all warm and fuzzy about her either, and was glad. A strand of Kate's honey-highlighted hair dropped across her face. She slowly reached up and tucked it behind her ear.

"Just mustard, please."

Rose marched away without so much as a thank-you. Her attitude, coupled with her oily, gray-streaked hair, did nothing for Kate's appetite. The spaghetti-like mass cemented her decision to deliver the food to Jake in the fields and make a sandwich for herself when she got back to Jake's trailer.

Kate had no problem getting to the Miller Farm. Out in the pasture there wasn't a four-legged animal in sight, just a big cloud of dust. She guessed it was Jake on his tractor. She honked the horn, hoping he would hear her without her having to get out of the car. He circled the field and waved his hand in acknowledgement.

Jake jumped out of the tractor and ambled towards Kate's Jeep. She got out of her car to come meet him. His eyes were bloodshot, and every square inch of him was covered in dust. Kate dove into his arms anyway.

"It's good to see you, hon. How was the drive?" Jake hated that Kate had to drive to see him, but the airfare to Rock Springs was unaffordable.

"Too long for such a short stay, but it was worth every minute to see you." Kate's eyes twinkled as she looked up at him. "I brought you some dinner."

"Thank you. I'm sorry I couldn't meet you, but I've got to get this field baled tonight."

"I figured. Don't you worry, I can take care of myself."

"Wanna take a ride?" Jake opened the Styrofoam container and wolfed down his burger. He didn't bother with the fries.

"You know, I've never been in a tractor. That would be fun!"

"In you go." Jake gave her a leg up into the small cab of the huge John Deere and climbed in after her.

"You're gonna have to sit on my lap," Jake said, so clearly happy to see her.

"I think I can handle that."

Kate settled on Jake's right knee. She was surprised to find that she felt excited. The huge machine made her feel powerful and strong.

"Now I get why men love running heavy equipment," Kate yelled over the roar of the engine.

"You wanna drive?" Jake yelled back.

"Are you kidding?"

"Nope." Jake shifted sideways and let Kate take the wheel.

"Oh my God—this is fun!" Kate screamed, as she looked back at the baler picking up hay as if it were a giant vacuum cleaner. A familiar tune from the old show *Green Acres* played in the back of her mind.

They went round and round the field like a spinning top. Unfortunately, it was too loud to have a conversation. The sun went down, and it became more difficult to see; the dust was thick as fog.

"How much longer?" Kate's enthusiasm had sunk with the sun.

"Not long, maybe two hours or so."

"Maybe you should drop me off. It's been a long day. I'm starved and I could sure use a hot shower, especially after this!"

Kate held out her arms. Her body was now saturated with sweat and dirt.

"No problem."

Jake stopped the tractor, helped Kate out, and walked her back to her Jeep. He then bent down and gently kissed her. Kate studied Jake as he headed back to his machine. Well-formed love handles and a muddy baseball cap had replaced his once–perfectly toned body and cowboy hat. He no longer looked like a young, strong, confident horseman. He had devolved into a tired, dirty farmhand.

JAKE CLIMBED INTO BED SOMETIME after midnight, only to get up at sunrise for another round in the fields. Through half-open eyes, Kate watched him pull on his jeans from the day before and put a wake-up wad of chewing tobacco under his lip.

"I'll make something nice for dinner." Kate reached out to touch his arm.

"Sorry, hon, I didn't mean to wake you." He bent over and kissed her. The mint from his chew tasted sweet.

"I don't mind." And Kate didn't. She hadn't come all this way to sleep. She wanted to be with him.

"I gotta go." He sounded defeated, like a dog beaten into submission.

"Already?"

"Yep." Jake grabbed his ball cap and headed towards the door.

Kate hopped out of bed and followed him. "How about I make you some coffee before you go?" She was desperate to have just a taste of time with him.

"Angus will be waitin' for me. I'll grab some coffee at the OT."

Kate walked back to the shotgun bedroom. The dingy brown floral curtains ballooned in the cool morning breeze; the craggy peaks of the Wind River Mountains looked like the razor-sharp teeth of a wild beast on the distant horizon. Kate lay back in bed and watched Jake, tired and hunched over, climb into the shiny new ranch truck. It was then that Kate realized it was Farson that had put a saddle on him, and it was he who was being broken.

Dirty Socks

KATE REVISITED THE DISTASTEFUL town of Farson for a week in August, and Jake's bottom was still stuck to the hot vinyl seat of a tractor. It seemed as if each circle Jake made in the fields took him farther and farther away from himself and Kate. Each bale that dropped behind that baler was a piece of him, and there were now hundreds dotting the fresh-cut fields.

Kate was driving to the grocery store in Rock Springs when she remembered the morning when Jake had finally reared back in frustration.

"I'm gonna take a tractor out into one of those damn fields and tie up a horse right beside it. Then I'm gonna bring old Angus out there and tell him, "This here is a horse, and this here is a tractor. I was hired to ride the horse!"

Kate had thought, *Thank God! He's finally come to his senses!* But then he simmered down, turned around, and to her astonishment, defended Angus.

"Oh, he's just seein' how tough I am," Jake said as he let out a hacking cough.

That was back in July, and Kate had not heard Jake complain since, not even a peep. It was Jake's pride that made him hang on, so Kate did all she could, offering her love, support, nasal spray, and Visine. The first few days, she hung out in the trailer and read most of the day, while Jake worked like a rented mule. At dusk he came home to a home-cooked dinner, but it certainly wasn't because Kate enjoyed cooking in the trailer. Cooking in the trailer was a challenge. The oven wasn't even deep enough to house a cookie sheet. When Kate brought this to Jake's attention, he remedied the situation by firing up the welding truck and cutting the baking sheet in half.

KATE PULLED THE OLD CHEVY PICKUP into the parking lot at Safeway. She had splurged and flown to Wyoming this time, but at least she didn't have to rent a car. The shopping list was written on a tiny yellow Post-it note and was stuffed in her back jean pocket. She couldn't believe she had to drive fifty minutes to buy the ingredients for twice-baked potatoes and a fresh vegetable. Luckily a liquor store was directly next door, and it carried a slim but drinkable selection of wine. Kate decided a merlot would pair nicely with the moose steaks already marinating back home. Kate would never forget Stella's reaction when Kate told her about Jake's new residence.

"I cannot believe you are living in a trailer." Stella's face had puckered up as if she smelled a stinky fart.

"I am *not* living in a trailer. It just happens to be where Jake lives now, and I visit."

"Yeah, right, a vision of things to come?" Stella was not a member of the Jake McComb fan club these days.

"Very funny. You know it's just a temporary thing."

Kate wasn't about to admit to Stella that she might be right. Jake almost seemed proud of the three-room trailer he called home, and favored cruising in the newer model, two-tone silver farm truck over the classic Chevy. The changes were subtle, but

Kate couldn't help but notice the signs of a little pocket change feeding his soul instead of his dream of riding and training horses.

Safeway felt as though it were trying to cool off the entire state of Wyoming. Kate was glad she had brought her long-sleeved denim shirt inside, and put it on over her tank top. To her delight, she found asparagus in the produce section. The long stems were thin, and the ends broke off with a nice snap. Kate picked a large bunch, then surveyed the potato selection, which turned out to be no selection at all. There were four large baskets, all holding big brown russets. Kate put two in her cart and moved on. The dairy section proved to be equally disappointing, with rows of Velveeta, sliced American, and Kraft block cheeses. Kate cursed under her breath. The Safeway in Jackson Hole would have had a display of everything from brie to manchego, not to mention fresh fish and an actual butcher. The two towns were separated by only 150 miles of highway, but they might as well have been on opposite sides of the world. Kate grabbed the cheddar and headed to the checkout.

Once back on the highway, Kate's spirits lifted. As much as she hated Farson and the neighboring town of Rock Springs, she still loved Wyoming. Today it was sunny. The sparkling blue sky cast dancing shadows on the clay-colored hills. Kate prayed for an afternoon storm. The trailer did not have air conditioning, and she desperately needed relief from the heat if she was going to use the oven.

As Kate drove, she thought about the Prickly Pear Ranch. From the moment she swung up onto that horse, the rhythm of her life had changed. She rocked in the saddle as if it were a chair on the porch of a house she had not visited for quite some time, but now realized the place was truly home. In less than an hour, Kate had realized she was not the woman in designer suits, sitting in traffic, on her cell phone, selling cars to faceless customers. Nor was she the traditional mother, running off to a PTA meeting or mothers' luncheons. She had put on one fabulous outfit after another, as if they were costumes for the role she was about to play. Kate had waited all her life for that one moment of enlightenment. But if those roles were not her, who the hell was she?

There were no quick answers, of that she was sure. Art was still the food that fed her soul, but it would not fuel her ultimate fantasy. If she really wanted her dream, the small log cabin and barn in the mountains, nestled in the trees, just like the one she stared at day after day in the little painting that hung on the wall back home, she would need money—lots and lots of greenbacks.

Farson had become the kick in the pants Kate needed. The longer she had to stay there, the more determined she was to make this dream a reality. Jake could live on the property full-time, and Kate decided she would just have to commute from St. Louis. Her job at Marino Motors would then at least be a means to an end. The real challenge was finding a place that offered affordable real estate and a grocery store with brie. Jackson Hole was undoubtedly out of the question. But a few towns flanked the playpen for billionaires, and Kate thought one of them might fit the bill.

Just as Kate pulled into Miller Farms, the sky swung open its arms and drenched the plains with rain. Kate smiled as she dashed back and forth between the truck and trailer, eager to create her special dinner. The rain would push Jake out of the fields early. If she hurried, dinner could be ready when he got home. Then they could relax, and Kate could share with Jake her plan to become a Wyoming landowner.

Jake arrived just after six.

"Perfect timing! Dinner will be ready in a minute," Kate said as she turned and kissed Jake's filthy face. Soothing fiddle music hummed from the boom box.

"Do I have time to shower?"

"If you want it hot, we'd better eat now." Kate smiled and plated the moose.

"Okay, let me just go wash my hands and face."

Kate put the silverware on the table. The last wildflowers she had picked days ago hung on in a Chianti bottle, and two votive candles softened the otherwise dark and confining room. Sitting down in the trailer was like being lowered into a hole. The windows were so high that no matter where you were seated, you stared at a wall. She turned the table and arranged the harvest-gold chairs so that they could at least look at each other.

She placed dinner on the table just as Jake walked in to sit down. Kate opened the wine, poured them each a glass, and then lifted hers in the air for a toast. Jake's head was already lowered, his hand steadily shoveling food into his mouth. He inhaled his supper in just under four minutes. The speed of Jake's eating was not an insult, more like part of his job. Farson had taught him how to eat quickly so he could get back out the in fields for more baling before the evening moisture set in. He pushed back the chair and went to the cabinet for a toothpick. "I tell you what, I ain't hayin' next summer. I said I'd give him a year and I'm goin' to keep my word. But I ain't ever doin' this again."

Jake sat back down. Kate parted her lips only to put another bite of meat between them. Something told her any comment at all would fall on deaf ears.

They did the dishes together, and then Jake headed for the shower. Kate cursed Angus Miller for the umpteenth time, and decided this was not the night to discuss her cabin-in-the-woods scheme. Instead, Kate boiled water for tea.

A mug of herbal tea was in her hand as Kate walked into the bedroom. The black sheets were cold, and the hot tea, of late, seemed to warm the chill beneath them. Jake stepped into the room with a towel wrapped around his thickened waist. He dropped the towel and climbed into bed. They began caressing each other, fingers following the paths along secret places that had become familiar only to them. Jake straddled Kate's slight frame. He was perched directly over her, eyes glued to the sight of his implement plunging in and out of her. Completely absorbed in himself, a faraway look on his face, he never missed a thrust, yet he never paused to take note of who or what the recipient was. It could have been anyone, or any number of things. His lack of focus made Kate feel sick.

It was slow yet quick, the force of it hitting her as if someone had dumped a bucket of ice water directly on her naked body. She lay frozen, the sinking feeling of loss heavy upon her. The circles he had driven had finally caught up with him. Farson, spineless and dirty, had possessed his soul. Kate could physically feel his lack of fight. He wasn't even fighting to keep her anymore. If he quit on her, she would surely lose herself with him. Kate lay quietly as Jake fell into a deep, exhausted sleep. Her fingers gripped his arm, holding on, as if she could save him.

THE NEXT MORNING, ROSE SAILED around the tables at the OT Café, filling the locals' coffee cups. Kate had chosen a booth next to the window with a scenic view of the semis heading east and west on Highway191.

"So, you want the eggs or pancakes?" Rose asked.

"Think I'll have the eggs this morning, scrambled, please. Oh, and could you melt a little cheddar on top?" Kate smiled sweetly, relieved that Rose had appeared to have washed her hair.

"Only have American." Rose snapped her gum and turned her head toward a big red Ford dually truck that had just pulled in.

"Skip it," Kate said, barely able to hide her disgust.

The muddy pickup belonged to Angus. He sauntered into the café as if he owned it. It occurred to Kate that maybe he did. He owned all the property around it. She watched Rose land on him like a fly on shit. He had a steaming cup of coffee in his hand before Kate even had the chance to say hello.

Angus could have been an attractive man. His eyes were the color of robin's eggs, his facial features were reminiscent of Robert Duvall, and his gray-flecked beard nicely trimmed. Unfortunately, the cases of beer he had consumed over the years hung around his middle like an all-terrain tire. He attempted to camouflage the girth by throwing his shoulders back, hoping his oversized silver rodeo buckle would hold up the rest. Kate craned her neck to check out the date engraved on the buckle as he turned to check out Rose's ass. The date put his trophy years many moons ago, in the late seventies. Kate calculated his age to be somewhere north of fifty.

Rose raced out from the kitchen. Today her clean hair was pulled back into a tight ponytail. Unfortunately, the new 'do highlighted her wrinkled and weathered face. But from what Kate saw, the men didn't seem to notice or care. Their eyes traveled farther south. Rose had what counted in all the right places. She filled out her cowboy-magnet, skin-tight, Wrangler jeans nicely.

"Just coffee today, Angus?" Rose said in a pathetic Marilyn Monroe breathy voice.

"Yep, that's it for now, but I might be back for lunch."

"Look forward to that." Rose placed his check on the counter. Her hand lingered just a moment too long.

"What's the special today?" Angus asked.

"It's meatloaf! With mashed potatoes and gravy, your favorite!"

Angus grabbed a toothpick and stuck it between his caffeine-stained teeth. He finally looked in Kate's direction and tipped his hat.

"I suppose I'll be back then," he answered nonchalantly.

It wasn't the words spoken between them, but the ones left unsaid that told Kate that Angus would indeed return. And she was pretty sure he'd be back for more than lunch. The dry eggs formed a stone in Kate's gut. To her, the whole town of Farson was beginning to stink like someone's dirty socks.

The red truck peeled off with a spray of gravel. Kate's coffee cup was empty, and Rose was nowhere to be found. Not that she felt like hanging around, but Jake's trailer was even more depressing. Stella was in Jackson Hole. Kate hated to leave Jake, but she really needed to talk to someone. Even though Stella wasn't crazy about Jake, she was definitely cheering Kate on to buy a place out West. Kate took out her cell phone; one bar glowed in the corner.

Stella answered, huffing and puffing. "I was out watering my flowers. How's beautiful Farson?"

"Well, I was thinking about taking a road trip, and I thought I'd see if you had plans tonight."

"Trouble in paradise?" Stella cackled.

"Yes and no. Jake is fine," Kate lied. "But I've definitely had enough of Farson. What I need is a vodka, any brand, on ice, with olives, in a real martini glass. And I could sure use some female bonding."

"I'd love to see you, but I'm going to Dubois this afternoon."

"Dubois, refresh my memory?" Kate vaguely remembered Stella mentioning the town.

"I've told you about Dubois. My friend Faith and her

husband, Robert, live there. They own the Flying V Ranch!" Stella said, exasperated.

"Oh, now I remember. It's not too far from the Prickly Pear, right?" The thought of the ranch made Kate feel even more depressed. She wished she could blink, and she and Jake would miraculously be transported back there right now.

"Yeah, actually Dubois is probably closer to Farson than Jackson Hole. Why don't you meet me there? It's only about an hour from Lander!"

Kate calculated quickly and said, "Well, it's about an hour's drive from here to Lander, so that is definitely doable."

"I'm meeting some friends for happy hour at five o'clock at the Rustic Pine Tavern. Why don't you meet me there? We'll have a blast!"

"Are you sure it's okay? I don't want to intrude." Kate needed to see Stella in the worst way.

"Of course it's okay! I'd love to see you, and since I'm certainly not cruising to that shit hole of a town, you'd better head to Dubois. And I am staying overnight at Faith and Robert's. I'm sure they won't mind if you stay with them, too. They've got plenty of room."

"Now I really feel like I'm intruding. Maybe this isn't such a good idea," Kate said, feeling so low she almost started crying.

"Don't be ridiculous. Faith is wonderful, salt of the earth. She won't mind a bit. And I know you will just love meeting her. This will be perfect!"

"Well, all right." Kate started to perk up. It was just what the doctor ordered: a night with her best friend, and she'd finally get to see the fabulous Flying V Ranch. Stella had been raving about the place forever.

"But please call me if there is a problem. I would totally understand."

"Trust me, there won't be."

"Okay, then, how do I get to the Rustic Pine?"

Kate paid Rose for her breakfast and left a 10 percent tip.

THE WIND TOSSED THE CHEVY AROUND on the two-lane highway like a small boat on a rough sea as Kate made her way back to the trailer. She parked at the front door. To the west she spied a neon-green speck moving silently against the flat, lonely horizon. Her watch said it was eleven o'clock. Jake would be in for lunch soon. She hopped out of the truck as Angus's rig rounded the bend. His eyes were glued dead ahead, never veering toward Kate. He sped off as if he were on his way to a fire, heading in the direction of Jake's tractor.

"Asshole," Kate muttered into the wind.

At noon, Jake unlatched the heavy, freezer-like door to the trailer. He removed his cap, hung it on the deer antler hat rack to the left of the door, and dropped into the kitchen chair. Flies bounced against the window screens like ping-pong balls. It was obvious that Jake was dog-tired, but he wasn't going to say a word. He'd been taught to "cowboy up" all his life, and this was no different. He flashed a weak smile at Kate who was across the room making his lunch.

"So, hon, what you been doin' today?"

Kate put a paper plate with a ham-and-cheese sandwich and Doritos in front of him. "Oh, nothing. I just went to the OT for breakfast." She really felt like saying, "Oh, I watched the grass grow," but bit her tongue.

"Oh," was all Jake said as he dove into his food like a starving animal.

"I saw Angus there."

"Yep, he said he'd seen you, too," Jake said between mouthfuls.

The curtains billowed out as a gust of wind blew through the trailer. Jake continued to chew, but this time Kate could tell he was digesting his thoughts. She waited for him to speak.

"You don't need to say anything to Angus's old lady about him and Rose."

So that was why Angus had rushed out to the field to talk to Jake. All Kate's suspicions had been confirmed.

"You know, I'm glad you said that. Angus was only there for a minute, but there was this quick little exchange between him and Rose. And you're right, I did get the impression that something is going on between them."

Kate waited for Jake to respond, but received only a good old Farson blank stare.

"I'm pretty sure infidelity isn't one of the codes of the West." Kate prodded but got no response, and her lame attempt at humor didn't seem to lighten the moment. The dust had either seeped into Jake's brain, or Kate was sure there was a stranger sitting in front of her doing a terrible impersonation of Jake McComb. The man Kate Marino had fallen in love with at the Prickly Pear Ranch was long gone. The man she fell in love with had morals, integrity, and intelligence. Even though Jake was young and still slightly slick, he had always stood on the right side of what was right and what was wrong.

"Yeah, well, don't say nothin' to nobody, because Angus will know where it came from."

Kate felt defeated. Things couldn't get much worse, so she decided to break her news.

"I'm going to Dubois to see Stella."

"Dubois? You're going to Dubois to see Stella? Hell, you're only here for four more days."

Kate was pleased. She finally had his full attention.

"I know, but I really need to get out of here. I've tried, I've really tried, but this place is suffocating me."

The pathetic look on Jake's face softened Kate.

"Honey, I know this isn't your fault. I'm trying to be supportive, but I have limited time off from my job and there is just nothing for me to do around here." Kate wanted to add that she was tired of watching him sit on that damn tractor all day, but didn't.

"You could paint." Jake spoke so quietly Kate could barely make out his words over the wind beating at the metal walls of the trailer.

"Honey . . ." Kate felt horrible but knew if she didn't go, she'd blow like Old Faithful in a matter of hours. "You know how I tried, but I've got to tell you, I'm not real inspired to paint here."

Her watercolors sat on a pile of papers in the center of the table; the oils were too cumbersome to travel with. When she first visited Jake in July, she had gone to Atlantic City, an old mining town about thirty minutes away, seeking inspiration—something, anything, interesting to paint. She worked on a few sketches, but they seemed as dull and flat as the town she had grown to hate. Jake had gotten her creative juices flowing, but Farson had dried them up.

"I'll just go for the night. I'll be back in time for dinner tomorrow night. You'll be working the rest of today and tonight and all day tomorrow. So really we'll only be apart for a few hours."

Jake studied the hole that was beginning to form on the bottom of his left boot. The toe of his right boot was already wrapped in silver duct tape.

"You're right. I know it ain't been much fun for you around here. Maybe I'll ask old Angus if I can get tomorrow night off. It's Saturday. We can go out. Have us a real date." He pulled Kate toward him, sat her on his lap, and gave her a playful kiss.

"That would be wonderful. I'll keep my fingers crossed." Kate rested her head on his shoulder. "You know how much I love you."

"I love you, too."

Jake lifted her head and this time kissed Kate long and deep. It was a kiss that reminded Kate of what the two of them had once shared and what she now had to fight to keep. She got up, picked up Jake's paper plate, and threw it in the trash can.

"I'm just going to grab a few things, then, and get on the road. Do you think the Chevy will make it to Dubois?"

"You betcha! Just keep her under sixty, Miss Lead Foot, and she'll do just fine."

An hour later, Kate was seated in the white flatbed. She grasped the big turquoise steering wheel; it felt sturdy and surprisingly cool to the touch. Jake stared at her as though she was leaving and never coming back.

"Jake, what's wrong?"

"I don't know what the hell I'm doing." He looked down and kicked at something Kate could not see.

"I don't understand." Kate took her hands off the wheel and reached for his hand.

She watched him shake his head as if he were waking from a bad dream. He looked up and finally said, "Never mind." He then leaned into the truck and placed a tender kiss on Kate's lips. "Have fun. I'll miss you."

"I'll miss you, too." For a brief second Kate considered turning off the ignition and blowing the whole trip off. Instead, she pushed the compulsion aside, reached for the black knob of the stick shift, and ground the truck into first gear. The gravel beneath the wide, worn tires popped and cracked as the truck slowly rolled forward.

"I love you!" Jake yelled over the wind as Kate pulled away. He reached up so he wouldn't lose his baseball cap.

If the Ring Fits

THERE WAS NO PROBLEM A GOOD drive couldn't solve. Kate's uneasiness subsided as she felt herself melt into the landscape. To the north, pine-covered foothills bordered the Wind River Mountains. The south was flanked by the breadth of the Great Divide Basin. Kate pulled over and got out her camera. It was difficult, to say the least, to capture one good shot of the panoramic scene. As she clicked away, she started to think about how the pioneers once crossed this very same country in covered wagons. The world seemed so vast and the shadows of doubt that darkened Kate's mind in Farson disappeared.

Once back on the road, the sun bounced off the chrome-trimmed truck, and the radio poured out classic country tunes, interrupted occasionally by static. Kate found herself singing out loud even though she didn't know all the words. Something about driving the big old flatbed made Kate feel as though anything were possible.

She began to think about Jake's marriage proposal. Was it convention that ruled her heart or her true feelings that kept her from moving forward? The age thing certainly bothered her. She looked as if she were in her late twenties instead of midthirties, but what would the mirror say in ten or twenty years? Would people think she was with her son?

"Stop it!" she screamed out loud. True love had nothing to do with age or looks. It was all about what you held in your heart. They were committed to each other and to building a life out West.

But what about Sam? How are you going to work that one out? Her heart whispered.

Kate couldn't ignore the very complicated issue of Sam. Michael could be so damned congenial when things were going his way. She wished she had never agreed not to move Sam out of the state without his permission. Michael would fight her tooth and nail if she tried to take Sam with her. Well, she was tired of kowtowing to his wishes, too. She had a life to live, and there just had to be a way she and Michael could work out some sort of agreement. The longer Kate drove, the deeper she dove into her thoughts. She grasped for the new woman who was fighting to surface, one that was just out of reach.

And then something strange happened. Her mind stopped. In the place where right and wrong had struggled was . . . silence. Kate felt light, as if her body were translucent, pulsing with a foreign energy, similar to the charge she felt when she was painting the wolf back at Willow Creek.

As the Chevy approached Lander, Kate got a clear vision of two platinum wedding bands sitting in a glass jewelry case. She had no idea if Lander even had a jewelry store, but as she drove down Main Street, there it was: Wind River Gems. A vacant parking space at the front door waited for her. She pulled in, got out of the truck, and walked into the store. A glass display case in the form of a U lined the walls. Kate headed for the wedding rings as if they were the sole purpose of her journey instead of a last-minute thought. A small sign in the corner of the case announced 50 percent off. It should have been a shock for Kate to see the his-and-hers, shiny, silver-colored bands, but instead it seemed like the most natural thing in the world for the small-town jeweler to carry the expensive platinum metal.

The smaller ring fit Kate perfectly, but the men's match looked to be too small for Jake. The owner of the shop, an older gentleman in a white Western shirt and Navajo bolo tie assured Kate it could be sized to fit him. When she explained that the purchase was also a surprise, he agreed to let her bring the rings back if they didn't work. Kate handed him her credit card.

"Well, I must say, your fiancé is one lucky young man!" he said as he handed her two pale-pink ring boxes.

"I'm the lucky one." She flashed a dazzling smiled and floated out the door.

Buttes, plateaus, and strange rock formations sprouted from the earth as Kate traveled west. As she got closer to Dubois, huge mounds of clay, deeply worn and wrinkled like the face of a wise old Indian medicine man, lined the highway. The great Wind River followed the twist and turns of the pavement through giant cottonwoods and willows. At the edge of town, the landscape changed again. Crimson faded to gold and the gentle rolling hills looked as though someone had draped them in velvet.

Kate arrived at the Rustic Pine Tavern a little after five. Happy hour was in full swing. The log-sided saloon was full of cowboys, young and old; tourists; and transplants from other lives and towns. Stella was perched on a stool about halfway down the old oak bar. She spotted Kate immediately and raced across the room to give her a hug.

"God, I'm so glad you decided to come. It's so good to see you!" Stella's eyes were glazed over, and Kate knew she was high as a kite. Stella took Kate's hand, pulled her over to her place at the bar, and waved down the bartender.

"My friend would like Tito's, on the rocks, in a martini glass with olives, please," Stella shouted.

"Thank you!" Kate was so drunk with happiness she felt as though she didn't really need that vodka after all.

"You just missed Faith. She had to go back to the ranch to make dinner. They've got a few paying guests in from New York."

"Are you sure it's not an imposition for me to stay there tonight?" Kate climbed up onto the bar stool next to Stella.

"I am absolutely sure. I told her we'd probably hang here for awhile, grab something to eat at the Horse Creek Café, and then head to the ranch. She's expecting us after dinner, sometime after nine. And knowing Faith, she probably baked something yummy for dessert. Maybe we can score some leftovers."

"Sounds perfect." Kate was famished. She spotted a bowl of pretzels within reach and took a small handful.

"So, how is life in that hellhole of a town? Is Angus still being a prick?"

"Angus is a lying son of a bitch, but I have to tell you, one good thing has come from all of this—" Kate paused. She wasn't sure how Stella would react to her news about the rings. Stella probably wouldn't understand, but then, how could she? Hell, at this point, Kate wasn't even sure if she understood what was going on. She just knew she had to do it.

"I did a little shopping in Lander."

"Oh, yeah, did it help? I know shopping always cheers me up!"

Kate chose her words carefully, knowing Stella was expecting an answer like, "I got a really cool pair of cowboy boots."

"You might say shopping in Lander was an out-of-body experience. I bought engagement rings." Kate let out a breath she didn't know she was holding.

"Oh my God." Stella's eyes bulged like a bug. "Why in the hell did you do that? Did Jake put you up to this?"

"Believe it or not, this is all my idea. Jake doesn't have a clue."

"Honey, let's be honest. Jake's been after you to marry him for months."

"And I've put him off because I was scared. That's all it was. It certainly wasn't because I didn't love him."

"Are you sure about all of this?"

"I am." Kate scooted back in her stool and took a sip of her drink.

"Your dad is going to shit."

Kate had no doubt that Stella was right about that. Stella's and her father's opinions never found their way to common ground, but on the subject of Jake McComb they agreed. They both thought Jake was after Kate's money. Kate always volleyed back, "What money? I know the balance in my checkbook, and it ain't much!" But Stella and Mr. Marino were referring to Kate's imminent inheritance.

"Look, I know how my dad feels about Jake, but I'm tired of living my life according to him! He's just going to have to accept Jake into our family, or he can kiss his favorite daughter good-bye."

"You'd better start packing your bags," Stella said.

Kate stared into Stella's now surprisingly clear eyes.

"My mom always used to say, 'Use what you got to get what you want.' Well, unfortunately, or fortunately, depending on which way you want to look at it, I've got the ace in the hole," Kate said with a sly smile.

"And what's that?" Stella leaned back on her barstool and crossed her arms.

"I've got Sam. I'll use him if I have to." Kate's smile faded as she realized that she was capable of manipulating people in much the same way her father had manipulated her. Frank Marino used money, and now his daughter would use his only grandson.

"Well, you've got a point. If your dad alienates you, he risks losing Sam. He'll never do that. What about the dealership?"

"I'm not going to be stupid. I'll need my job more than ever if I'm going to buy a place out here for me and Jake."

"Holy shit! You're finally going to do it?" Stella jumped out her chair and hugged Kate.

"I told you one good thing happened out of all of this mess," Kate laughed.

They huddled at the bar discussing Kate's criteria for a small ranch. The property had to feel as though there were an inordinate amount of space even though her budget wouldn't allow her to buy a big spread. Kate wasn't sure if she was up to building a house, so they decided it would be easier to find an existing cabin or house, and she could mold it to her taste and Jake's needs for a horse-training facility.

"And the town has to at least have a grocery store. One or two decent restaurants would be a bonus." Kate was firm about a few city conveniences.

"What about here? I love Dubois. If I could find a job that paid even close to what I make in Jackson I'd move here in a heartbeat." Stella had been working as a personal assistant to a wealthy developer in Jackson and had been doing very well.

"I was thinking the same thing! I really haven't seen much of the town, but it's certainly beautiful."

"Like the T-shirt says," Stella looked at the cotton shirt dangling from a hanger behind the bar, "Dubois, Wyoming. It's Where God Spends His Vacation!"

"Well, there you have it!" Kate couldn't believe her dream of owning a cabin in the mountains was about to come true. "Do you have any idea what land goes for around here?"

Stella pointed to a bearded man in a straw cowboy hat at the other end of the bar. "There's my good friend Lane Stuart. He owns High Country Real Estate. I'm sure he'd love to show you around Dubois and fill you in on the local real estate market. I'll introduce you."

The next thing Kate knew, she had an appointment with Mr. Stuart to view properties the next morning.

The girls went to Horse Creek Café for a celebratory dinner, arriving at the Flying V Ranch near ten o'clock. Not a light was on in any of the cabins. The ranch was completely dark except for one little light glowing on the porch of the main lodge.

"Geez, people do hit the hay early around here!" Kate said.

"I am sure the dudes are plumb tuckered out. And Faith, well she's up at the crack of dawn. She cooks three meals for the guests, coordinates the cleaning, helps with the horses and stock, and who knows what else," Stella whispered as they walked up to the front door. There was a note. Faith had left it telling them to bunk in Columbine, the closest cabin to the creek, and that she would see them the next day, bright and early, for coffee. Kate and Stella grabbed their bags, crossed the lawn by the light of the moon, and found their beds for the night.

The following morning was cool and clear, and the smell of sagebrush hung heavily in the air. The Flying V was a magical place, with turn-of-the-century log cabins edged with flower beds planted with columbine, larkspur and wild roses. There was a bathhouse behind the cabins with two antique claw-foot tubs. The buildings were nestled on the gentle sloping banks of Horse Creek. Rocking chairs perched on the porches invited guests to sit, relax, and listen to the sounds of the rushing water and musical wind flowing through the pines. Faith and Robert Voss lived in the main lodge, a modern log home that sat just east of the cabins.

By the time Kate made her way to the lodge, she found Stella and Faith, coffee cups in hand, busy catching up on all the local gossip.

"Sorry, I've never been an early riser," Kate said.

Faith jumped up to greet her. "I am so glad to finally meet you. Stella has told me so much about you!" Faith's blue eyes sparkled with kindness.

Kate sensed there wasn't an unkind or insincere bone in the woman's body. "I hope it's all good!" she chirped.

"Of course, all good. Would you like some coffee? Or tea perhaps? I have herbal or caffeinated."

"I'd love some coffee, and full octane please!"

Kate followed Faith to the pot, watched her pour the ebony brew into a ceramic mug, and then joined Stella in the dining room. Sunlight poured through the huge glass windows. Sheep grazed peacefully in neon-green pastures. In the distance, the Beartooth Mountains stood watch. Kate thought if she were God, she'd spend her vacation, or better yet, the rest of her life, at the Flying V Ranch.

"How about a quick tour?" Faith suggested after they finished a breakfast of pancakes smothered in fresh blueberries, and thick slabs of bacon.

"Are you sure you have time?" Kate answered.

"I have a little time before I have to start lunch," Faith said as she cleared the table.

"You've got to show her the garden and your new peacocks!" Stella gushed.

As they walked the grounds, Kate fired off a list of questions that would have exhausted any normal human being, but Faith answered each one thoroughly and with the patience of a saint. Kate learned that the ranch was a working ranch, home to cows, horses, and sheep. The Vosses took in guests in the summer months to help make ends meet. Faith cared for the animals, cooked, and cleaned cabins, while her husband Robert handled the more "manly" chores. Kate knew it was all hard work, but a job she would give her right arm to have.

"This is just unbelievable. You are so lucky to have all of this," Kate said as she picked her way across the stepping stones in Faith's huge vegetable garden. There was a fifteen-foot bed planted with leaf lettuce, spinach, and chard, and three others had more vegetables intermingled with beautiful flowers.

"We are fortunate. Robert's had several ranches in Wyoming. They were all beautiful, but I must say, the Flying V is very special."

Stella had told Kate that Robert hired Faith as kitchen help when he owned a ranch in Cody. She worked for him for five years before he finally married her. They had just celebrated their ten-year wedding anniversary.

Kate looked at her watch and frowned. "I really hate to leave, but I have to meet Lane at the drugstore in twenty minutes."

"If you are going to the drugstore, you have to have a milk shake. The raspberry is my favorite," Faith said.

"Kate, I forgot to tell you," Stella broke in. "The drugstore has an old-fashioned soda fountain. It's so cute. And Faith is right—the milk shakes are the best, worth every last calorie."

"Just what I need! I already feel like I'm going to pop right out of these jeans!" Kate said as she put her hands on her hips and inhaled.

"I don't think you need to worry. You look great. And I am so glad that we finally met!" Faith said.

"Me too. The ranch is just beautiful! Thank you for letting me crash last night."

"Yes, thank you." Stella put her arms around Faith and gave her a good long squeeze. "And I've got to run, too. Mr. Money Bags is having a big dinner party tonight. I've got a ton of errands to run."

"Well, I wish you both could stay longer." Faith turned to Kate. "But I understand you need to get back to your beau—congratulations again!" Faith hugged Kate and whispered in her ear, "I'd like to meet him sometime. Come back and visit soon."

"It might be sooner than you think! Keep your fingers crossed, maybe I'll find my dream ranchette today."

LANE PICKED UP KATE IN FRONT of the drugstore at eleven o'clock on the nose. They spent the rest of the morning and the better part of the afternoon touring properties, but nothing looked or felt right. Either the house was nice but the view was all wrong, or the view was spectacular and there wasn't a house at all.

Lane had one last place to show her. The sales sheet sat on the console between them. The house was made of hand-hewn logs, with a massive wraparound deck and a sky-blue metal roof. The barn was new, and a roof in the same shade of blue was topped with a cute moose weather vane. The home was built on the side of the mountain, three miles above town. It looked almost too new for Kate's taste, yet the photo showing an expansive view of the valley and a curiously shaped mountain peak captured her attention.

"That's Ramshorn Peak," Lane said after he rolled down his window and spat out a wad of tobacco-colored mucus.

"It does look like a horn, now that you mention it." The view was priceless, yet the asking price was within reason. The voice of her father rang in her ears, "If it seems too good to be true, it probably is."

Lane looked at the digital clock in his dash. "I've got to meet another client. It shouldn't take long. Why don't you go get a sandwich and we can rendezvous at say, four o'clock?" Lane swiveled in his seat, pushed back his cowboy hat, and gave her a toothy smile.

"I appreciate the offer, but it's getting late. Why don't you give me directions and I'll do a drive-by. If I'm interested, I'll give you a call."

"Are you sure?" Lane looked at Kate as though she weren't capable of finding her own ass in the dark.

"I'm sure." Kate smiled sweetly.

The road leading to the house was a combination of black-top, mud, and gravel, in poor shape and full of potholes. The old Chevy strained as the four rear tires slipped on the rocks. Kate kept it in second and took it slow as she wound around switchback after switchback. She kept an eye on her odometer. Lane's directions told her to go three miles and then turn right on Bachelor Gulch. Everything got smaller and smaller until she saw nothing but fence and horizon against a cloudless blue sky. Kate felt as if she must be driving to the top of the world. Finally, at exactly the three-mile mark, Kate saw a tiny green sign that said Bachelor Gulch.

The truck's wheels found the well-formed ruts that led down the steep terrain. As the road dipped to the left, Kate slammed on the brakes.

The photo didn't come close to doing the property justice. The view was truly spectacular. Wavy red hills spilled into the valley below, and she could not only see Ramshorn Peak, she felt as though she could see all the way to Montana.

Kate turned her head slightly and then noticed the house and barn. She stopped breathing. The house was almost an exact replica of the cabin in the small painting that hung on her wall back home. She inched the truck forward, absorbing every detail. As in the painting, the road bent to the left, leading to a log home nestled in a grove of pine trees. The only thing missing was a curl of smoke drifting up from the river-rock chimney.

Kate made a right, followed the long gravel driveway, and parked the truck in front of the double-door garage. Wood steps wound up to the deck and front door. A pine-cone wreath with the word "Welcome" still hung in its center. She walked around the gigantic deck, peering into each and every window, jumping up and down like an excited child. The interior was completely refurbished. The floors and walls were covered in honey-colored knotty pine, massive beams supported the vaulted ceilings, and the open floor plan complemented the stone fireplace. The kitchen held pristine white appliances wrapped in pine and glass cabinets. Kate walked to the far end of the deck and looked into the huge master bedroom window. The room was perfectly situated to take full advantage of the stunning views. She walked to the other end of the deck and went down the stairs. The house had a finished walkout basement with large windows as well. Through the curtain-framed windows, she could see another large bedroom and large room next to it with a wall lined with built-in book shelves. *This will be Sam's bedroom, and we can make the other room into a playroom!* There was no need to drag Lane up there for a walk-through. Kate had seen enough to know she was going to buy it.

Before she left, Kate took a quick tour of the barn. It looked as if a horse had never stepped a hoof in it. The cement floors were scrubbed clean and the tack room and workshop were also immaculate. Outside, a weathered split-rail fence circled a round pen and small riding arena. Jake would be thrilled.

Kate ran back down to the truck. As she drove away, she turned around and took one last look at the property. Finding it wasn't an accident. Something powerful was at work. Kate had stared at that little painting in her room, saying to herself, *This is all I want*, thousands of times. The fact that the house was identical to the image was mind-blowing. There was no way she could figure out the how's and the why's; she just knew her desire was becoming reality.

It was nearly four when Kate got back to Dubois. Kate tried Lane on his cell phone and got his voice mail. She left him a message telling him that she had to get back to Farson, but to call her about the Bachelor Gulch house. As badly as she wanted to call Jake, there was no use; he'd still be out in the fields.

The sun ducked behind the red hills as Kate steered the Chevy back down Highway 287. As she drove, she decided she would try Jake a little later and see if he wanted to meet her for dinner in Atlantic City. The old Western mining town didn't do much for her artistically, but it did have a wonderful steak house. If she could catch Jake in the trailer, he could be there in under an hour. The restaurant was a favorite for both of them and might just be the perfect spot for Kate to break her news.

Once again, Kate's cell phone read "No service." Thirty minutes later, she pulled into the Exxon gas station in Fort Washakie. An Indian man with long, blue-black braids sat behind the register. Kate asked him if there was a pay phone, and he directed her to the rear of the store. Kate fished out some change from her jeans and dialed the trailer.

"Hello!" Jake sounded excited.

"Hi there, honey, how's it going?"

"Great! Guess what?"

"What?" Kate couldn't imagine what could have occurred in Farson that could possibly cause such excitement.

"Old Angus finally gave me the rest of the weekend off! I don't have to be back to work until Monday at noon!"

"No kidding! That's great. Does that mean you could meet me at the Merc for dinner?"

"I was thinking the very same thing. Where are you?"

"I'm in Fort Washakie, at a gas station."

"Well, I'd say you're about an hour away. I'll grab a quick shower and then hit the road."

"No need to rush." Kate felt tiny butterflies flutter in her stomach.

"Well, I'd like to get there before you if I can—don't want to keep my best girl waiting!"

Jake was full of enthusiasm. He suggested they take a ride to Jackson Hole the next day, maybe even get a room and spend the night, his treat. Cecil had landed a job on a big ranch and he thought it might be fun for all of them to go out and really hit the town. Kate thought it was a wonderful idea, happy to spend the rest of her visit anywhere besides Farson. Before they hung up, Kate told Jake she had a secret. Jake loved and hated secrets. He questioned her endlessly.

"You'll just have to wait and see!" Kate chirped nervously.

Kate didn't see Jake's truck when she pulled into the Mercantile, so she took a moment to brush her hair and apply a fresh coat of primrose-pink lip gloss. The butterflies in her belly were gone, only to be replaced by an elephant sitting on her chest. She picked up the ring boxes, put them in her leather backpack purse, and got out of the truck.

The hostess led Kate through the bar to a table in the rear of the dark, cozy dining room. A server introduced herself and offered Kate a drink. She ordered a vodka and club soda with a slice of lemon. *Liquid courage*, Kate said to herself. She felt a chill even though she was seated in front of a large, open barbecue grill that looked more like a giant fireplace. Glass oil lamps placed on each table were the only other source of light in the room. Kate loved the old Western feel, scanning remnants of previous lives, photos and tools of the pioneers who had settled the land. She sipped her drink, thinking of the hardship those people had suffered. Survival was what it was all about, which put the moment in perspective. The drink softened the tight muscles in her chest. Yet a moment later, her uneasiness returned. Pioneers or no pioneers, Kate wondered how in the hell men dug up the nerve to propose to a woman.

A tall cowboy in a black felt hat and a perfectly pressed khaki dress shirt walked in the dining room. Kate squinted in the dim light. As he moved closer, Kate recognized the handsome figure to be Jake. He was clean, shaved, and wearing a big smile. Kate felt like running into the bathroom and throwing up. Jake pulled her to her feet and gave her a reassuring kiss.

"How's my best girl?"

"Just fine," Kate lied.

"Well, you sure look better than fine. Have I told you lately how pretty you are?"

Kate blushed. His words gave her the courage to stay seated at the table and go ahead with her plan.

"I see you have a drink. Think I need to play some catch-up!" Jake signaled the waitress over and ordered a whiskey.

Kate sat back and absorbed Jake's jovial mood, relieved to see a glimpse of her old beau. He ordered steak and lobster for the both of them and ran on about how much fun they were going to have the next day. Kate picked at her salad and barely touched her entrée. What she could chew was washed down by a big swig of her drink. Jake ate as if he hadn't eaten for weeks, oblivious to Kate's sudden lack of appetite.

"How about some after-dinner drinks?" Jake asked the waitress as she cleared away their dishes.

"What can I get you?" the all-smiles waitress asked.

"Honey, what's that stuff called you like to order when we are in Jackson?" Jake looked at Kate like she hung the moon.

"Cognac." Kate couldn't drink another drop if her life depended on it. She felt sick again. She knew it was showtime.

"We'll have two of those please," he said to the waitress, then turned his attention to Kate.

"Now darlin', tell me about your surprise!"

Kate could barely speak; her throat felt dry as a desert. She reached behind the back of her chair and opened her purse.

"I did a bit of shopping when I was in Lander," Kate said as she put one of the pale-pink boxes in front of Jake and put the other in front of her snifter. A silence passed between them. It wasn't that obstinate Farson silence, more like the kind of silence that brings truth. It took a minute for Jake's mind to catch up with the moment. When it did, he reached out, as if in slow motion, and opened the lid of the ring box. Kate burst out crying.

Jake sprung into action as though he'd just been catapulted out of a buckin' chute. He jumped out of his seat and rushed to Kate's side. He lovingly pulled Kate from her chair, brought her back to his, and sat her on his lap.

"Now, now, why are you cryin'?" He spoke in a slow, buttery

drawl, a voice he used to gentle young, scared horses. This usually calmed Kate, but this time it made her bawl even harder.

"Ah, honey, nothing can be that bad." Jake wasn't prepared for this unexpected turn of events. He had no idea why Kate was so upset. He tried one more time to get out of her what had brought on her tears.

"Honey, please tell me what's wrong?"

Kate felt as if her feet were slipping from underneath her and that she was about to take the hardest of falls. She burrowed her head into Jake's shirt and finally muttered, "I'm afraid you'll say no." A fresh stream of tears flowed, drenching Jake's once–perfectly pressed shirt.

"What are you talking about?" Jake forced a laugh, "Now, why in the world would I say no! I've been trying to marry you since the day we met!"

He sounded so convincing that Kate lifted her head and began to laugh right along with him.

"Of course I'll marry you!" Jake said.

Kate heard what she wanted to hear, closing her ears to the nervous apprehension in his laughter. She also ignored how his limbs were as tight and strained as the strings on the fiddle as they danced to "The Lovers' Waltz," played in their honor. Kate held on tight to Jake's hand as they talked about setting a date, and folks in the bar bought rounds of celebratory drinks. Kate was ready to pull the trigger, right then and there. She even suggested she extend her stay and marry him that very week.

"I'm only getting married once. I want my mother, grandparents, and Cecil to be there!" Jake said.

Kate couldn't argue with his reasoning. After all, she had had a fairly big to-do her first time around with Michael. It would be selfish for her to deny Jake the opportunity to share his wedding day with his family and friends.

"I understand," Kate finally said, although inside she felt like she was slipping again. A horrible feeling tugged at her heart. It told her if she got on that plane a single woman, the marriage would never take place.

Kate wasn't surprised to find that the ring did not fit Jake when he finally tried to put it on. No matter how much he tried to force it, it just wouldn't slide over his knuckle. In the end, he threaded the band on the larger ring of the zipper on his plaid wool jacket and ordered a Lord Calvert and Coke.

Too Much

BACK IN ST. LOUIS, THE SALES attendant pulled a clear plastic bag over the vintage 1940s pale-apricot lace dress as Kate signed the sales receipt. The tea-length dress oozed romance, and Kate planned on pairing it with her chocolate-colored lizard cowboy boots. It would be the perfect outfit for their old-fashioned country wedding. Jake would wear jeans, boots, a Western-style tuxedo shirt with a matching jacket, and a cowboy hat. The ceremony would take place in a meadow. A horse and carriage would transport them to the reception. Kate crossed her fingers that it would be held in their new barn.

After Kate's surprise proposal at the Mercantile that night, she told Jake about the property. Jake was just as excited as Kate had imagined. They took the long way to Jackson Hole the next morning, making a stop in Dubois to view the cabin and barn. Jake drank in every detail, yet a perplexed look stretched across his face.

"How am I going to make a living here . . . ?" his voice trailed off.

"You'll train horses, silly!"

"It's not that easy to get into the horse-training business. You need clients."

"Don't you worry, we'll work it out!" Kate had visions of Jake standing in the center of the round pen with horses running in circles all around him.

When Kate got back to St. Louis, she put her house on the market. It would have to be sold before she could close on the place in Dubois. Kelly, the listing agent, assured her that someone would snap it up faster than she could call a mover.

"Houses in this price range, on a golf course, are few and far between," she said as she held out the six-month contract. Kelly was tall and leggy with a year-round tan.

"I hope you're right," Kate smiled, wanting to believe her.

Nearly a month had passed. There had been a lot of traffic through the house, but no serious buyers.

Kate stood on the front porch, her wedding dress draped over her arm, staring at the "For Sale" sign that was now the focal point of her yard. She then looked down at her left hand. The platinum band looked dull against her milky-white skin. Jake's ring hadn't come back from the jeweler in Lander yet. Kate had sent it to be sized before she left Wyoming. Kate wondered for the umpteenth time if she really was getting married. She stared at her ring often, as if it were a guarantee.

Once again, Kate felt like kicking herself. She had allowed her and Jake's last parting words at the Rock Springs Airport to be less than loving. She replayed the scene over and over again. It wasn't pretty.

"Now, don't you go taking off that ring when you have one of those city fellows chasing after you!" Jake had said, only half-joking.

"Well, I'll do as I please until you pay for it!" Kate said loud enough for everyone to hear as she walked through the security gate.

It was one of the meanest things Kate had ever said to Jake, and it had popped right out of her mouth before she even knew what she was saying. Kate could have stopped right then and there and apologized, but she didn't. She had a thorn in her side, and it had nothing to do with who paid for the rings.

Truth be known, Jake had passed on the elopement, and her feelings were deeply hurt. It didn't matter that he had every reason in the world to want his family and friends there. His words felt more like excuses. Instead of confronting him, she lashed out and hit him where she knew it would hurt most.

Kate unlocked her front door and walked up the stairs and into her bedroom. She hooked the wedding dress on the closet door. The delicate lace shift hung motionless and Kate wondered if she would ever get the chance to wear it.

The temperature dipped unseasonably low for September that night. After she put Sam to bed, she climbed into her own. Remorse made her rest heavily on her pillow. She had never apologized for being such a bitch that day at the airport. She had let it sit and resonate. Kate wished with all her heart she had not done so now, and wanted to call Jake to set things right. But Jake could not be reached. He was on a hunting trip with Cecil somewhere near Jackson Hole.

When sleep finally came, Kate began to dream. Jake was in a seedy hotel room. He wasn't alone. There was a woman she didn't recognize getting into the bed opposite his. It was dawn. The motel room was bathed in lamplight; the sun hadn't risen yet. Jake and the faceless woman were awake. She kneeled in front of him and unzipped his pants with a look of such adoration it caused Kate to scream out. It was bizarre. Kate felt as if she were awake and in the room with the two of them. Another figure, an iridescent female form with long, wavy hair and a tail like a mermaid, stood next to Kate, watching her yell in horror. Kate kept on screaming, waking herself up. Jake and the woman were gone, but the spirit-like woman was still there, next to her bed. She touched Kate's shoulder and said, "What did you expect?" and then disappeared.

Kate didn't move. The dream made no sense at all, but she felt as if it had all really happened. Something was terribly wrong; she felt it in every fiber of her being. Her body was heavy, drained of all energy, as if she had the worst hangover in the world. Nothing like this had ever happened to her. Synchronicity was one thing, but visions were a whole other ball game. Kate decided Betty was about the only person she could call for a reality check.

Kate rolled out of bed, put on her sweats, and went to Sam's room to make sure he was still asleep. He was out cold, curled on his side, legs twisted around his Thomas the Tank Engine sheets. Kate pulled a blanket over him and tiptoed out.

The kitchen clock read twelve minutes after eight. It was an hour earlier in Colorado—early, but not too early for Betty. She would just be finishing her sunrise yoga and meditation. Kate measured two scoops of Italian roast coffee into her espresso machine. As she waited for the thick stream of caffeine, she tried to shake off the dream hangover. But the negativity hung on. After she steamed the milk for a cappuccino, Kate dialed Betty's number.

"Thank God you're there!" Kate said in a hushed voice.

"Why are you whispering?"

"Sam is upstairs sleeping, and I don't want to wake him up. I've got to talk to you!"

"What's up?" Betty was all ears.

Kate poured out her story with not so much as a pause for a sip of cappuccino.

"You know, Kate, you are pretty in tune with your sub-conscious."

"But this is crazy!"

"Native Americans have visions all of the time!"

"So, you're saying that it was real?" Kate dropped her head. Betty might as well have said she was dying of some god-awful terminal disease.

"I'm saying it is possible."

"So, what am I going to do?"

"Have you tried to call him?'"

"No. I think he's still out on that hunting trip."

"Why don't you try him anyway? Maybe if you talk to him, you'd feel better."

"You're right. I guess I could try and track him down."

Kate didn't have a clue how to get ahold of Jake. She tried calling him at his trailer the minute she got off the phone with Betty. Two days later, she was still dialing and not getting an answer. She tried Cecil in Jackson Hole. The answering machine was on, but nobody picked up.

Pain and frustration squeezed Kate with a viselike grip. She sat in the middle of her walk-in closet and yelled, "What do you want of me?" at something she could not see. Her face was twisted and wet from crying. The wedding dress still hung on the door, looming over her head. She hadn't eaten or slept in days. Kate had come so far, but never felt so lost or lonely.

In desperation, she called the OT Bar. Candi answered the phone.

"Have you seen Jake around?" Kate asked with a light, friendly tone, as if nothing were wrong.

"You know, I did see him at the Eden Bar last night." Candi spoke slowly. Kate could tell she was picking her words carefully.

Eden was a spit-in-the-road town about twenty minutes from Farson.

"Oh, good, I tried him last night and got a busy signal for hours. I finally called the operator, and found out the phone was off the hook!"

"Really?" Candi replied nonchalantly.

"Yeah, isn't that funny! Jake can be so absentminded sometimes. If you see him, please tell him to hang up his phone!" Kate laughed the fakest laugh of her life.

"Sure thing." Candi laughed back an even faker laugh.

"This is bullshit!" Kate screamed after she hung up. It was obvious Jake was avoiding her. She couldn't take it anymore.

Kate called Marino Motors and told Janet to tell her father she was sick with strep throat. Janet asked her when she would be in, and Kate told her she wasn't sure; she'd call in on Monday and give her an update. Kate then went to her purse, pulled out her wallet, and called the airlines. The next call was to Michael.

"I've got an emergency. I've got to fly out to Wyoming. Can you take care of Sam for a few days?" Kate worked hard to hold her emotions in check.

"It's already Friday, no problem. I'm home all weekend, and he's with me for the next two weeks anyway," he said, and then offered Kate a ride to the airport.

JAKE WASN'T SURPRISED WHEN HE got the message Kate was in Denver waiting for a connecting flight to Rock Springs. He finished his chores, hopped in his truck, and went to pick her up at the airport. He greeted her with the same tired, defeated look he had worn the months before their engagement.

The drive from the airport back to Farson was about as much fun as a root canal. Jake and Kate didn't talk much, although there was so much to say. Kate noticed the last of the gold-colored bales had been hauled away as they parked in front of the trailer. Hay season had finally ended. Jake got out of the truck first and went around to the passenger side to help Kate pull her bag from the cab.

"I think I'll just go inside and freshen up." Kate forced a weak smile. If Jake was going to call off the wedding, she wanted to be sure she looked her best, a beautiful snapshot of what he was going to miss.

The tortoiseshell hairbrush she had left behind sat on the tiny vanity top. Kate was meticulous about removing any hair before and after she used it. Jake hadn't been as careful. The clear bristles held a tangled mess. Kate began pulling out long, copper-colored locks. The hair was definitely not hers. She felt as though someone had just punched her in the stomach. After several deep breaths, anger pushed out the pain. Kate marched out of the bathroom waving the brush in her hand as if it were a gun.

"Okay, you asshole, who the hell is she?" Kate yelled.

"What do you mean?" Jake looked shocked.

"Who is it? She left her hair in my brush, you idiot!"

"I—I don't know what you're talking about." He stuttered like a child caught lying.

"Do I look like I'm stupid?" Kate trembled, she was so angry. If the brush were a gun, she was sure she would have used it.

"Honey . . ." Jake got up from the velour couch and moved toward her.

"Don't you dare call me 'honey'!" Kate hissed. She backed away as if he were a rattlesnake.

Jake stood in front of Kate. Genuine tears of shame poured from his eyes. In between sobs, he attempted to tell Kate what happened.

"She came by here looking for a job."

"Who? Who came by looking for a job?" Kate tried her best to keep her voice even.

"It was Candi."

"Why wouldn't she just call Angus? He's in the OT every day!" Kate screamed, losing her patience.

"I don't know. I guess she hadn't seen him for awhile, and she knew I worked for him, so she came by the trailer and asked me how to get ahold of him."

"Like I'm supposed to believe that?"

Jake swore it was the honest-to-God truth and that nothing had happened between them.

"So why are you looking so guilty then?" Kate pressed. Half of her wanted to know; the other half didn't.

"Well, I did run into her when I was in Jackson," Jake said just above a whisper.

The blood drained from Kate's face. She stood there, unable to speak.

"I swear to you, nothing happened. She knew I was engaged!"

"*Was* engaged?" Kate felt a rush of blood return to her brain. She was torn between running to the bathroom to puke and going to the closet for the thirty-ought-six.

"Well, when I was out hunting, I rode and rode. And the more I rode, the more I thought—I think this is all just too much," Jake moaned.

"What do you mean, too much?" Kate felt like she was having an out-of-body experience. This had to be someone else's life. One look at the pain on Jake's face told her it was not.

"The wedding, the place in Dubois, settling down in one place—well, it's just too much!" And he continued to cry.

Kate slammed down the brush on the Formica table and counted to ten, willing herself to maintain some control.

The wind howled, the metal trailer groaned, and then came an eerie silence. The reality of the situation hit Kate. She walked over to where Jake was sitting and climbed onto his lap. His agony became her own. She could not speak, although her gut reminded her she had felt this coming on for a very long time.

Jake whispered, his voice barely audible. "If I don't pursue this, her, I'll always wonder. I'll never forgive myself."

"You want to *date* her?" Kate said, shaking her head in disbelief.

"I think so."

And then Kate told Jake about her dream.

"I can't believe you really dreamt that!" He then admitted most of it had happened, every gory detail. He and Cecil were at The Cowboy Bar, throwing back a few whiskeys, when they ran into Candi. She said all the motels were full of hunters and asked if she could bunk with them. But Candi did not kneel in front of him and pull down his zipper. He was adamant about that.

"But she wanted to," Kate choked out.

Jake didn't answer. Instead he said, "If you love me, you'll let me go."

Kate was incensed. Jake had begged her to marry him for over a year and now that he was faced with the possibility, he was falling apart. The trailer trash that left her hair in the brush was just another excuse. Jake had arrived in Farson a man, and now the town, the land, the fields, and the dust had reduced him to a scared little boy. Kate saw that fear had gotten stuck in Jake's throat, and he was choking on it. The old Jake would have swallowed hard instead of spitting it out.

OVER THE COURSE OF THE NEXT week, the two circled the situation like the tractors that had gone round and round the fields outside the old metal trailer. They dissected, hashed, and rehashed their relationship. The days were filled mostly with tears, and the nights brought lovemaking, arguing, and little or no sleep.

Finally, they decided to give the relationship a three-month break. Neither of them was ready to completely sever the cord that had tied them together for so long. They had grown so close, they did not know how to function apart. The hiatus would give Jake time to explore what he had to seek out, and Kate prayed that in the end he would come to his senses.

"You are a part of me, Kate Marino. You have a part of me that no one else will ever have. I don't want to lose you."

"You'll never lose me," Kate said, and meant it. He, too, held a part of her that she was sure would never come back.

But in the end, Kate learned what too much really was.

Besides finding out about Jake's new love interest by seeing her hair in Kate's very own hairbrush, too much was walking into the Eden Bar her last night in Wyoming and watching as the bartender slipped her now-ex-fiancé a note from "the other woman" with a hawk feather attached to it. Too much was then staring at the foul feather dangling like a trophy from the rear-view mirror of his truck, the very same truck Kate had bought him with her money. Too much was being in bed in a sexy black teddy, desperate to keep his love, watching him scan her body, and then listening to him say how beautiful she was.

"I love you," Kate said.

"I think I'm in love with Candi," he replied.

Now that was too much.

The next morning, Jake took Kate to the airport. On the way, Kate watched the hawk feather swing back and forth on the mirror like the yellow caution light that swung at the only intersection in Farson. As if sealing their fate, when she got back to St. Louis, Kate backed out of the contract on the house and barn in Dubois. She did not tell Jake.

It was shortly thereafter that Kate stepped up her daily routine of walking and started jogging, feeling the need for speed, convincing herself she was moving toward something instead of running away.

Loose Ends

THEY HAD AGREED THEY WOULD NOT communicate with each other unless it was absolutely necessary. Kate thought about calling Jake about every other minute, which reminded her of why she wasn't supposed to call, which then made her think about Jake being with the red-headed bitch from hell. It was all her fault. If Candi hadn't come sniffing around, throwing herself at Jake, none of this would have happened.

Four tortuous weeks passed, and Kate wondered how she was going to survive another two months. In the past, the combination of working all day and chasing Sam around had thoroughly exhausted her. Now, she still dropped right off to sleep, but by two in the morning she was wide awake, thinking about Jake all over again.

Uncertainty seemed to cloud everything Kate did. If things didn't work out with Jake, she wasn't so sure she wanted to live in the mountains alone. Since she was no longer buying the house in Dubois, she decided it didn't make sense to keep her house on the market in St. Louis.

But musical houses seemed to be a popular tune. Michael decided to sell his.

"You know, I think Sam and I just need a bigger place. And

I know this is weird, but I've always wanted a swimming pool," Michael explained.

"You work hard. You should have everything you want! I think it's great you're building a new home." Kate knew the long hours Michael put in.

"Well, the thing is, I already have a buyer for this house."

"You're kidding!" Kate was a bit jealous her place hadn't sold so fast, but then her heart said, *There's a reason for everything; it wasn't meant to be.*

"Yeah, this couple basically knocked on my door and told me how much they loved the house and wanted to know if I would consider selling. That's how this whole thing started."

"That's wild. I suppose you got a great price?"

"Let's just say the price was right, so right I agreed to close in a month."

"But where will you live?"

"I guess I'll rent an apartment until the new place is finished."

Kate envisioned Sam and Michael in some small, bland, two-bedroom rental.

"Why don't you move in here?" Kate blurted out.

"I couldn't do that!"

"Why not? Sam already has his room all set up, and you can stay in the guest room."

Kate thought about how lonely she had been. It would be nice to have Sam there every day. And Michael would be off to his office before she even got out of bed. It was nearly six when he returned home, and many nights he had to entertain clients. They'd probably never see one another. She'd have to move her studio to the basement, but it didn't matter. She had painted only one piece since her "pause" from Jake, as she called it. The painting depicted the figure of a Shoshone woman, a papoose strapped to her back. The figure stood in a gold, grassy field, a stormy sky hung above her, and a scarlet bleeding heart dripped from her hands. Kate had cried and cried while she worked. But after that, there was simply nothing. The spiral notebook where she recorded her deepest thoughts now sat untouched as well. Kate couldn't bear to face the pages for fear of what might come out.

"I don't know," Michael said slowly.

"Come on. It'll be better for Sam to live here. You don't need to move him to a strange apartment, then move him again into a new house. He moves around enough as it is." Kate was practically begging.

"Well, you're right about that."

Kate could tell he was warming up to the idea.

"Of course I am. I'm hardly ever home, and you know how much I like to travel. It will work out fine. It's not like we don't get along, for Christ's sake."

"The builder did say the house should be ready by the end of January. So if I let these people close in November, I'd only be staying with you for maybe a month or two."

"So, it's settled. You and Sam can move in with me. It'll be fun."

Kate hung up, wondering how bizarre her life really was. She was dating a cowboy barely out of puberty and was going to live with the man she had divorced five years ago.

Kate poured herself a see-through, a vodka martini on the rocks, and called Stella.

"Life gets stranger and stranger." Kate took a sip of her ice-cold drink.

"And it just got stranger," Stella said in mysterious voice.

"Oh God, now what?" Kate couldn't bear any more drama.

"This is a good thing. You'll never guess who is having a show at the Circle JD Gallery!"

"I'm not in a guessing mood," Kate said.

"Ah, come on, you can't stay sour forever. Who's your favorite artist?"

"Earl Conifer," Kate shot back without a second thought. One of his original oils, a dreamy scene of a Shoshone Indian hunting party on horseback gathered around a watering hole, hung over her mantel at home. She stared at it almost as often as she stared at the flames in the hearth below it.

"Bingo!" Stella acted as though she had just won the lottery.

"No kidding!" Kate would kill for an opportunity to meet the artist.

"Yep, right here in Jackson Hole. Why don't you come out? I miss you!"

"You have no idea how much I miss you. When is it?"

Kate caught Stella's excitement. Earl Conifer was her idol. She loved everything about him—his subject matter, wild colors, and impressionistic style.

"The artist reception is November twenty-seventh, the Sunday after Thanksgiving."

"It's my turn to have Sam for Thanksgiving. Michael will have probably moved in by then. Maybe I could spend the holiday with them and come the day after."

"That would work. Come on, you deserve a trip out West!"

The word "West" brought a pang of sadness. Kate shoved it down deep and focused on the trip. It would be good timing. Michael could have some time alone in her house to get settled while she got some time with Stella.

"Well, I'd have to drive. There's no way I'd get a cheap fare on a holiday weekend."

"Whatever it takes. You've got a free place to stay, and we can cook in and drink out." Stella sold hard. "Come on! We need some female bonding time!"

"That's an understatement. Why do all of my best girlfriends live out of state?"

"Because St. Louis sucks. That's why."

Kate laughed a long overdue laugh.

"So you'll come!"

"What about Jake?" Jackson Hole was a big small town. Half of her was dying to see him, but the other half dreaded a confrontation of any kind, especially if he was with that trailer trash.

"Who in the hell cares! Anyway, Angus will be keeping him busy in Farson, you can be sure of that. And you certainly aren't going to run into him at the Conifer opening."

"You're right. It sure would be nice to get away from Dad. God, he drives me crazy!"

"Business as usual at Marino Motors?" Stella joked.

"Oh, sure, Dad and James are thick as thieves." The more Kate thought about it, the more she wanted to get out of Dodge. The drive to Wyoming would do her good. A familiar voice called out to her, and it yearned for something other than a man to fill her up.

Stella rambled on, reliving her days working for her father. "God, I am just so glad to be out of there. I don't know how you stand it."

"If I could figure out a way to live in Wyoming and still be with Sam, you know I'd move in a heartbeat!"

"Well, in the meantime, just come visit me!"

"All right, you win."

"Yes!" Stella shouted.

Kate smiled, her brain already spinning a traveling plan. She could make it as far as Denver in one day but she had nowhere to crash for the night. Betty had moved to Texas to study with her guru. Then she thought of Ted.

"I guess I could always crash at Ted's in Denver. He's never there anyway."

"Why not? He doesn't have a problem calling you for World Series tickets."

Ted had remained consistent in one arena. He would not let Kate forget about him. And to muddy the waters even more, in addition to buying all of his Jeeps from her, he was now referring friends. It didn't matter that they didn't live in Missouri. Kate directed them to go a nearby Jeep dealership, pick out what they wanted, and then call her. Kate would then order the vehicle from the factory and have it delivered to their door. These were sales Marino Motors would have never gotten if it weren't for Ted. Needless to say, their business association made it difficult for her not to take his calls.

"He's sold quite a few cars in Colorado for me. I owed him a favor."

"You don't owe him jack shit. If anything, he owes you for being so nice when he was such a dick."

Kate chose to ignore the remark. "I'll give him a call and see if he's single these days or has a live-in of the month. If he's solo, he'll probably let me stay there."

"It's the least he can do."

The receptionist stood at Kate's door waving a fan of pink paper.

"I'd better run. I'll talk to you later."

"Call me after you talk to Ted!"

"I will," Kate promised, and hung up.

She thumbed her way through the message slips. Most of the

calls were from her radio and TV reps, all begging for business. Daniel, her Fox Sports rep, had become a good friend. She would return his call first, but not before she phoned Ted. If she didn't try him now, she knew she might lose her nerve. Her fingers reached for the phone and dialed the 303 phone number she knew by heart.

"Is Ted in?" Kate asked hurriedly.

"Is this Kate?" Ted's secretary of ten years answered the phone. She knew all about Ted and Kate's history.

"It is. How are you doing, Fran?"

"Great! The weather is just gorgeous out here. The aspen trees are just starting to change."

"Fall is so beautiful out there," Kate said impatiently. She just wanted to ask Ted if she could crash at his place and be done with it.

"It's my favorite time of the year. Let me see if Ted is available," Fran said, and put Kate on hold. She was back on the line within seconds.

"He'll be right with you!"

My, how times have changed, Kate thought. Music played as she waited for Ted to pick up.

When he did, Kate was smart and charming, answering all of Ted's questions about the car business like the expert she was. Ted proceeded to tell her all about the condo he had bought in Aspen and a trip he was planning to Bora Bora. She listened patiently until she found an opening for her question. He finally gave her one, and she spit it out as fast as she could.

"Marino, don't you ever stay in one place?"

"Look who's talking!" Kate thought about Jake. If she stayed at Ted's, it would drive him crazy. Well, if he could screw the redhead, she could certainly stay with her old boyfriend.

"Sure you can stay. Isn't that Thanksgiving weekend?"

"It is. I'm going to spend the holiday with Sam and leave Friday morning. I'd probably get there around seven."

"I might be skiing in Aspen. I won't know until the last minute. I'll just leave the key in the barbecue pit."

"Perfect," Kate said, thinking how typical it was for Ted to be so elusive. She was relieved she was no longer a Tedaholic, and even more relieved that he did not bring up Jake.

Kate put the phone on the cradle and felt a surge of relief. She was going back to Wyoming and would most likely not run into Ted or Jake. That was, of course, if Jake got off his ass and mailed the box of winter clothes she had packed up before she left. She would need her snow boots and ski jacket. If he didn't send them soon, she would be forced to call and remind him. She did not want to make that call.

Three weeks passed and no box. Kate was incensed. November wasn't exactly a busy month for Farson farmers, unless they were hunting every day or completely obsessed with a new girlfriend. Kate broke down and called Jake and got the answering machine. She left a message, and he didn't call back. Kate thought maybe the red-headed bitch got the message and didn't pass it on. She called again. This time Jake returned the call, but instead of calling her back at work or on her cell, where he knew he could reach her, he left her a message at home. He said he was sorry he never got around to sending the clothes, so he guessed he would have to meet her somewhere on her way to Jackson Hole.

Kate was pissed. She did not want to see Jake, and she definitely did not want to see dandy Candi. But he had left her with no choice. She didn't have the money to waste on new winter gear.

"What an ass!" Stella screamed over the phone.

"I'm telling you, it's that bitch." Kate still refused to say Candi's name.

"Well, you're just going to have to meet him and get your things. It'll take two minutes."

Kate played phone tag with Jake the next few days. They never spoke to each other but made a plan via messages to meet at the gas station in Eden late Saturday afternoon. Kate would call him when she was in Rock Springs, which would give him plenty of time to meet her.

Thanksgiving Day was filled with football, food, and happy sounds of a family that got along. Michael's mother and father joined the Marino clan at Kate's, since Michael had just moved in. Kate cooked a twenty-pound turkey. Everybody else brought a dish, except James, who came empty-handed. But he redeemed himself by not creating any drama. The company kept him in line. Sam was in seventh heaven with both sets of grandparents hanging on his every action.

After everyone left, Kate loaded her Jeep with water, iPod, self-help CDs, her laptop, and enough clothes for a month. In the morning, she made a thermos of cappuccino, packed a cooler with food, and ran upstairs to kiss a still-sleeping Sam good-bye.

Once on Interstate 70, she set the cruise control just below eighty miles per hour. The iPod remained unplugged and the CDs sat in their cases; the peace of the open road was the only sound she needed to hear. Her mind rolled with the hills of Kansas, but as the landscape flattened, so did Kate's thoughts. She stopped only twice for gas, and before she knew it, she had crossed the Colorado border. She had driven this drive so many times in high school and college, she could do it with her eyes closed. But she didn't. At the Colorado Springs cutoff, Kate scanned the western horizon for the familiar sight that made her spirit soar.

The Rocky Mountains sat waiting in the distance as if they were the pearly gates to heaven. And for Kate they always would be. The drive should have been exhausting, but it wasn't. She felt like she was sixteen again, full of energy, and in awe of the massive rocks that rose from the earth. Anything was possible all over again.

What she wasn't ready for was the music that filtered from Ted's house when she pulled into his driveway. It never occurred to her that he would be home. He had never married again but always had some feline lurking about. And he just told her he was now spending his weekends in Aspen. Kate was pissed. Ted and his infamous game playing wasn't part of the plan. She had looked forward to a nice quiet evening in his beautiful home— alone. She popped the tailgate, unloaded her overnight bag, then locked the car.

Limestone slab steps led into a Spanish-style courtyard. Soft spotlights illuminated the patio, which was surrounded by glass sliding doors leading into the house. The interior was lit up like downtown Las Vegas on a Saturday night. Ted stood with his back to Kate at the kitchen counter. It looked like he was arranging cheese on a platter. He turned his head to reach for a glass of white wine. His profile was much more angular than she had remembered. He had lost weight. And his once-longish dark hair was shaved into a short silver crew cut. There was obviously no need to search for the key.

Kate's heart felt as though it were going to leap out of her chest as she moved toward the door. She cursed herself for being nervous. Ted turned and motioned to her to come in.

"I'm shocked and amazed!" Kate announced as she stepped into the house.

"I live here, remember?" He smiled slyly.

Kate noticed that he had indeed shed at least twenty-five pounds since she had last seen him. The gut was gone. He looked fit and younger despite the gray hair.

"Well, yes, I know that, but you said you were going skiing." Kate smiled back, wondering what the hell he was up to.

"How was the drive?"

"It was good. I made great time." She looked at her watch; it was six thirty. "It only took me about eleven hours."

Kate stood there in a T-shirt and black leggings, with a sweater tied around her waist. She hadn't bothered with makeup and hadn't seen a mirror since she left her house at 6 a.m. She had no idea how she looked, but she guessed it wasn't a glamour moment.

"Still a lead foot, eh? Would you like a glass of wine?"

"I'm thinking I'd like something a little stronger, if you don't mind. I'm feeling a little road wired." Kate wanted to add, "and pissed off," but knew being rude wouldn't fix the mess she had gotten herself into. She wondered how she could get away for a moment to regroup.

Ted walked to the bar. "You still like tequila?" He opened the cabinet door and grabbed a strange-shaped bottle.

"You have a good memory!" Kate watched Ted pour her a glass of the honey-colored liquid into a delicate snifter.

"Ever tried this?"

"Can't say that I have."

"It's Herradura tequila. It's pretty good stuff. I think you'll like it."

Kate took one sip. "It is good, smooth." She put down the glass, hating that she was slightly impressed. It wasn't just the expensive booze; it was the whole package. Ted looked great, his house was gorgeous, and he was definitely more seasoned.

"You wanna go to the hockey game?" he asked casually.

"Huh?" Kate's mouth hung open like an idiot.

"I have tickets to the hockey game; would you like to go?" Ted stared at Kate.

Kate had to think fast, which was a real challenge after the 950-mile drive.

"I'm sort of tired," Kate lied. "Could I take a bath and see how I feel?" She needed to get away and think. They had not done this dance for a long time, and she wasn't so sure if she could or wanted to follow.

Ted led Kate to his bedroom suite. "It has the only bathtub in the house," he explained as they walked down the long hall.

His bathroom was beautiful. Mexican porcelain tile covered the walls of a decadent open-air shower, and an enormous sunken tub ran the length of the room. Ted set out fresh towels and left. Kate turned on the water and poured in lavender bath salts, leftovers from some other woman, of that she was sure.

The tequila she sipped on started to take the edge off. Her brain wasn't as sharp as it should be, yet it didn't miss the humor in the bizarre turn of events. She hated to admit it, but she was flattered. It was obvious Ted had skipped going skiing in Aspen to see her. For a moment, a picture of Jake and Candi shot through her mind like a bullet. It was a direct hit to her already-bruised ego.

What the hell, let's see what old Ted's got up his sleeve! She laughed defiantly. It was entertaining as hell, and what could it hurt?

They arrived late at the hockey game. Ted had season tickets, excellent seats, of course. Ted was very attentive; he fetched beers and warm pretzels, and explained what was happening in a game Kate never took much interest in. Kate looked down at her hand

and wondered how it had gotten wrapped in Ted's. The halftime buzzer sounded, and the crowd got up to stretch.

"I know it's been a long day for you. How about we get some dinner?" Ted looked at her as though he was really concerned about how she felt. Kate thought for a moment that maybe he had changed.

"That sounds good." Kate shoved her full warm beer under her seat.

"What are you in the mood for: trendy, or great Mexican food at a hole-in-the-wall?"

"What do you think I would choose?'

"White tablecloth, trendy."

Kate threw back her head and laughed. "See, you don't know me at all. Let's head for the Mexican joint!"

"Remember the Eagles concert in Vail?" Ted said on the way to the restaurant, his eyes sparkling with excitement.

"How could I forget?" It had been a wonderful weekend. She had flown in from St. Louis, and Ted had immediately whisked her away to Vail. Ted knew all the hot spots and toured Kate through one fabulous meal after another, in between walks and lovemaking. On Sunday morning, he told her he had a surprise. He slid an envelope under her cappuccino cup. Kate opened it.

"Oh my God! Tickets for the Eagles concert tonight! You've got to be kidding me! That show has been sold out for months!" Kate jumped out of her seat and ran to give him a hug. The Eagles were her all-time favorite band.

"The concert starts at eight. I thought it might be fun to try that fondue restaurant before the show. We have a six o'clock reservation."

That was Ted; he always had tickets to every event worth going to, and they were always the best seats in the house. Kate started to soften. She sat back and listened, chuckling at the appropriate moments. He was being so nice, and she needed someone to be kind to her.

Finally they pulled in front of a dumpy building with "La Cantina" flashing in neon over the front window. Ted turned into the dimly lit parking lot, parked the car, and turned off the ignition.

"Okay, I can't stand this anymore!" He jumped out of the car, ran around to Kate, and grabbed her as she got out of the car.

"What are you talking about?" Kate barely got the words out before Ted planted a passionate kiss on her pursed lips. He held her tight, as though he had been waiting for the moment for years. Kate gently pulled away.

"I think we better go inside," she said politely, not ready for so much intensity. Her mind was spinning. *This guy has killed you over and over again; he's a jerk.* But her heart yelled, *Jake is a jerk too. He's with another woman. Two can play this game!*

Ted's taste in food was still right on target. La Cantina served excellent chili rellenos and silky smooth guacamole. Kate relaxed and began to enjoy the conversation and Ted's company. He told her about his bike trips to France, dinners in New York, skiing in Vail and Aspen, and his upcoming fiftieth-birthday celebration in Bora Bora. That was one of Kate's dream destinations. Ted didn't outright ask her to join him, but he dangled the trip like a carrot.

"You still like driving your Jeep?" Kate steered the conversation to a safer subject.

"It's great, but I'm thinking about buying a Mercedes, a sports car, something fun to drive around when the weather's nice."

"The sporting goods business must be good!"

"It's great. We just opened our twelfth store in Kansas City."

"That's wonderful, congratulations." Kate stifled a yawn.

"I think it's time to get the check," Ted said as he waved to the waiter.

"Let me get this!" Kate reached for the black leather binder.

"I don't think so." Ted pulled it back, opened the binder, then threw in three twenties.

"I really wanted to buy you dinner. It's the least I can do. You're letting me stay at your place and you took me to the hockey game."

"Marino, it was no big deal. Let's go."

When they returned to Ted's place, he built a fire. Kate tentatively took a seat next to him on the couch. She could smell him, his scent so familiar but scary at the same time. She no longer knew where her heart was. The conversation turned more personal, and so did Ted's intentions. It wasn't long before Ted started kissing Kate, then swiftly and expertly unbuttoning her suede shirt.

"Hey, whoa!" Kate took his hands off her chest and leaned back.

"Whoa?" Ted looked thunderstruck.

"Yeah, whoa, like, slow down. You're gonna have to give me a moment to catch up." Kate's confusion evaporated.

"Catch up?" Ted still looked stupidly confused.

"You know, I just can't keep up with you! One minute you want me, and the next minute you run away."

Ted closed her shirt and pushed her away. Kate could tell he hadn't expected any resistance. He really thought he could just crawl right back into her life and pants. Ted screwed his face into an ugly grimace and looked at her as if he were seeing her for the very first time. It was at that moment Kate realized how much Ted had stolen from her. He had taken not only her heart but her pride. She could never be with a man that used love in such a wicked way.

"Where do you want to sleep?" Ted spit out like the spoiled child he was.

"Is this a trick question?" Kate asked, utterly amazed by his ego. She had never intended to sleep with him.

"I think you better sleep in one of the guest rooms," Ted said it as if it were punishment.

If Kate weren't so surprised, she would have burst out laughing. In a way she felt sorry for him. He would never get it.

"I think I better just go. There's a Hampton Inn right down the road."

Kate collected her things and walked out the door.

THE NEXT MORNING, A THIN LAYER of snow had fallen on the streets of Denver. As Kate traveled west, the roads worsened into an icy slush. But she felt strong and unusually clearheaded, happy to be driving with the mountains surrounding her again. The signal on her phone went out but picked up again as she neared Laramie. She dialed Jake to let him know she was on her way. Snow was now floating from the sky like big down feathers. Kate was relieved she would soon have her heavy Carhartt jacket, Sorel boots, and snow gear. The painting she had painted that was hanging over Jake's bed and a few pairs of jeans were the only things left at the trailer. Jake loved the painting. Kate had painted it the summer before, her interpretation of a photograph of Indians on horseback taken by Edward Curtis. Kate figured he could keep it for now.

The phone rang and rang, but Jake's machine didn't pick up. She tried again in Rawlins and still got no answer. By the time she hit Rock Springs, she was furious. The parking lot at the

Eden Bar, their agreed-upon meeting point, was only thirty min-utes away.

At 7:30 p.m., she drove through Eden. There was no sign of Jake's truck in the one-bar town. Kate knew this was no time for a surprise entrance, but Jake wasn't leaving her much of a choice. It was snowing harder now, and the dual highway was slippery as an ice-skating rink. Kate gave Jake one last phone call when she arrived in Farson. When he didn't answer, she headed for his place.

A light flipped on in the dark mobile home as she pulled up to the front door. A strange horse trailer was hitched to the back of Jake's ranch truck. The old white Chevy she bought a year ago was parked to the side.

Jake stepped outside. He was in a hurry, pulling on a shirt and making his way to Kate's car in his stocking feet. Another figure stood up, then ducked behind the curtains.

"I tried to call you a million times!" Kate rolled down her window and screamed.

"Yeah, I know, I forgot to turn on the machine and I was out riding, on a pack trip. I was just fixin' to meet you in Eden."

"You're a little late, don't you think? The least you could have done was call!"

"Kate, you've got to believe me! I just got home, and I tried to call you from the road, but everything closed up early because of the storm." Jake couldn't look Kate in the eye. He stared at the ground, lifting one foot then the other, shaking off the thick, wet snow.

"Go get my things. Now," Kate said as evenly as she could. To have to see Jake's lover in his trailer, the trailer they once shared, was almost unbearable.

Jake walked over to the Chevy, opened the passenger door,

and took out a big brown cardboard box, all taped up and ready to ship.

"How long have you had that in your truck?" Kate knew that Farson had a post office, and with a population in the double digits there was never a wait.

"Kate, I'm sorry, I just never got around to sending it." Jake kept looking down at the ground as if it could open up and he could drop out of sight.

"You son of a bitch! This is all your fault! How could you put me in this position?" Kate was too furious to cry. "Go get the painting."

"The painting?" Jake asked stupidly.

"You know the one; it's hanging over your bed." Kate blocked out the image of Jake and that trashy bitch screwing under her lovely piece of art. "I want *my* painting and the rest of my stuff."

"It'll take me a minute," Jake mumbled.

"I'll wait." Kate hit the rear tailgate remote unlock. "Put the box in the back."

Jake did as he was told and picked his way back to the front door.

Kate sat back and wondered how in the hell this had all happened. She felt like someone was squeezing all the breath from her. She knew what to expect, but it didn't make it hurt any less. Her heart ached, and tears threatened. She fought them back, refusing to give the bitch inside the satisfaction of seeing her fall apart.

Jake walked back outside. Two tiny black puppies followed at his heels. He carried a trash bag filled with clothes in one hand and the painting in the other. He placed them in the back of her car, closed the tailgate, and came around to her car door.

"Kate, you said we'd give it three months."

"Three months! I don't need three months! I am done! You are not the man I fell in love with anymore. You've changed, Jake. Where are your morals? Your integrity?"

Jake just shook his head and said nothing.

"Besides, Michael's moved in with me." Kate couldn't believe the words that spilled from her lips.

"Really?" Jake took his hands off Kate's car and stepped back.

Kate glanced at her left hand, which was resting on the top of the door. The platinum band was still wrapped around her finger. She put her hand down to her side.

"Yeah, at first it was just a temporary thing. He was staying with me while he finished building his new house. It's got a pool. Anyway, things are good between us. And Sam is thrilled."

"No kidding." Jake glared at her.

"Well, stranger things have happened." Kate became an actress in a scene she just wanted to end. Lie upon lie flew out of her mouth like vomit. It was her only defense. After all of their talk of friendship, after him sobbing in her lap and telling her how afraid he was of losing her, Jake had hurt her in a way no one else ever would. She felt like a fool.

Kate didn't stop to cry until she got back to Farson. She pulled into the Texaco gas station, pushed the hazard button on the steering wheel, and sobbed until no more tears would come. The barely visible yellow caution light, at the intersection of Highways 191 and 28, caught her attention. It flew back and forth chaotically in the blizzard-force wind. Kate's eyes followed the swinging motion of the blinking light for a long time, mesmerized, as if she were hypnotized. Finally, she shook her head.

The road and landscape blurred into a solid white sheet. Kate had to make a decision quickly, a decision she did not know she had to make until now. To the left the road led to Jackson

Hole, her planned destination. To the right was Dubois. With a spirit she did not know she possessed, she turned off her flashers, looked both ways, and then turned the wheels of the Jeep to the right. Jackson Hole and Earl Conifer could wait; there was one more loose end she needed to tie up.

Water Woman

WHERE FARSON WAS BARREN, DRY, AND unforgiving, Dubois was rich in texture, full, and generous. The community was an interesting mixed bag of ranchers, artists, retirees, and trust-fund babies. Everyone was kind and willing to help. Kate would meet someone in the tavern or store, and they'd get to talking. They'd ask how her move was, and she'd say fine, but she was having a hard time hanging a large mirror or painting. Next thing she knew, she'd get a call and that very same person would offer to come help her. The few neighbors she had dropped off fresh-baked bread and cookies. She felt as though she had landed in a flock of angels and they had miraculously taken her under their wings.

For a while, Wyoming's rare breed of people, the move, and the business of settling in a new town kept her occupied. It was the first time she had been out on her own, living away from home, other than her brief stint at college.

"I feel like I'm finally growing up at the ripe old age of thirty-eight!" Kate said to her mother after her move that spring. Her mother had gently prodded her to buy the property in Dubois.

"What is the worst thing that could happen if you buy the cabin?" her mother had asked.

"Maybe it doesn't work, and I can't afford to go back and forth." Kate was scared, and that was all there was to it. She hadn't sold her house yet, and when she did, she had no idea where she would live when she came back to Missouri to be with Sam.

"I've got plenty of money. If worse comes to worst, I'll pay for the house in Dubois. You're going to get it when I die anyway, so I might as well put it to good use now."

It was an offer Kate couldn't refuse. She called Lane Stuart and made an offer on the cabin that very next morning. Michael and Sam had already moved into their new home, so she was free to put her house on the market. It sold two weeks later. The last dangling detail was where to hang her hat when she came back to St. Louis. It was Michael who came to her rescue.

"Paybacks are a bitch!" he said to Kate when he offered up the guest room in his new home. "My room is on the first floor, so you and Sam will have the whole second floor to yourselves. And I'm long on square footage and short on furniture, so bring whatever you want."

Kate couldn't believe her good luck. Everything had fallen into place as if it was meant to be. She moved a few things to Michael's, but most of her and Sam's belongings went on the big United Van Lines truck to Wyoming.

The majority of Kate's furniture was traditional in style. When she started placing the pieces in the cabin, she was thrilled with the contrast of the formal elegance against the warm pine walls and floor. Her favorite piece, a Chippendale mahogany sideboard, was placed along the dining room wall. She put a Waterford lamp on one side and an old lead crystal decanter and two brandy glasses in the center. Her dining room set, a burl-inlaid table with six Queen Anne–style chairs, looked perfect on the blue-and-gold oriental silk rug. The rest of the main floor was filled with her comfortable down sofas and chairs, Navajo rugs, a few antique pieces, and her small but exquisite art collection. Downstairs was Sam's space. His bunk beds were separated into twins, at his request. The spare room off his bedroom became the playroom. There was a TV set up with Sam's PlayStation, and plenty of room for his books, toys, and games.

"It's like having my own apartment!" Sam said.

Although she loved every inch of the house, Kate's favorite place was the master bedroom. There was a huge panel of windows that faced north and ran the length of her king-sized bed. Every morning the light was different—sometimes a fiery red, other times a pale lemonade yellow—painting beautiful and inspiring dawns. There were days Kate stayed in bed until noon drinking coffee, soaking in the ever-changing sky and patterns in the valley below.

Kate bounced back and forth between St. Louis and Dubois through the summer. The cabin had become her home; all the boxes were unpacked except for one, which remained untouched in the basement since her move that spring. She couldn't bring herself to go near it. A frightened inner voice told her it was better left closed and forgotten. But the box stared at her in defiance each time she walked downstairs, as if daring her to open it.

Finally Kate gathered the courage to face the contents. She went to the basement, tore at the thick brown tape, and went through the books and towels that were packed inside. Finally her fingers found the stack of letters she had tried to avoid. A folded piece of yellow loose-leaf paper with singed edges hung out the side. At one point she had tried to burn it. She unfolded the note. The words caught her all over again as she went through the E. E. Cummings poem line by line.

Tears blurred her vision so badly she could barely see Jake's handwriting. Pain, agony, and loss racked her body as she reread the poem and then his words. He had loved her, really loved her. Why hadn't she just given him the three months? Why did she let him go? Deep inside, Kate knew the answers. It just wasn't meant to be. It was hard to digest, but Jake probably needed to be with someone closer to his own age.

It had been eight months, and Kate still couldn't bring herself to go out on a date. Men asked her out right and left, in the city and Wyoming, but she refused. Ben, who was a part-time Dubois resident, was the only male she felt comfortable with. She had met him at a dinner party at Faith and Robert's ranch earlier that summer. He was far from a cowboy in his Patagonia khakis and hiking boots. He never admitted to Kate that he'd been recently dumped, yet Kate could tell that he'd had his share of broken hearts and romantic disappointments.

Ben was from Texas but had been summering in Dubois since he was a child. His grandfather had bought their ranch in the early 1900s, and it was on the Registry of Historic Places. Ben's light-gray eyes sparkled with intelligence. He had a degree in history and architecture. Kate was fascinated with his stories about Dubois. She could listen to him talk forever. They started to meet a few times a week for coffee or a walk. Eventually, they added a drink at the Rustic Pine, then an occasional dinner. Ben verged on nerdy, but in a good way; he was kind, sensitive, and undemanding of her heart. He just seemed happy to be in her company, and Kate felt safe with him. It was Ben who took Kate to Torrey Lake to see the ancient petroglyphs.

The weather was perfect that May afternoon, cool enough to wear a jacket, but warm enough to go without a hat and gloves. Kate watched Ben climb around the boulders scattered on the hillsides like a bighorn sheep, finding and pointing out hidden etchings carved into the rocks. He explained the spiritual and historical meaning behind each one.

"Who do you think did them?" Kate was in complete awe. She had never seen anything like it. Some of the images looked like aliens from another planet. Others were more realistic, resembling animals, birds, or deer.

"The so-called experts think the Shoshone Indians made them. But the Shoshone say their people had nothing to do with them; they were in the valley before they came here. So then the experts said, 'Oh, it must have been the Sheepeaters!' It's all conjecture, really. No one really knows."

Ben led Kate over to a huge panel with three drawings, all variations of the same figure.

"Now that's called Water Woman," Ben said.

Kate was strangely drawn to the figure, like iron to a magnet. The oval-shaped body would have been monsterlike, but long, flowing hair softened the creature, making it clearly feminine. Its arms reached out like branches, the fingers small twigs. Smaller creatures, about a fourth of her size, floated around her spindly feet.

"Maybe the spirit drew itself," Kate said in a trancelike voice.

"You know what?" Ben studied the rock for a few seconds and cocked his head.

"What?" Kate couldn't take her eyes off Water Woman.

"That's exactly what I think."

Kate turned and looked at Ben, who was smiling.

"I've got a story for you about my brother, William. A spirit that looked just like Water Woman appeared to him late one night when he was laid up in bed with a broken leg out at the ranch. He said this being put its hand on his leg, and then these little creatures began pulling at his legs as if trying to get him out of his bed. He got the distinct impression they were trying to pull him through the wall and away to the lake. And then the Water Woman spirit said, 'No, it's not his time.' Then she just disappeared."

Kate looked at Ben like he was crazy. This was way out there, even for her.

"You've got to be kidding me! Was he on painkillers or something?" Kate's mind flashed back to the dream of Jake in the motel and the gossamer figure that floated next to her bed.

"Well, sure, I guess he was on something for the pain."

"Maybe he was hallucinating?" Kate paused, then added, "But William seems pretty levelheaded. He doesn't seem like the type that would make something like that up." William was just as conservative and straight-arrow as Ben.

"No, he wouldn't, and to be quite honest, I believe him. And his leg healed much quicker than the doctor anticipated. You know, they say the spirit is evil. But I'm not so sure." He shook his head and shoved his hands in his pant pockets.

The wind kicked up suddenly and whipped around them with such force that Kate's chest tightened to the point of discomfort. She grasped for a rational explanation for her dream and William's eerie experience, but came up with nothing. Kate looked up at the sky. Steel-blue clouds were building in the east, swirling and moving very quickly, so quickly it was almost surreal.

"The Water Woman can heal or kill you; that's how the legend goes," Ben said.

Kate thought about the Water Woman as she rolled through town and up the steep switchback that led to her house. The etching was almost identical to the mermaid-like figure that haunted her bedroom last fall. It was beyond weird. The hair on her arms stood up. She took a centering breath, made the sharp right that led down to her house, then stopped, as she often did. Kate paid homage to the valley below, now blushing in high colors of rose and orange. The Absaroka Mountains in the distance were lightly kissed with snow. She looked toward her property and knew that there was a presence out there, in nature and all around her. The cabin and barn that stood in front of her was proof of that. There had to be a spirit, or energy—call it what you will—and it was far more powerful than she had ever realized.

It was after five when Kate started to marinate the salmon. She had brought the ruby-red filets packed in ice in a cooler all the way from Missouri. They were a special treat for Faith and Robert, who were coming over for dinner. The fish had been caught by her father in Alaska the month before. They had finally come to an understanding. Joseph Marino had accepted her purchasing the ranchette after Jake was out of the picture. He even came out for a visit with Sam earlier that summer to check on Kate's "investment property," as he called it.

"I don't know what you *do* out here," he repeated over and over again. He would then find something in or outside of the cabin that needed repairing, and run to town for a tool or supplies.

"Dad, can't you just sit back and enjoy the mountains and this incredible weather?" Kate finally said after one of his excursions to the Coast to Coast hardware store. It was over one hundred degrees back in St. Louis and a delightful seventy-five in the shade on her deck. Mr. Marino handed Sam a hammer and showed him how to pound in the loose nails sticking up on the deck.

Her father just laughed, then said, "Well, don't you get bored?"

"With all of this to look at?" Kate turned toward the incredible view. "No. Never."

Sam, on the other hand, was easily entertained, playing underneath the boughs of the lodgepole pines or in the hayloft at the barn. And his usual pleas to watch more TV or play a video game were almost nonexistent. Sam's new favorite activity was riding in Kate's nearly new big blue pickup truck. Kate bought the used truck after she bought the house, and she loved the macho half-ton machine as much as Sam did. The truck was an instant shot of testosterone, even for the all-female Kate. She and Sam would go for rides back on the forest service roads, collect wood, and haul whatever caught Sam's eye.

Kate added more soy sauce to the oil-and-vinegar marinade, a recipe passed down from her father, and went to the refrigerator to get a red onion. She got her chef's knife and began slicing thin slivers. She couldn't help thinking of Sam and the first time she let him drive Big Blue, a name he came up with for the truck. When she offered to let him take over the wheel, he was so excited Kate thought he would explode. He was too small to operate the gas and brake, so Kate let him sit on her lap and steer. His smile went from ear to ear. It was one of Kate's fondest memories, that and the look on her father's face when he took Sam fishing that same trip.

"How about we go up to Ring Lake and see if we can catch some dinner," Kate suggested, determined to show her father that Wyoming was indeed where God spent his vacation.

"Now, that's a good idea! Would you like that?" Mr. Marino looked at Sam.

"You bet!"

"I only have one fly reel," Kate said, knowing her father would jump at the chance to run to town and fetch whatever they needed.

An hour later, he came back with more gear than a fishing guide. Kate looked at the rods and reels, lures, and weights, then at her father, who for once wasn't complaining.

"What's that for, Grandpa?" Sam said, pointing at a red cooler.

"That's for all the fish we're going to catch!" Mr. Marino said as he lifted Sam into the truck.

When they got to the lake, Kate watched as her father showed Sam how to cast. He stood to the side, his arm an extension of Sam's, then squatted behind him when the line hit the water.

"Just sit still and wait for that bobber to go under." Joseph Marino put both of his arms around Sam to help him support the rod. Grandfather and grandson stood on the shore together as if they were one. All traces of tension and disappointment vanished from the man who was broken by pain. His face radiated peace and joy. He then turned to Kate and smiled.

It was a beautiful moment, and once again Kate was reminded how different her father must have been before her brother's death. Underneath the gruff personality hid a kind and gentle heart. He loved too much; that was his problem. Kate put the salmon back in the refrigerator and took out tomatoes, fresh mozzarella, and basil, and began preparing a caprese salad.

After the salad was made, Kate moved to the dining room, where she set the table with green-and-white Herend china, Baccarat stemware, and linen napkins. She placed new candles in the silver candelabras and then stood back to admire the room. Ralph Lauren couldn't have done a better job. Kate smiled and went to light the fire.

The evening was a huge success. Robert watched football while Faith helped Kate in the kitchen. Faith was an extremely talented, self-taught chef. Her philosophy was to use the freshest ingredients possible and keep it simple. She had brought chard from her garden to sauté as a side with the salmon.

"It's really not that hard. Just use a good olive oil, a pinch of nutmeg, and throw in a splash of white wine right at the end," Faith said as she flipped and tossed the leafy greens in a pan like a true professional.

"You make it look so easy. But I'm sure *that* was a little more complicated," Kate said, eyeing the home-baked rhubarb pie.

"I made that this morning. It's not difficult, but it's definitely more time-consuming."

"I'm sure! And you, of course, made the crust." Kate knew it wasn't store-bought. Faith made everything from mayonnaise to bread from scratch.

Faith giggled like a little girl. "I did. But it's really no big deal."

After they sat down, Kate leaned forward, looked around the table, and silently thanked God for giving her what she needed most.

"To new friends and good health!" Kate raised her wine glass, filled with a delicate pinot noir.

"And to fresh fish in the land of beef!" Faith chimed in.

Robert let out a low, throaty "For sure," and smiled a rare smile.

Faith winked at Kate. It wasn't easy winning Robert over. He was a man's man, and Kate was thrilled that he appeared to enjoy her company. To have the "A" couple dine with her, a single woman and a "newbie," was a real accomplishment. Kate knew that it was her background in the car dealership that gave her credibility. Robert respected her as a businessperson, and that was just fine with Kate. Faith had become a dear friend, and it was important that Robert approved.

Kate waited until her guests left to clean up. It was nearly midnight by the time she climbed into bed. At about 2 a.m., Kate was jolted out of a deep sleep as four tiny feet scampered across Kate's pillow, skimming her hair. She screamed, jumped up, stood on the bed, and fumbled for the light switch. Her heart pounded to the beat of terror.

"It's only a mouse, you fool. It can't kill you, for God's sake!" Kate yelled into the empty house. Yet she wished she had a gun or weapon of some sort to hunt down the ugly varmint. The only home defense she had was the can of bear spray she kept in the top drawer of her dresser. She looked wildly around the room. Finally she got up the nerve to check under the bed, the armoire, and the chintz-covered loveseat. There was no sign of the mouse.

Kate waited a good fifteen minutes before she turned off the light. Once again, there it was, only this time the minute claws were scratching on a paper shopping bag she had left on the floor. She got up, turned on the light again, and put the bag on the couch. The light was left on as Kate tried to close her eyes.

Sleep came just as the sun rose. By nine o'clock, the dryness of the altitude and the red wine they had consumed with dinner forced Kate to get out of bed and rehydrate. She guzzled a glass of water, then made coffee.

"Okay, my friends, we're going to have a shoot-out," Kate said, mentally preparing herself for the war of the rodents.

She didn't waste time with breakfast. She hopped in Big Blue and headed for the hardware store. The sales clerk warned her that if she used poison, there was a chance the mice or rats would crawl into the walls for warmth initially, then die. The stench in the spring would be awful. Kate listened to his advice while she pictured stiff furry creatures with their bodies smashed in traps. Neither scenario was appealing, nor were mice running across her head. She left with traps and poison, thinking she'd use both if she had to.

That night it was all quiet on the Western front. In the morning when Kate went to check the d-CON box, it was licked clean. Kate calculated that there had to be one very large mouse lurking about, or her bed partner had a whole lot of friends.

Time to bring out the big guns, Kate said to herself as she smeared peanut butter on three traps and placed them in the kitchen, dining room, and next to the door of her bedroom.

Each morning she checked the traps, and each morning she found dead mice. She put on tan leather work gloves for the disposal process. One by one she emptied the traps, turning her head from the dead carcass while she ran outside. She would then squeeze the plastic clip-like contraption and fling the gooey mess over the deck railing. It was an ugly job. But by the end of the week, all three traps sat unsprung. Kate felt proud and self-confident. She had won the battle of the mice. Unfortunately, the victory did not provide a refuge from the emptiness that chased her.

Running no longer provided escape. The mountainous terrain forced Kate to slow her pace to nothing more than a quick walk. But the lack of speed made her notice and study every flower, rock, and tree. She became an antenna of awareness, and it showed in her painting. Her landscapes became more detailed, the colors and texture more refined. When using her talent, absorbed in creating, Kate's focus shifted. Time ceased to exist, and peace found its place in her soul. It was in the evening, after she cleaned her brushes and put the caps on the tubes of oil, that the awful melancholy would return.

It was Thursday evening, and her visit was coming to an end. She had to return to Missouri the following week. She made a cup of tea, wrapped a blanket around her shoulders, and went out on the deck. The Wyoming moon peeked its wide face over the dark hills behind the barn; its lonely blue light pulled at Kate like the tides. She stared at it for a long time.

Suddenly Kate stood up, bored with what had become her nightly ritual. She picked up her tea, took it inside, and replaced the blanket with a down jacket. The gift Ben had given her came to mind. On an impulse she went to her bedroom, opened her jewelry drawer, and pulled it out of the soft leather pouch. The Old Pawn coral-and-turquoise Indian necklace was exquisite. Kate lifted it over her head. It felt heavy, not from the weight of it, but from what she feared it represented.

"Ben, I can't accept this. It's much too extravagant," Kate had told him when he gave it to her three weeks ago. The two of them had been out to dinner, celebrating her upcoming birthday.

"There are no strings attached to this," he said as if reading her mind.

"Ben, I don't know." Kate felt as though their relationship was changing before her very eyes. The necklace was very expensive. They had never discussed each other's financial situation. She guessed Ben was comfortable, but not a jet-set millionaire by any means.

"I don't want to argue about this." Ben looked hurt.

"We are not arguing. We are having a discussion." Kate put a chunk of prime rib on her fork, swirled it in the creamy horseradish sauce, and popped it in her mouth. She chewed slowly. Ben had helped her through her mourning process. Yet Kate got the feeling that Ben was mourning something or someone too. She had never questioned him. But she walked with him and listened. Somehow it seemed as if that was enough.

"Okay, let's discuss it. I saw it next door, at the gallery, and it reminded me so much of you, with your paintings of the Indians and all. You're not going to be here for your birthday next month. It's my gift to you."

The dark circles under Ben's eyes were more prominent in the candlelight. He looked as if he was about to lose his best friend.

"Okay. I'll keep it." Kate smiled and hoped she wasn't losing hers.

"Now, if you don't like it . . ." Ben leaned forward, his eyes wide open with expression.

"Are you kidding? It's gorgeous! It's just this receiving thing is new for me. No one has ever given me such a lovely gift."

"Well, don't you think it's time for you to learn to receive? You have given me so much."

Kate thought about the truck she had given Jake, and how he and his new girlfriend were probably out cruising in it right now.

"I suppose you're right," Kate said.

Kate floated out of her bedroom, the coral and turquoise strands still resting on her chest. As she passed through the dining room, she caught her reflection in the gold gilded mirror. The necklace looked like a large noose hanging around her neck. A bitter laugh bubbled from her belly, and she imagined pulling the coral strings tight, allowing it to strangle her. It didn't take long to figure out where she needed to go. The necklace was at her throat.

Big Blue's lights cut through the dense fog, a blanket suspended in space over Torrey Lake. The stars barely blinked through the mist. Kate rolled down her window and let the wet wind bite into her face.

Beethoven's Symphony in A Major blared from the truck's speakers, making Kate feel as though she were part of a funeral procession. Two red eyes glowed in the headlights: a wild animal in the brush. The melody built, and so did her thoughts of Jake making love to her, completing her, filling her up like no other. It all came back to her like a car crash being rerun backwards in a film clip. The music climaxed, tearing at her heart. The dark thing that had been eating at her soul bared its ugly fangs and told her it was easier to just give up. She was empty; she had no purpose.

She pulled over to the far end of the lake, killed the engine, and opened the car door to get out, fear long gone. Kate stood with her hands out to her sides as if her palms were nailed to a cross, her face distorted by pain, beckoning whatever power was out there.

"Okay, Water Woman!" Kate screamed at the whitecaps that beat against the shore. "If you're out there," she sobbed, "heal me or kill me because I don't want to feel like this anymore!"

KATE SLEPT WITH THE WINDOWS open that night. A wolf's eerie howl woke her. She wondered if it was calling to her or its pack. Kate tossed and turned, then finally fell back into a sound sleep.

In the morning, she woke to a silent snowfall. She curled up under the down blanket, feeling strangely happy and light, as if she were one of the beautiful snowflakes dancing down from the heavens.

Thoughts of a hot cup of coffee and a long talk with Betty finally lured Kate from the warm cocoon of the bed. She put on her fleece robe and walked into the ice-cold kitchen. She dialed Betty's number in Texas as she measured three heaping table-spoons of coffee into the bright white coffee filter. Betty was the only one who would understand.

"I am so proud of you! You're learning to let go!" Betty

gushed. By the way she spoke, you would have thought Kate had just given birth to twins.

"Oh, come on! It's really no big deal. Now, what you've done is a big deal!" Kate thought about how Betty had sold her house, car, and pretty much anything that didn't fit into a few suitcases to move to Texas. She was in a full-time state of bliss following her guru. It wasn't the life for Kate, but she was happy for Betty.

"Kate, baby steps, remember? You don't just wake up one morning totally enlightened. It's a process. We constantly learn, grow, and change. That's life."

"I know, I know. But I want to be like you. Doesn't anything *bother* you?"

Betty laughed deep from her belly. "There are many things that bother me, but you have to learn to let it go. And you are learning how to do that!"

"I'm not so sure," Kate said wistfully.

"You always have choices. Let me ask you something, but I don't want you to answer right away. What exactly do you want to let go of?"

Kate let Betty's question resonate.

"Once you know, I want you to write it all down and then this is what I want you to do . . ."

What Betty suggested was beautiful and so simple, but Kate avoided the exercise like the plague. She came up with every excuse in the book—she was busy painting, she had to clean the house, she had to go to dinner with Faith, or Stella, or anybody that would keep her from doing what she needed to do.

It was a card she picked up at the Water Wheel gift store in Dubois that gave her the push she needed. On the cover was a picture of an angelic woman with a quote from Emily Dickinson penned underneath.

Hope is the thing with feathers
that perches in the soul
and sings the tune without the words
and never stops at all.

Kate thought about those words over and over again as she drove home. They gave her courage to ask herself the tough questions. What precisely did she want to let go of? What scared her the most? She had to let go of parts of herself that had been with her most of her life. What would replace them? How would she cope if she couldn't crawl into the frightened child inside and bury her head in its tiny arms?

A strange voice in her head answered immediately. *You will be embraced by the arms of a strong, wise, confident woman. You will touch many, and you will help others find their calling in this lifetime.*

The calm inner voice was so loud and so real that Kate could not ignore it. She picked up the pen that sat on the table in front of her, opened the card, and began writing.

The words came out without any effort at all, with love, giving the scared child inside permission to heal and let her go. And the new woman, strong, confident, wrote: *You will not walk in the shadows but will be graced with light and wisdom, with the ability to touch many a heart.*

The pen floated across the page as if it had a mind of its own, granting forgiveness to Ted, to Jake, and finally to her father.

Kate closed the card, set it in a ceramic pot, then lit a match. The flame licked the corners of the card. Kate watched the paper's edges curl and turn black, her intentions sealed in the cinders.

The next step of Betty's ritual called for water, and Kate knew the perfect spot. It was dark, but Kate could find her way to Torrey Lake blindfolded.

She pulled off the gravel road and marveled at the power of the night. A glass jar with the ashes rested in the center console. Kate picked it up with her right hand and grabbed a flashlight with the other. Her boots crunched on the snow as she carefully walked around the sagebrush, skirting most of the large rocks but occasionally stepping on one to help her cross marshy areas. Finally, she came to the spot where the water flowed freely from one lake to the other. It was there that she poured the ashes. The light-gray gossamer particles were carried away in the swift current as if they never existed.

To the east, a large red boulder etched with a spidery image hung on the side of the cliff. And Water Woman looked down at Kate with silent approval.

Never Sweat

FAITH HAD ASKED KATE TO HELP move the cows, knowing Kate loved any opportunity to jump on a horse. Faith rode point while Kate lagged behind the herd with Travis and Jason, two cowboys that worked for Faith and Robert.

Sorting and moving cattle made Kate think about running and hiding. Cows and calves were all mixed up in the herd, as if the rider and animals were playing an intricate game of hide-and-seek. Some of the cows could be pretty calculating. They had a way of knowing how to lose themselves in the calico quilt of brown and black fur. Kate was beginning to see how so many people were just like the cows, running and hiding, too.

It was one of those glorious fresh spring mornings, the horizon an unbroken circle around the corral, the cloudless cobalt sky a dome above them. Jason worked the stock, moving slowly amongst the herd, trying to pair up the mama cows with their calves. The chorus of moos, in the same low monotonous tones, had a sleepy effect, like a lullaby.

Kate sat on Blossom, a big, beautiful paint horse, excited to be a part of the moving and sorting of pairs. Kate was positioned at the gate. She turned her horse, but not soon enough to head off a pair that slipped out. She tried to chase them back, but they were too quick for her.

"You have to pay attention. You can't just sit there and look straight in front of you, 'cause sure enough, one of those cows is gonna sneak right out behind you," Robert scolded her like a child.

Robert, like most of the ranchers, didn't have any problem treating a woman just like a man. If you were out there to do a job, you damn well better be able to do it. There were no excuses, and forgiveness was not dished out in any quantity. Ranching was his livelihood, not fun and games or a hobby.

"Sorry, Robert—it won't happen again." Kate backed her horse to the fence so she could see all the way around. Now she knew why Faith made herself invisible when Robert was around. He was the king. And instead of playing queen, a title Faith certainly earned and deserved, she bent to him as if she were his servant. It was so backwards—and so Wyoming, the roles they played.

Jason and Travis moved the herd with ease once the cows were through the gate. As instructed, Kate counted the bovines as they passed through. She counted eighty-four. They were to move them to the south pasture, about a mile over the sandy hills dotted with the stubble of brown, dormant sagebrush.

"I'll get the gate. You wait and push them from behind." Travis masterfully swung the green metal gate closed while mounted, as if he and his horse were perfectly timed dance partners.

This is what she loved, what made her feel alive. Kate removed her camera from her saddlebag, took the lens cap off, and began photographing the cowboys, denim jackets pulled high on their necks, hats low on their heads, colorful silk scarves billowing in the wind. They directed the herd silently and gracefully.

Kate grew somber as she focused on Travis's young face.

How long would he be able to do this? How long before the Vosses' ranch got eaten up by taxes or dropping beef prices? How long before living expenses would force Travis to get a "real" job? Kate felt her calling course through her as she snapped picture after picture, trying to freeze a way of life that was so quickly disappearing.

When she ran out of film, she put the cap back on the lens but kept the camera strapped across her shoulder. Her mind flashed back to a scene long past: Jake, crouched in a corner behind the chutes at the Jackson Hole rodeo. He was bowing his head, in deep meditation, imagining himself riding the bull he had drawn.

"I guess I always thought it just took a lot of balls and no brains to ride one of those big sons of bitches," Stella had commented to Kate while she watched the scene.

Kate knew better. The rider tried to put himself into the animal's head, figure out how the bull was going to move. The rider formulated a plan for how he was going to respond and outsmart the beast. The mental picture, mingled with the smells and visuals—leather saddles, ropes, gloves, and spurs—were all strangely romantic for Kate, with or without Jake in the picture. She remembered the night she ran into Jake's old rodeo idol and her once-upon-a-time crush.

A man with flashy tan chaps, bordered and fringed in hot pink and green, was warming up behind the bucking chute at the Dubois rodeo. Kate had her head behind the camera, watching him put his leg up on the back of the bucking chute, leaning to the side to touch his toe as if he were a ballerina. Kate felt her pulse quicken, not from attraction to the man, but from the excitement of capturing the moment of the all-male cowboy stretching in such a feminine, beautiful way.

The strange man climbed over the rail to mount his horse just as Kate zoomed in to get a shot of his face. The rider must have sensed a presence, because he turned and looked directly into the lens. It was J. P. Benton. Kate lowered the camera, feeling like a Peeping Tom. J. P.'s lips formed a quick smile before he refocused on the fifteen-hundred-pound bronc he was about to ride.

Kate knew J. P. had tuned out all distractions, so she started shooting again, advancing the film, catching every detail: J. P. checking his cinch, pushing his hat down on his head, his gloved hand making a fist, gripping and re-gripping the bareback rigging.

The voice over the loudspeaker roared. "Folks, our next rider is one of our very own, born and raised right here in Wyoming, a PCRA winner three times over. He's gonna be ridin' a powerhouse called Thunder. Let's give a big round of applause to J. P. Benton!"

The crowd, cranked with beer, soda pop, popcorn, and cotton candy, whistled and shouted.

J. P. shook his head up and down as if he had a spring-loaded neck, letting the cowboy working the gate know he was ready.

"Outside!" J. P. cued.

The gate flew open. J. P.'s right hand was glued to the rigging. His left arm waved up and down like a giant bird in rhythm with the bucking horse. His legs were thrust forward; his body moved with every twist and turn. For those eight seconds, he was the horse.

The loud buzzer sounded. A pickup man galloped beside J. P. and J. P. grabbed his waist, then dismounted. His boots hit the ground, and Kate's heart pounded. But this time it wasn't for the man; it was for what she had just captured on film.

"Hey, Kate!" Robert yelled out, interrupting her reverie. "What's the count?"

"Eighty-four," Kate shot back confidently. She knew she could count better than she could ride.

"All right, I think we're finished here. Let's head back," Robert called out to Travis, Jason, and Faith.

Kate's thoughts returned to J. P. After the rodeo that night, she searched through the rows and rows of dually trucks and Circle J horse trailers for him. She found him sitting in an aluminum lawn chair, next to his candy-apple-red Ford, drinking a Miller Light.

"Hi there," Kate said shyly.

"Hi there yourself," he said, not making a move to stand up.

"Long time no see." Kate walked up to him and set her camera bag down in the dirt. "I think I got some good shots of you. I could send you copies if you'd like."

"That would be real nice," J. P. answered with little enthusiasm.

"Well, all I need is your address." Kate wasn't sure what she expected, but it wasn't this. She thought J. P. would at least try to hit on her, or at the very least make some crude remark.

J. P. got up and went to his truck. After retrieving paper and a pen, he opened his Playmate cooler and took out another beer. He didn't offer her one. He scribbled quickly and handed the information to Kate.

"I hear that old boyfriend of yours moved to Idaho and is shacking up with some gal he met in Farson."

Kate's blood simmered. So that was what this was all about; he was still pissed off about the truck deal.

"That's what I hear," she said breezily. There was no way she was going to let this sour cowboy get to her.

"Well, it's his loss. Of that I'm sure. I met the gal at the Cowboy, and she didn't hold a candle to you." J. P. sat back down in his folding chair, put his beer in a coolie cup, and popped back the metal tab. His face showed no emotion.

"That's nice of you to say. I'm a firm believer that everything happens for a reason," Kate said, thinking what a strange bird this man was.

"So, what brings you to Dubois?"

"I bought a house here a few months ago. I go back and forth between here and St. Louis. I still love Wyoming—" She almost said, "even though Jake doesn't love me."

"Well, maybe you and me can go for a ride some time. I come over here for the rodeo when I don't feel like being in Jackson. God, there's just so many damn tourists!" He raised his voice. "Those squinty-eyed Japs hopping on and off those big, stinky buses, running around taking pictures, and you can't understand any of their gibberish!"

"Yeah, you're right. It's a little crowded over there." Kate stuffed his address in her pocket and picked up her camera bag. "Give me a call next time you're in town. If I'm around, I leave my answering machine on. If I'm in St. Louis, it's off."

Kate knew she'd never hear from him. And even if she did, there was no way she'd ride out into the wilds of Wyoming with him. Thankfully, the attraction she had felt months ago was completely gone. Kate was sure she was cured of cowboys. They made wonderful artistic subjects but surly partners.

Faith rode up beside Kate.

"I'm sorry about Robert yelling at you like that back there. I hate it when he does that."

"You don't have to apologize—I know by now that's just Robert," Kate replied, sensing discontent in Faith.

"I know, but sometimes he can be so rude."

"Well, he's got to be a tough one to live with. I know I could never be married to him." Kate paused and quickly added, "I mean, he's a wonderful man. I'm just too sensitive; he'd probably hurt my feelings all the time."

"It's a challenge all right."

Faith's tan face and sun-streaked hair complemented her soft blue eyes. She was a natural beauty, sitting tall in the saddle with perfect posture. Kate thought her to be very regal in more ways than one. Faith was a gracious hostess, kind, unassuming, and intelligent. She listened more than she spoke. When she did speak, it was always well thought-out and full of meaning. Faith never wasted time with small talk.

"Did you get any good pictures? I saw you out there with your camera." Faith switched the subject, clearly not wanting to talk about her marriage any longer. She turned her horse toward the ranch.

"I think I did. I won't know until I get into the darkroom."

The women rode side by side. Kate tried to emulate Faith's perfect horsemanship, but it was no use. Kate didn't ride enough to have the strength or knowledge. She had taken a few dressage classes, but she found she really didn't enjoy it. Kate just loved to ride. Horseback riding got her outdoors, allowed her to explore the landscape, and enabled her to travel to places she couldn't get to on foot.

"So, tell me about the show! I think it's so cool you still shoot film, haven't given into all that high-tech digital stuff none of us understand. You must be excited. Isn't it next month?" Faith asked.

"October eleventh," Kate said slowly. She was still unsure about her new creative medium, but she knew Faith was some-one she could confide in. "I know I should be excited, but I'm really nervous. When somebody looks at my art, I feel like I'm standing in front of them naked!"

Faith laughed. "You are too funny! Kate, you have nothing to worry about—your photographs are beautiful."

Kate sat back in her saddle. She must have still looked unsure of herself, because Faith pressed on.

"Kate, I've lived here most of my life. You have the eye. I love your paintings too, but your photographs are very special."

"I hope you're right."

Kate had decided to put aside her bright oil paints and put all of her energy into photography when she sold her house in St. Louis and bought the cabin in Dubois. She found her camera more portable and black-and-white film more suitable for her subject matter. She was never without the old 35mm Olympus. Her work wasn't exactly cutting-edge, but she had fallen head over heels in love with the West. And above all, she wanted to share her love affair with those who may or may not have the opportunity to experience it. She wanted to teach the world that some people held on to something hard, yet simple, because they loved it and believed in it. And making money was certainly not their primary purpose. She had miraculously landed a one-man show at a small bookstore in St. Louis. It wasn't a big, fancy gallery, but it was a start.

"So, are you going to happy hour?" Kate asked, knowing Faith usually didn't go to town for the Friday evening event. It was one of the few times Robert and all the hands left the ranch at the same time. Even though Faith enjoyed the big Friday night social event, she craved the quiet time even more.

"I doubt it."

"Please come. Stella's coming over from Jackson. She's going to stay the night, then shuttle me to the airport in the morning."

"I haven't seen Stella in ages. Maybe I will go . . ." Faith's voice trailed off.

"Please come! I'm leaving tomorrow, and who knows when I'll be back! We can all have dinner afterwards and celebrate my show."

Faith smiled. "Well, I couldn't miss that!"

An hour later, Kate was elbow to elbow with the usual Dubois suspects at the Rustic Pine tavern. It was shoulder to shoulder, three deep at the bar. The local guest ranches had shuttled in their dudes, all dressed in jeans, expensive boots, and Western shirts. Stella made a dramatic entrance swathed in a gorgeous butter-colored suede fringed jacket, her infamous white-streaked hair hanging long down her back. She spotted Kate and rushed right over.

"God, it's so good to see you. I wish you didn't have to go back so soon!" Stella said as she gave Kate a crushing hug.

"I know. But I've been here two weeks. It's enough, and I want to get back to Sam."

"The kid factor. Sam's great, but I'm glad I'll never have to deal with that." Stella removed her jacket, revealing a white silk shirt and stunning Swarovski crystal Western belt buckle. "Let's get a drink; I'm parched."

Kate waved a twenty across the bar, finally getting the busy bartender's attention.

"Linda, can I get two margaritas with Patrón, please?"

"That'll be five dollars, Kate."

"You gotta love these Dubois prices! If I could afford the gas, I swear I'd move here," Stella said.

Kate looked at Stella's belt, exasperated. "Is that new?" If Stella would curtail her spending, she could probably afford to live anywhere she liked.

"Oh, yeah, but it was on sale at the Bootlegger!"

"Yeah, right, like it was a thousand dollars marked down to five hundred? You are unbelievable!" Kate laughed. Stella was a shopaholic, always had been and always would be.

"How's the new apartment?" Stella expertly changed the subject.

"It's good. I'm not sure how long I can handle not having a yard, but it's right across the street from Shaw Park."

Michael's place had worked out beautifully. But when Kate started dating again, it got too weird, even for her. She never allowed a man to pick her up at her ex-husband's house. Kate thought Sam was confused enough. There wasn't anybody special in the picture, which was fine. She had accepted the fact that she would probably never meet a city slicker that dreamed of living on a ranch. But she did enjoy fraternizing with members of the opposite sex from time to time. Fortunately, interest rates took a dive south, so the mortgage on the cabin and rent on a small apartment became affordable. She had just moved out of Michael's place a few weeks ago. The lack of green space and a yard drove her a little crazy, but the park gave her the nature fix she craved for now.

"Well, it's got to be awesome to be able to walk to all the restaurants and shops in Clayton."

"It is. I was really afraid Sam would freak out, but he likes the new apartment more than I do. He thinks he's living at a hotel, with the doorman and restaurant. And there is a private screening room you can reserve. Sam invites friends over on the weekends all the time. They eat popcorn and watch movies on their own giant movie screen. And best of all, they don't mess up my apartment! It's actually perfect."

"I'll say! And how about your dad? How's he adjusting to all of this?"

"He's staying true to dysfunctional dealership form. I actually think he's happy that I am going back and forth. I guess he feels less threatened or something."

It was true. Joseph Marino was happy as a clam with his daughter there when he needed her and gone when he needed to play Chief Joseph, King of Marino Motors Land.

"And I'm sure he's thrilled now that Jake is history." Stella drained her drink.

Kate hated that Stella still gave her trouble about Jake, but refrained from hitting back.

"Look at it this way. If I hadn't met Jake, I would never have spent all this time in Wyoming. And if it wasn't for him, I know I would never have had the guts to buy my house in Dubois." Kate leaned close to Stella and said softly, "And if you think about it, in a roundabout way, Jake is responsible for you moving to Jackson Hole!"

"*How* do you figure that?"

"How soon they forget. Don't play stupid because I know you're not. You wouldn't have moved here if it wasn't for me being out here dating Jake."

"Interesting." Stella leaned forward toward the bar and yelled, "Two more of the same, Linda!"

"Well, then, we must toast to Jake!" Stella grinned like a Cheshire cat. "To Jake—thank you for bringing us to Wyoming!"

"To Jake!" the girls said in unison, then took long pulls off the sweet green drinks.

Faith walked up and gave them a puzzled look. "What are you two up to?" she said in her motherly tone.

"We're toasting to Jake!" Stella said.

"Really?" Faith looked mildly shocked.

Kate noticed Faith looking at her ring finger on her left hand. The finger was bare.

"Well, did you know, originally the town of Dubois had another name?" Faith looked right at Kate.

"No, I didn't." Kate wondered why in the hell Faith was quizzing her on Dubois history when they were knee-deep in her history with Jake. This had been one wild ride, and she was tired.

And even though she would always hold a soft spot in her heart for Jake, she prayed to God she never, ever, laid eyes on him again.

Faith leaned in toward the girls and lowered her voice as if she had some deep, dark secret.

"Dubois used to be called 'Never Sweat.'"

"Oh, come on!" Kate shouted.

"You've got to be kidding me!" Stella screamed.

"I am dead serious." Faith raised her voice and said, "I propose another toast," she paused for effect, "to Never Sweat!"

"To Never Sweat!" They laughed. They all realized that life was really just one uncontrollable event after another. And the trick was not to fight it, to go with the flow, and never, never sweat.

AND NOW, FAR FROM FARSON, SAM is encircled in Kate's arms. She sighs and closes his storybook.

"Time for bed. You want me to tuck you in?" Kate feels the warmth of his body nestled up to hers and regrets his having to go off to his room.

"Yes," Sam slowly crawls out of Kate's bed.

Kate follows Sam to his room and pulls the covers up to his chin. "I love you," Kate says.

Sam sits up and gives her a hug. "I love you, too."

Kate gets up, turns out the lights, and walks across the apartment to her bedroom.

The platinum band circles her left ring finger once again, a symbol of love, but not for Jake. It is a constant reminder that she promises to love and cherish herself and her art.

Love and happiness. It had been there all the time. And like her camera, Kate carried it with her, inside, wherever life took her.

Reading Group Questions and Topics for Discussion

1. Why did Kate invite her father to join her and Sam on their vacation to Wyoming after her father hurt her so badly?

2. Why did Joseph Marino choose to believe his son James's accusations in regards to Kate's behavior?

3. Ted is a thorn in Kate's side, yet she still carries on a relationship with him, claiming he's a good customer. Is this just an excuse? Are there any similarities in her relationship with her father that she is playing out through Ted?

4. At the airport, Joseph insults Kate in front of Sam, and he continues to dish it out throughout the the majority of the trip. What is his motive? Why does Kate continue to accept it? What kind of role model does this communicate to Sam?

5. When Jake spots Kate checking in to the Prickly Pear Ranch, he thinks to himself that she is clearly, romantically, out of his league. What makes him take a chance and deliver a cup of coffee to her cabin?

6. Young boys still dream of being cowboys, but few really pursue that career choice. What is the draw for Jake? Why are some people more comfortable with animals than humans?

7. Kate has been burned by many men. Why is Kate attracted to Jake?

8. It has been said many, many times that opposites attract. Kate and Jake come from very different backgrounds, but are they really opposite?

9. What is it about Wyoming that helps Kate get in touch with her authentic self? What makes you feel more creative or in touch with your true self?

10. Women have a lot of pressure to fit in to certain stereotypes. Kate is used to putting others first. Why is it so hard for many women to put themselves first, even for just a short amount of time?

11. Kate and Michael are divorced, yet they have a good relationship. How do they accomplish this when so many other couples fail?

12. At the wedding, Kate meets another handsome cowboy, J. P. Benton, and is surprised when she finds that she is attracted to him. Kate laughs it off, thinking to herself she might be a "cowboy addict." Why are so many women attracted to the cowboy type?

13. There is an uncomfortable encounter at the Bear Track Ranch between Jake, Kate, and Cecil. Halfheartedly, Kate expresses some responsibility, yet inside she blames it mostly on Jake and Cecil. Is it really their fault?

14. Friends and family members can be mirrors of our own personality. Is that true for Kate and her friends and relations in the story, e.g., Jake, Stella, Betty, and Faith? Think about your own relationships. Do you see any aspects of your own personality—positive and perhaps not so positive—in the people with whom you socialize?

15. Throughout the novel, Kate begins to believe "there are no coincidences," especially after her experience with the wolf painting at Willow Creek. Do you believe that a higher power is at work, giving you direction? Share your belief or disbelief. Do you recognize coincidences in your own life?

16. Fear drives both Jake and Kate to do many things they regret later—Kate gets an abortion for fear of her father's reaction; Jake pushes Kate away for fear she is going to leave him anyway; Kate gives up her art for fear of not being good enough; when Jake is finally offered his dream job of training horses, he's afraid he's not good enough. How does fear control your life? How can we all help each other act out of a place of love instead of fear?

17. The author uses metaphors throughout the story. In the chapter "First-Time Heifer," do you think the cow giving birth to a dead calf foreshadows what's to come in the future for the lovers?

18. The author is very sensitive to her surroundings and even goes as far as giving towns, like Farson, human characteristics. Do you think people are affected by places? Do you feel that certain places affect how you feel—calm, agitated, energetic, or depressed? Do you feel the town of Farson plays a part in Jake's personality change?

19. When Kate goes to see Stella in Dubois, Kate, driven by some unknown energy, feels compelled to stop at the jewelry store in Lander and buy wedding rings. Some people call this strong urge "intuition." Kate also gazes at a painting for many years repeating to herself, *This is all I want,* then decides to go look at real estate and finds her dream ranch. Have you ever felt like you had to or needed to do something that made absolutely no sense at the time, but you followed through on that feeling anyway? If so, what was the outcome? Have you ever visualized something you desired and later it was manifested? Or, if the exact "thing" wasn't realized, was the outcome something even better?

20. Jake agrees to marry Kate. At the airport, before Kate leaves for St. Louis, she delivers a low blow—a comment in regard to the rings. Do you think that is the reason Jake strays? Do you think things could have turned out differently if she had not made that comment?

21. Kate experiences a strange dream that turns out to be reality. Do you pay attention to your dreams? Do you believe dreams are a direct link to the subconscious?

22. In Dubois, Ben points out to Kate that receiving is as important as giving. Discuss how "letting go" can clear the pathway for receiving. Why is it hard for some people to receive?

23. At the end of the novel, Kate fights off the sadness of losing Jake. But does she really lose him? As it turns out, who becomes the real cowboy? Discuss how men and women look to or allow other people to complete themselves. Is this a good thing?

24. *First Rodeo* explores many life lessons, including the idea of self-love and "calling." Think about your own calling, or purpose, and discuss.

Acknowledgments

I WANT TO THANK MY MOTHER, June, who dragged me to a Jackson Hole Writers Workshop many moons ago, where I met Literary Agent, Charlotte Sheedy. At that time, *First Rodeo* was a short story entitled *Far From Farson.* Charlotte looked me in the eyes and said, "this is not a short story, this is a novel. You are a good writer; write." Talk about a spur in the side—I have the utmost respect for Ms. Sheedy—so let's just say I listened!

It took me over a decade to finish this novel, but I did, with the help of a few editors over the years. Amy Scholder, Katherine Rankovic, Lois Standing, and Wayne Parrish - I deeply appreciate every one of you, for your support, encouragement, and advice. Behind every good writer is a great editor and I had a pose!

Thank you to all of my friends in Wyoming—Tracey and Renny, Michele and Butch, Frank, Bill, Joe, James, John, Kate and Robin, and the rest of the Dubois gang. The list could go on and on— the entire town roped my heart, squeezing it with love, generosity, and kindness. I am so grateful that there are still ranchers, cowboys, communities, and organizations dedicated to family and tradition, keeping the West alive. Thank you for sharing your knowledge, stories and answering all of my endless questions.

This novel would most likely be sitting in a file in my computer had it not been for David Dirks, who passed the manuscript on to Peter and Mary Kershaw. They approached me 3 years ago and asked if I would consider adapting *First Rodeo* into a screenplay. Peter already had a world renowned screenplay writer, Helen Jacey, interested in the project. It was their faith in me, as a story teller and writer, that gave me the courage to wade into the murky waters of publishing.

Thank you to Stephen Lee who was so kind and generous, leading me to Crystal Patriarche at Booksparks. Her team, Lauren and Brooke, are incredibly talented, patient and dedicated. Sheila and Jeanie at PenPower put the 'friendly' back into user. They are uber creative and professional, and get an A Plus in hand holding. Without them I would have never been able to hop on the social media train! I appreciate all of you so much and thank God for your great sense of humor!

There is no doubt that I am blessed with many amazing people in my life; the entire Hennessey family, my husband Timothy, whose love and understanding of my free spirit allows me to do what I love to do—create entertaining stories. He's a cosmic cowboy and the love of my life. Chris, my ex-husband; I can not thank you enough for being an incredible father to our son, supporting me when I started writing years ago, and still supporting me to this day, by reaching out and helping with PR. My cup runneth over! Catherine, you will be my wing-woman forever—I am so glad you are back in St. Louis! Julie, you are the rock star travel guru. Jill and Jeff, Astrid and Bob, Sally, Kelly, Lori, Tracy and Amy—thank you for reading, listening, laughing and having that emergency cocktail with me. Cheers!

About the Author

JUDITH HENNESSEY was in the automobile industry for twenty-five years, operated her own advertising agency, and is now a full-time writer. Her works have appeared in multiple magazines and newspapers, including the *St. Louis Post-Dispatch*. Actively involved in the film industry, she was executive producer of *20 Ways*, an award-winning short film; has served on the board of New Mexico Women in Film; and is a partner in the New Mexico–based production company, White Crow and Raven Productions. She is also the cowriter of the screenplay adaptation of *First Rodeo*. Judy lives on an organic farm with her husband in Missouri.

Website address: www.judithhennessey.com
Facebook: @AuthorJudithHennessey
Twitter: @SpurSeries

SELECTED TITLES FROM SPARKPRESS

SparkPress is an independent boutique publisher
delivering high-quality, entertaining, and engaging
content that enhances readers' lives, |
with a special focus on female-driven work.
Visit us at www.gosparkpress.com

Learning to Fall, by Anne Clermont. $16.95, 978-1940716787. Raised amidst the chaos and financial insecurity of her father's California horse training business, Brynn Seymour wants little more than to leave the world of competitive riding behind. But when her father is trampled in a tragic accident, she struggles to save the business—and her family—and is forced to reckon with the possibility that only the competitive riding world she's tried to turn away from can heal the broken places inside of her.

The Balance Project, by Susie Orman Schnall. $16, 978-1-94071-667-1. With the release of her book on work/life balance, Katherine Whitney has become a media darling and hero to working women everywhere. In reality though, her life is starting to fall apart, and her assistant Lucy is the one holding it all together. When Katherine does something unthinkable to her, Lucy must decide whether to change Katherine's life forever, or continue being her main champion.

The House of Bradbury, by Nicole Meier. $17, 978-1-940716-38-1. After Mia Gladwell's debut novel bombs and her fiancé jumps ship, she purchases the estate of iconic author Ray Bradbury, hoping it will inspire her best work yet. But between her disapproving sister, mysterious sketches that show up on her door, and taking in a pill-popping starlet as a tenant—a favor to her needy ex—life in the Bradbury house is not what she imagined.

So Close, by Emma McLaughlin and Nicola Kraus. $17, 978-1-940716-76-3. A story about a girl from the trailer parks of Florida and the two powerful men who shape her life—one of whom will raise her up to places she never imagined, the other who will threaten to destroy her. Can a girl like her make it to the White House? When her loyalty is tested will she save the only family member she's ever known—even if it means keeping a terrible secret from the American people?

CPSIA information can be obtained
at www.ICGtesting.com
Printed in the USA
BVOW04s2244041216
469789BV00001B/2/P